LEVI PRINCE SERIES

THE FALL OF THOR'S HAMMER

BOOK TWO

Amy C. Blake

HALLWAY PUBLISHING

Hallway Publishing
45 Lafayette Road #114
North Hampton, NH 03862

www.hallwaypublishing.com
Contact Information: info@hallwaypublishing.com

The Fall of Thor's Hammer

COPYRIGHT 2017 by Amy C. Blake
First Edition, August 2017

Cover Design by Hallway Publishing
Typesetting by Odyssey Publishing

ISBN: 978-1-941058-69-5

Published in the United States of America

For the glory of Christ alone

For my husband Charles
And for our four blessings from God:
Elias, Charis, Jonas, and Lukas

Chapter 1

On the Precipice

Levi Prince stood on the edge of Castle Island's northern precipice and willed solid wood to fill the empty space in front of him. Fighting dizziness at the hundred-foot plunge to Lake Superior, he scanned the cloudless sky and squinted against the low sun in the west. *It has to be here.* He strained to see through the falling shadows in the east. When a squawking seagull passed directly in front of him without crashing into any invisible barriers, he huffed.

"Come on, show up." He knelt on the rocky ledge and groped the air for some sign of the bridge.

But there was no drawbridge. Just a gust of moist wind that nosed at his fingers like his hyperactive puppy Cerberus begging for a biscuit.

He sighed as he stood upright. He'd ended last summer feeling so good in the knowledge that God was with him everywhere, even in Terracaelum, a world most people had no idea existed. But as the months at home dragged on, he'd found it harder and harder to hold on to the newfound maturity he was sure he had gained. Before long, his siblings were annoying him worse than ever, and his parents' rules seemed ridiculous for somebody who'd battled a demon sorcerer and lived to tell the tale.

Not that he could take credit for the victory. God had been responsible for the violent windstorm that had saved him and his friends from Deceptor. And he hadn't told anybody the tale, especially not his folks. If he told them his summer camp was a haven for mythical creatures, at least one of whom wanted to kill him, they'd never have let him come back. So he'd brooded in silence while his guilt and aggravation grew to monstrous levels. By the time he'd left for camp a few days earlier, the rift between him and his family had grown to a chasm even more vast than the one separating him from the castle. Because of that rift, Terracaelum had come to represent his only hope of regaining any sense of peace.

The longing almost choking him, he studied the empty air. What if the drawbridge wasn't lowered? Or what if it only appeared when he'd been invited? After all, people could only enter the castle if Mr. or Mrs. Dominic admitted them. He plucked his Camp Classic invitation from his pocket, unfolded the dog-eared paper, and waved it as proof to the empty air. "They did invite me. See?"

Nothing happened. He drew in a deep breath and gagged on a whiff of rotten fish.

Shoulders slumped, Levi peered behind him through the scraggly trees at the trail leading downhill to the cabins, a good thirty-minute hike away. He didn't see anybody on the trail. Not that he expected any of his friends to want to be around him right now, especially after what he'd said about Mr. Dominic at breakfast. Here he'd spent all school year wanting to get back to Camp Classic and his friends, and now he'd made them all mad. He should've kept his big mouth shut, especially in front of Sara. But between being crowded into three small buildings for five days with eighty campers and the pranks *somebody* in the boys' cabin kept playing, he was downright aggravated. This morning's green Jell-O in his shoes had pushed him beyond the breaking point.

He considered all the mean jokes additional proof that he was right about Sara's dad doing a bad job as camp director—this summer at least. Last year, Mr. Dominic had been awesome, but this year he'd disappeared right after the campers arrived and had yet to return. Still, Levi should've kept his opinions to himself because with Sara and the others mad at him, life in the cabins would be worse than ever.

Yet another reason he needed to get back into Terracaelum. So where was the drawbridge? Why was it keeping him out? Why couldn't he catch at least some shimmer of the rainbow lights that always appeared when the castle materialized?

Fists clenched, he stomped like his baby brother throwing a tantrum. Chunks of dirt fell, and he froze, breathless. Would the debris land on the bridge? Then he'd know where to cross, invisible or not.

But no, the dirt dropped straight into Lake Superior.

The path to Terracaelum had to be there somewhere. "Come on, God, show it to me, please."

Wait. What if he needed to prove he believed in the drawbridge for it to materialize? What if he needed to act on that belief? To show faith?

He peeked down at the water shattering against the rocks, and his stomach churned. Okay, fine. He could do this. He closed his eyes and inched one foot out over nothingness. "I know you're there. Let me in." If he could only touch the bridge with the tip of his toes—

"Get back!"

The scream from behind shot adrenaline through his veins. He teetered. His eyes flew open. His balance shifted from the solid earth beneath his left foot toward the thin air beneath his right. A huge wave slurped upward as though eager to snatch him into the lake's maw. He shoved backward with every ounce of his weight but still wobbled on the brink, his mind frozen on a single thought. If he fell, would the drawbridge catch him?

Or the rocks?

A sudden yank to the hem of his jacket had him flailing backward, and he landed on the ground with a grunt. For a moment, he sat there, eyes fixed on the empty sky. He clenched his jaw against a wave of nausea. When it passed, he twisted around.

Who had kept him from Terracaelum?

A small, pink-jacketed girl with jet-black hair stood in the shadow of a massive oak tree, her chest heaving. "Are you okay?"

"Yeah," he croaked.

Reproach crept into her pale blue eyes. "What were you doing? Trying to kill yourself?"

"Of course not." Levi stood on shaky legs and stared pointedly at her hand still clutching his Cleveland Browns jacket.

She blushed but was slow to let go, as if worried he'd leap the moment she released him.

He raised both eyebrows. "It's not like I was gonna do a Peter Pan or anything."

"If you're sure . . ."

"I'm sure." Yeah, he was going nuts in the cabins, but he wasn't that far gone.

"I'm Morgan." The girl was tiny, like she belonged in second grade or something, but he knew she had to be at least thirteen or they wouldn't have let her come to camp.

"I'm Levi," he finally said. "You're new, right?"

She nodded. "You were here last year?"

"Yeah."

"Then shouldn't you know better than to stand half-on, half-off a cliff?" She scrunched her lightly freckled nose. "What were you trying to do anyway?"

"Nothing." He wasn't about to tell her he'd hoped to make a castle magically turn up in the sky.

"Oh." Morgan scuffed her silver Reebok through the grass, her dark hair curtaining her face.

He'd hurt her feelings. Still, he couldn't tell her anything about Terracaelum. Most campers who'd attended last year hadn't known their summer camp for classically-educated kids was in a realm suspended a hundred feet above the lake like a gargantuan tree-covered Goodyear blimp. They had no idea the camp staff was made up of creatures they'd only read about in myths and legends. He hadn't known, so how could he expect this new kid to have a clue?

Instead, he forced a bright smile.

Too bright, apparently, because she stepped closer to him, her eyes sparkling like he was her new best friend. "I've been watching you. You're so good at everything."

Should he be creeped out? Or flattered? Neither, probably. Any second she was bound to bust out laughing: *Just kidding, you're really pathetic! Ha!*

When her admiring look remained for a solid minute, he cleared his throat. "Uh, thanks." He was better at fencing and archery than last summer and didn't look like quite as much of a doofus building a campfire or pitching a tent, but *good* was stretching things. Still, the compliment felt nice, especially after his year at home.

He couldn't do anything right with his mom and dad lately. Home-schooling, which he'd always liked before, had been torture this year because he could never escape the pressure of knowing he should tell his parents about Terracaelum. He'd never kept secrets from them before.

Morgan edged even closer to him, a goofy smile on her lips.

He sidestepped away, turning toward the lake where sunset painted purples and oranges across the vast, clear sky. At the faint whisper of her jacket sleeve brushing his, he squeezed his arms tight to his body.

She breathed out a dreamy sigh, the kind his sister Abby gave when she watched a sappy-sweet movie. Levi strained his eyeballs to catch a glimpse of her expression without giving away that he was looking.

Yep. She looked just like Abby watching Daddy Warbucks and that secretary woman smooching at the end of her favorite movie, *Annie*. But Morgan wasn't staring goo goo-eyed at the sun setting on the water. She was staring at him.

Oh boy. It was definitely time to head back to camp.

Levi and Morgan reached camp as twilight fell. Sara's roommate Lizzie confronted them beside the dining hall, both fists planted on the hips of her skinny jeans.

"Where have you been, honey?" Lizzie's soft Southern drawl didn't mesh with the pink-tipped claws she dug into Levi's arm.

Now what had he done wrong? "Just hiking." He wrenched his arm away.

"Sara's been lookin' all over for you." Lizzie's glare slid from him to Morgan and back.

"Okay. What does she want?" Probably to yell at him. No, Sara wouldn't yell. All she had to do was give him a disappointed look, and he'd melt through the ground in a pathetic puddle of misery.

"It's about Mr. Dominic."

Maybe Lizzie would do the screaming. She was good at that. And if their other roommate Monica joined in, she'd scold him in six-syllable words. *Yay.* Too bad Ashley hadn't come back this summer. She was too nice to yell.

Mouth tight, Lizzie cut her eyes toward Morgan, telling Levi he'd better think of a polite way to get rid of her so his friends could tell him how horrible he was.

Morgan turned her oblivious smile on him. "Mr. Dominic's awesome, don't you think?"

"Yeah, um . . . I need to go now, Morgan."

"No problem." She squeezed his wrist then skipped toward the girls' cabin, silver shoes glowing in the semidarkness. "See you later, Levi."

"Okay, bye."

Lizzie slapped his shoulder.

"Hey, what was that for?" He rubbed his stinging skin.

She whipped around close enough that her long blond hair smacked him across the face, burying him in a heavy cloud of perfume. "Just come on."

Letting loose a violent sneeze, Levi followed her past the dining hall. He wished he could go inside for a piece of the fried chicken he smelled, but he knew he'd better face the firing squad first. So he moved toward the woods and the faint glow of Sara's golden hair, almost hidden in the shadow of the trees.

As soon as he reached her side, he said, "Look, Sara, I'm sorry for what I said, I just—"

"Hush." She snagged his hand and pulled him a few paces within the tree line.

Okay, so they wanted to scold him in private. Hang on, where did Lizzie disappear to?

Stopping behind a particularly large tree, Sara whispered, "Dad's back, and he says it's time."

Levi's mind blanked. "Huh?"

"We're going in the morning. To Terracaelum."

"Really?" Excitement touched his belly. Then he shivered at how idiotic he'd acted a mere hour before, almost falling off the cliff in his impatience to get there on his own.

"Yeah, but remember not to say anything around the new kids."

He nodded. Like Morgan, lots of campers were new this summer. Only a little over half from last year had returned. "Did your dad say where he's been all this time?"

"Yes . . ." She nibbled her lower lip. "Apparently he's at it again."

"Who?"

"Deceptor, of course."

Deceptor. Levi's throat went dry. "So he's still . . . alive then . . . and out there?" Cold sweat tricked down his spine.

"He is." Sara's chin trembled. She had to be thinking about Deceptor kidnapping her last summer, a memory that had given him nightmares all year long. He'd never explained to his parents that bad dreams were why he dragged himself from bed, exhausted and cranky, so many mornings.

"What—Um, what's he up to this time?" Why couldn't Deceptor have died that night? Mr. Dominic had said the shape-shifting demon sorcerer would return, but Levi had still tried to convince himself the director was wrong. He needed Terracaelum to be a safe place.

"I don't know all the details. Something about a group of dwarves who live way up north. And then some weird creature one of the scouts spotted near the Medicollis."

"The Medicollis?"

"You know, the mountains you see from the field south of the castle. Near where you fought him . . ." A haunted look crawled into her eyes.

Levi swallowed hard. "I assumed he lived there. With that cave and all."

She shook her head. "My dad usually keeps him and his army

restricted to the far northern tip of the kingdom—as far from the castle as possible."

"Oh."

"Anyway . . ." Sara straightened her shoulders. "Dad and the others handled the problem with the dwarves, and things are quiet again. He says it's okay for everybody to come up."

"That's why the delay? So the campers would be safe?" Of course it was so the campers would be safe. He'd been an idiot to doubt Mr. Dominic's leadership.

"Yes, that's why." Sara's sad smile showed she still felt the sting of his earlier criticism. "He isn't just Prince of Terracaelum, you know. My dad's also a really great camp director."

Chapter 2

Back to Terracaelum

After breakfast the next morning, Levi trudged up the hill north of the cabins with his friends, who, thankfully, had all forgiven him—even Lizzie. Behind them hiked a pair of new kids, identical twins named Braden and Brock. They kept horsing around, shoving each other and laughing hysterically. Levi hoped they quit before they got much higher, or one of them might fall off the cliff. He knew what a long drop that was.

Trevor cast a glance over his shoulder at the pair. "Have you noticed how much those two look like you?"

"A little, I guess." Levi shrugged. They were short and skinny like him. They also had his coloring—pale skin covered in bright red-orange freckles—but their hair was more strawberry blond than red. Plus, it was stick-straight and spiky, while Levi's curls were the bane of his existence, especially in humid weather when he looked a lot like Ronald MacDonald with his finger in a light socket.

"'Course, they're younger," Trevor said with another backward glance. "And they look sorta like rejects from the 'hood."

Levi peeked at the two and nodded. It wasn't so much the crotch of their jeans hanging between their knees with their boxers poking out the top or the thick gold chains around their necks. It was something about their eyes—especially Braden's—that said it wasn't wise to turn your back to them. Brock's expression was fuzzy, like his twin had punched him in the head too many times when they were toddlers.

Levi hadn't said anything to anybody, but he suspected the twins were the practical jokers in the boys' cabin. Last night, he'd entered the otherwise empty cabin to find them on the wrong side looking guilty. When he went to bed later, something like a water balloon burst under his pillow and soaked his bunk. Yells from all around the cabin told him the other boys had the same presents under their pillows. The problem was he couldn't prove Brock and Braden had anything to do with it, especially since there weren't balloon remnants in anybody's beds. He had no idea how they'd managed the trick, but he'd been relieved to have his suspicions diverted to the twins.

Before that, he'd wondered about Trevor. Under the influence of a new friend at his private school, Trevor had really gotten into practical jokes. During one of the weekends he'd spent at Levi's house, he'd hidden rubber roaches in Levi's underwear drawer. During another visit, he'd stolen Levi's towel while he was in the shower, so he had to dry off with his dirty clothes. At Christmas, he'd given Levi a huge, gorgeously wrapped gift box filled with sand from Lake Erie. Annoying, yes. But Trevor had never done anything to cause a serious mess like the culprit in the boys' cabin.

Right then, their chunky roommate Steve pushed between him and Trevor. "I can't wait to sleep in my old bed at the castle." Sweat plastered his dark blond hair to his forehead despite the fact they'd been hiking only five minutes.

Trevor stretched his muscled arms above his head, rubbed both hands through his brown hair until it stood on end, and let out a yawn that popped his jaw. "Yeah, my feet hang off the end of those little cardboard things they call bunks."

Levi bit back a laugh. He knew full well the snoring duet those two put on every night hadn't lessened any in the cabin, but he was looking forward to his cushy castle bed, too.

Their other roommate Tommy squeezed his thin frame between Steve and Trevor. "I still don't get why we stayed down there so long." He hooked a thumb toward the camp they'd left at the base of the hill.

From her position further up the path, Monica sent them an imperious glare. "Sara already informed us of the situation. And of the necessity of keeping silent about it." She cocked her chin toward the other campers then turned forward with her nose in the air.

Tommy rolled his eyes. Lizzie, walking next to Monica, glanced back at the boys and moved her glossy pink lips in mocking imitation. Levi and Trevor exchanged a grin. Sara's roommates always grated on each other's nerves. Though Sara didn't turn around, Levi saw her mouth twitch with suppressed laughter.

Levi chuckled. His friends hadn't changed much over the school year. He sure was glad they weren't mad at him anymore.

As they climbed, the hardwood trees and underbrush squeezed the dirt path into a narrow trail. With no room to walk in a clump, his friends paired off, and Levi walked alone behind Sara and Monica. The nearer they got to the cliff, the queasier he felt. What if the castle didn't appear today? What if the trail ended in the same sheer drop to the lake? What if Mr. Dominic decided Terracaelum wasn't safe after all?

When only one bend remained, Sara dropped back beside him. She didn't say anything, just fell into step with him, offering the support of her presence. Or maybe she was seeking support from him. Either way, he appreciated the gesture.

As they rounded the curve, his stomach jolted—this time with joy. The castle stood before them with its glittering gray stones and thick wavy windows. High on the four tower rooftops, red pennants fluttered in the breeze. Waving her welcome, Mrs. Dominic stood in the doorway, enveloped in the soft multicolored lights of the stained-glass windows.

In front of Levi, campers clustered beside the extended drawbridge, the waters of the moat smooth as mirrors on either side. Birds twittered in the surrounding oaks, but there weren't any seagulls screeching. The new kids' gasps mingled with the excited chatter of last year's campers as a smile tugged at Levi's lips.

They were back in Terracaelum.

"Come on in, everyone," Mrs. Dominic called.

Even from across the drawbridge, Levi could see the deep wrinkles and bluish tint to her nearly transparent skin. He knew she was one hundred and forty-three years old, so he shouldn't be surprised at how ancient she looked, yet it worried him a little because she was the Princess of Terracaelum. Her kingdom needed her. Not to mention Sara, who needed her mom. He glanced at his friend, but Sara looked perfectly content. As Levi returned his gaze to the castle, Mrs. Dominic smiled, transforming her face into that of a much younger woman. Her wispy, pure-white hair shimmered in the sunlight like an angel's wings. Relief trickled through him. She was fine. Had to be.

As Mrs. Dominic turned to speak with someone inside the castle, Lizzie and Tommy started across the drawbridge with Monica and a waifer-thin new girl, who kept casting nervous glances at the moat. Steve and Trevor flanked Levi and Sara, and the four stepped onto the weathered planks together.

When they reached the midpoint, a commotion drew Levi's attention behind him. Braden and Brock had apparently shoved through several campers and now pushed their way onto the thin slats on either side of the bridge, their arms outstretched as though on a high wire.

He frowned. What were they thinking? The moat could be dangerous.

With his fox-like face contorted into a sly smirk, Braden jostled Trevor, who yelled, "Watch it, man."

Monica made a disapproving noise in her throat. Sara sucked in a sharp breath.

Levi called out, "Hey, you guys don't wanna fall into that moat—"

Before any of them could react, Braden scooped up the scrawny girl beside Monica and flung her out toward the water as if she weighed no more than a feather. Trevor belly-flopped onto the wood as he grabbed for her, and Braden scampered toward the castle, snickering like a little rat.

At the same moment, Steve let out a bellow. Brock rammed into him as if to shove him into the moat on the opposite side of the bridge. Only Steve, much larger than the girl Braden threw in, didn't fall so easily. Brock tried again, grabbing onto Steve's neck and hurling himself toward the edge of the bridge. Steve wobbled, tripped over his own boat-sized shoe, and dropped to his knees. Brock splashed into the water, still latched onto Steve's head like an octopus. Steve's upper body went underwater while he scrabbled with toes and fingers for a hold on the slick drawbridge.

Levi dove for Steve's legs and got kicked in the chest. Air left his lungs in a whoosh, but he managed to hug his friend's ankle. Tommy snagged Steve's other leg, and they yanked. Slowly, with plenty of grunts and groans, he and Tommy dragged Steve onto the bridge with the twin still clutching his head.

Steve shoved Brock off and flopped against the wood, sucking in air. "What's wrong with you? Why'd you try to push me off?"

Brock blinked stupidly then sputtered, "I . . . I . . . what're you talkin' about? It was your fault, loser."

As Steve's face reddened in fury, Levi remembered the new girl and wheeled around to see if she needed help. But Trevor had rescued her. His roommate hunkered next to her, awkwardly patting her back. Water flowed from her blue-black braids, and tears streamed from her eyes.

Monica and Lizzie knelt beside her.

"What's your name, sweetie?" Lizzie smoothed a strand of hair from the girl's forehead.

She sniffled a few times. "Yasmin."

"Don't you cry now, Yasmin." Lizzie's voice soothed like warm honey, even as her eyes flashed fire. "We'll get you inside and dried off right quick."

Lizzie and Monica helped her stand. Trevor jumped up and squeezed out his t-shirt, clearly relieved the others were comforting the girl so he didn't have to.

At that moment, Mrs. Dominic reached them, a hand on her chest. She stooped to Yasmin's level. "What happened, dear? Was the wood damp? Did you slip?"

An angry snort drew Levi's gaze to Sara, who stood with her fists on her hips, glaring at the twin who'd thrown Yasmin off the bridge. Still perched on the slat, the twin grinned across the crowd at Hunter, Levi's least favorite person. Surrounded by his cackling friends, the bully saluted the twin.

A groan worked its way through Levi's lips. So the twins were Hunter's new pet thugs. Perfect.

"Excuse me, what's the holdup?" Mr. Dominic skirted the big pine tree and squeezed through campers clogging the trail. When he pushed between Hunter and Martin, his gaze shot to the sopping-wet Steve and Yasmin. "What happened here?" His shoulder-length white hair flapped around his tanned face as he strode onto the drawbridge.

Levi scowled. The Dominics hadn't seen a thing. That meant Hunter and his buddies probably wouldn't even get a slap on the wrist.

Sara stomped over to her dad and tapped his arm. He leaned down and she whispered in his ear. After a moment, he questioned her quietly. She pointed at the twins, one dry, the other dripping. Levi's eyebrows shot up. This was new. What happened to Sara avoiding the Dominics so no one would suspect her of being their daughter?

After a moment, the director straightened to his full height of well over six feet and stalked to the twins. "Come with me, you two. You're about to receive an education on how to behave at Camp Classic." He took each boy by the arm and marched them into the castle.

Good. Maybe Mr. Dominic would keep Hunter and company under control this summer.

But he knew his nemesis too well to count on it.

Chapter 3

Rules and Regulations

Later that morning, Levi sank onto the lush grass of the castle courtyard and drew a relaxed breath for the first time in days. Months, really, but now that he was back in Terracaelum, he didn't have to worry about all that. He could simply enjoy a guilt-free summer with his friends.

Leaning back on his elbows, he let the sunshine and soft breeze warm his face. On either side of him, Trevor and Sara waited for Mr. Dominic's welcome-to-the-castle speech. Beside Sara sat Monica and Lizzie. On the far side of Trevor sprawled Tommy and a now-dry Steve.

A shadow fell over Levi. He looked up, squinting against the sunlight at a small form.

Morgan again. And she had that same sappy smile fixed on him. "Hi, Levi."

"Uh, hi."

"Can I sit here?" She pointed at the spot between him and Sara.

"Um, I, well . . ." He glanced around the courtyard. Maybe it was a little too hot in the sun after all. Maybe he should find a spot in the shade.

"Of course you can." Sara scrunched up to Monica and patted the grass beside her. "Levi would love that. Wouldn't you, Levi?"

He tried to nod, shake, and shrug all at once. Trevor's snort told him he looked as ridiculous as he felt, but Morgan bounced into the open spot, grinning like she'd been offered a throne.

Levi decided it was a good time to study the new wooden platform that stretched the entire north side of the courtyard. As he peered over the other campers' heads, he pretended he couldn't feel Sara, Lizzie, and Monica staring at him. *Please, Mr. Dominic, start now.*

Within seconds, the director stepped onto the platform, drawing all eyes. Thankfully. When the campers quieted, a broad smile played on Mr. Dominic's leathery face, making him look far more like an old sea captain than a prince. Or, with his purple-flowered Hawaiian shirt, more like a retired surfer.

"Welcome to my home." He extended his arms in a gesture that took in the huge castle. "The staff has prepared a short play both for your amusement and to help you understand the rules here at Camp Classic. Before they begin, I will pray and ask the Great Sovereign's blessing on each of you. *Oremus.*"

Latin for *Let us pray.* Levi bowed his head.

"Holy Lord of all things on, above, and under the earth," Mr. Dominic prayed in his unique way. "I thank you for giving us safe passage into this place. I beg your blessing on each of these young people as they learn and grow this summer. Help them grasp the importance of the rules put into place for their wellbeing. I praise you with every portion of my humble being. In the name of your precious and holy Son King Jesus, amen."

Levi looked up.

Mr. Dominic's eyes twinkled. "Now, enjoy the show." He waggled his eyebrows, bent low in an exaggerated bow, and stepped from the stage.

Giggles and murmurs turned to full belly laughs as a stern-faced Miss Althea stalked onstage, dragging a scarlet-cheeked Dr. Baldwin. The petite pixie woman (dressed in a frilly pink gown) and the stumpy, stodgy dwarf (in gym shorts and a tank top) carried a large sign between them: "Boys and girls must stay out of each other's dorms."

Because Dr. Baldwin was his friend, Levi tried to keep a straight face. But the sight of those knobby knees and the hair sprouting around that awful orange tank top made him burst out laughing along with the rest of the audience.

When a scream silenced the laughter, Levi rose to his knees for a better view. A snorting creature with a bull's head and a man's body ran across the stage in pursuit of Mrs. Drake. The elf woman waved a red cloth with one hand and clutched a poster in the other: "Don't tease the minotaur."

The two disappeared from the stage before the screaming died out, but Levi's gaze flew to Mr. Dominic, propped against a pillar at the far end of the stage with a nonchalant smile on his lips. Throughout the crowd, people whispered together. A few laughed hesitantly.

Tommy leaned around a slack-jawed Steve and caught Levi's eye. "What's he playing at?"

Levi shook his head.

Lizzie whispered, "Sara, I thought this stuff was a secret."

Sara shrugged. "It is."

"Who cares?" Trevor grinned. "That was totally sweet."

Levi cared. Did Mr. Dominic actually *want* the whole camp to know about this place? Wasn't it his job as Prince of Terracaelum to keep his kingdom secret? To protect its inhabitants? How could he be so irresponsible?

Then a new boy in the row ahead of Levi said, "That's gotta be the best mask I've ever seen."

The girl beside him shivered. "Yeah, and did you hear him snort? You'd almost think he was real."

In the clamor over the minotaur, Levi almost missed the next tableau. The dwarf Mr. Austin, his face and hair dyed pure white, stumped along dragging a ratty door with another rule painted on it: "Stay out of the cellar . . . or else." Levi remembered that rule from the previous year, but it hardly compared to the minotaur or to what came next.

A woman he'd never seen before, but who was so willowy she had to be an elf, strolled onto the stage carrying a plate of pink cupcakes in one hand and a sign in the other: "Don't feed the harpies . . . They're dieting."

"No way," Levi murmured.

A plump creature with flowing black hair and small blue wings swooped in and snatched the entire plate. The elf's marble-like face didn't even twitch as she strolled from the stage, but the campers squealed louder than they had when the minotaur passed.

"Cool animatronics," a kid near the stage hollered.

Watching the bird-woman scarf the cupcakes in mid-air reminded Levi of his Papa Levi's story about the harpy that stole his lunch one hundred and fifty years ago when he attended Camp Classic. He couldn't stifle a grin. So that was what a harpy looked like—a long-haired pig with hummingbird wings.

After she devoured the cupcakes, the harpy shot the campers a sour look and chucked the plate. Kids shrieked and backpedaled. The plate shattered near the edge of the stage—just a few feet from Levi's pixie friend Albert, who bellowed "Watch it!" and swatted at the sky with his poster. The harpy released a giggle so shrill Levi had to cover his ears. She soared away as Albert stomped across the stage with a dunce cap on his head. He carried a blackboard with the scrawled words, "No cheating."

Trevor elbowed Levi. "Look at Albert. Ha!"

Levi doubled up with laughter. "I can't wait for him to show up in our room tonight." Albert had a habit of planting himself on the boys' beds, chowing down on chips and sodas, and playing cards for hours on end. It drove Levi crazy.

Steve giggled until tears streamed down his cheeks. "It'll be so easy to beat him at Spades after this."

"Yeah, all we have to do is squawk and flap around and—" Tommy flailed his arms and fell onto his back cackling.

Mr. Drake came on stage at that moment, carrying a sign that read "No swimming or boating without a staff member present." He walked alone, wearing his Camp Classic polo and khakis. He looked completely normal.

"What's the trick?" Trevor said into the silence.

"Don't know." Levi scanned the sky. Seeing nothing, he looked toward the shadowy wings right and left of the stage.

Just as the other campers started muttering, a huge green creature with purple spots appeared stage right. A couple of girls squealed, but most people chuckled at the ridiculous, rubber-suited thing that hobbled a few feet then fell on its face. Mr. Drake hauled it from the stage by a flipper.

The laughter came to an abrupt halt as Mrs. Forest ran screeching across the stage. The kitchen boss's tiny pixie wife was gone almost before Levi had time to read the rule she carried: "Don't leave your room after lights-out!"

Stunned silence followed her screams. Then came the sound of rattling chains and a rotten smell, sort of like the time Levi had forgotten a roast beef sandwich in his backpack for three weeks.

Cold fingers of dread closed around Levi's throat as Mr. Austin and Dr. Baldwin dragged something manacled across the stage. A brown hood covered the creature's face, except for eyeholes, which showed red glowing eyes. The cuffed hands were hairier than any he had ever seen, and the long, yellowed fingernails made him want to run and hide.

Beside him, Morgan gasped. "What is that thing?"

The Asian boy in front of them twisted around and gave her a look of disdain. "It's just to scare us into obeying the rules. Hollywood tricks like the other stuff."

Levi plucked at his lower lip, eyes narrowed. Would the campers really dismiss all of these bizarre creatures as mere Hollywood tricks?

"You stay in your room at night. I mean it." The cold voice Levi hated more than any other—Hunter's voice—came from the row behind them. Levi whipped around.

Hunter was glaring at Morgan. Or was he talking to Sara? The bully's gaze flicked back and forth between the girls. Both Sara and Morgan had tight mouths and lowered brows as they frowned at Hunter. Levi's mouth turned down at the corners, too. Why did Hunter feel he had the right to tell either girl what to do? Not that he thought wandering the castle at night sounded like a good plan for either—

A sudden roar pulled his attention to the sky. Two massive creatures covered in glittering scales soared overhead, the black one ridden by Mr. Drake, the blue one by Mr. Sylvester. Both men held long, thick wooden poles with sharp tips. Mr. Sylvester balanced a sign on his saddle: "No dragon jousting without permission."

The campers cheered, stuff like "Awesome!" and "That has to be the coolest hologram I've ever seen!" But Levi couldn't seem to close his unhinged jaw. What in the world . . . ?

Hot breath tickled his neck as Hunter's whisper invaded his ears. "You and me, Prince. Name the time."

Dragon jousting? Seriously? "Yeah, right." As if people really tried to knock other people from the backs of dragons with pointed sticks.

Yet what would be worse: Riding a fire breathing dragon? Or facing the tip of Hunter's lance?

"Scared, aren't you?" Hunter's blue-gray eyes were the color of iron. His upper lip curled. "You know I'll knock you off your dragon, runt."

A burst of riotous applause saved Levi from having to think of a good comeback, something lame like, *Uh-uh, my mom won't let you.*

Instead, he turned to see Mr. and Mrs. Dominic standing center stage, arms around each other's waists. Mrs. Dominic held a sign in her free hand: "Chapel attendance is mandatory. Don't forget your Bible."

"I hope you've enjoyed our little performance," Mr. Dominic said over the cheering. When everyone settled down, he continued, "Even though we did this to entertain you, I hope you'll remember the rules." He shot a significant look toward the back of the crowd, seemingly straight at Levi.

He flushed. Did the director mean him? Had Sara told her dad what Levi said about his skills as a camp director? Maybe it was against the laws of Terracaelum to criticize the prince? He glanced at Sara, but she had her eyes on her parents.

Loud thuds and a collective gasp drew his gaze back to the stage. A gigantic man, triple the height and four times the width of Mr. Dominic, stomped up behind the elderly couple. The platform trembled with his every stomp, but the wood didn't crack. The Dominics waited with serene smiles on their faces.

"One final rule." The director indicated a poster clutched upside-down in the giant's fists. Mr. Dominic tapped the hulk's elbow and made a twirling motion with his forefinger. Square jaw hanging wide, the creature knitted his thick brows and blinked his dull eyes in a way that reminded Levi of Hunter's sidekick, Martin. But the giant must've been smarter than Martin, because he rumbled "oh" and turned the sign right side up. On it was a single word, "Excelsior."

Mr. Dominic patted the creature's forearm fondly then faced the campers. "Remember our motto. Excelsior. Ever higher." Pointing at the poster high above his head, he peered at the kids, eyebrows raised as if he expected a reaction. "Get it?"

After a moment, Monica said, "Oh, that's an awful joke."

Sara giggled, and Levi groaned. Most of the kids stared at the giant in obvious confusion.

"A little Latin humor?" Mr. Dominic gave another hopeful poke skyward. "Excelsior? It means 'ever higher,' remember? Like him . . . high?" He waited. "No?"

His wife flashed him an indulgent smile and shook her head.

The director heaved a sigh. "Ah, well, as I was saying . . . Seek to do ever higher, strive always to do better than you think you possibly can." He beamed at the campers. "Follow these simple rules, and I'm certain you'll have an outstanding summer."

Moments before room check that night, Levi stood in the open kitchen doorway. "Hello?" He knocked on the doorframe and stepped into the vast room, still steamy from supper. "Anybody here? Mr. Forest? Mrs. Forest?"

No one answered. Levi grunted. It figured the place was deserted. Steve should've come down for clean sheets himself, since he was the one who'd slopped water all over Levi's bed.

Now what? He scanned the room. The industrial-size stove, stainless steel refrigerator, and massive central island didn't really fit with the soot-gray stone walls, lit torches, and huge fireplace, but he couldn't imagine caring for a castle full of people without the generators, hot water heaters, and other conveniences Mr. Dominic had added for the camp. But the modern kitchen didn't help him with his mission: finding clean sheets.

He turned toward the adjoining laundry room. Bangs and rattling sounds halted him. He whipped around. Nobody was there. Nothing was out of place. Not a single pot had shifted, despite the precarious way they were stacked on shelves along the back wall.

The pounding resumed, more ferocious than before. There—a door hidden in a dark alcove at the farthest corner of the kitchen. Was it a pantry? Or a closet maybe? Had Mr. Forest locked himself inside?

Wait. What if this was the cellar Mr. Dominic warned them to stay out of? Even if it was, Levi had no intention of going *into* the cellar, just of letting poor Mr. Forest *out*. Who could blame him for that?

As he touched the knob, it twisted violently. The door shook so hard he thought it might burst. Heart hammering, he fell back against the wall. The pounding ceased.

Levi forced a chuckle that sounded hollow in the sudden silence. "Calm down, already. I'm gonna let you out." He grasped the handle.

A shriek from behind him stilled his hand and almost stopped his heart. "Get away from that door, you foolish boy!"

Chapter 4

Caught in the Act

Levi wheeled around. Mrs. Forest, the kitchen boss's pixie wife, stood behind him, her eyes even bigger than normal behind her thick glasses. A tray of dirty dishes rattled in her hands.

Afraid she would drop it, Levi took the tray and set it on the island. "What's the matter, Mrs. Forest?"

The door clattered again.

Mrs. Forest's tiny hand fluttered to her throat, but she stepped between him and the offending door. "Do not open that for any reason. Ever."

He glanced from side to side. Had Trevor put her up to this? He was way too into practical jokes these days. "I . . . I just thought you or your husband might've gotten closed in down there . . . accidentally."

"Well, we didn't." Two bright red patches appeared on her cheeks. "And even if we did, you have no business opening it. You know the rules. Don't go in the cellar, period."

"I wasn't going in." What was this, the third degree? He was just trying to help. "Besides, I didn't even know for sure it was the cellar."

Her eyes narrowed. "Likely story. There's always one that thinks they should flout the rules. Always one who thinks it's funny to disobey."

He opened his mouth to defend himself, but the furious pounding kicked up again, and Mrs. Forest leapt away from the door.

Levi's scalp tingled. "What's going on down there?"

"Come." She grasped his earlobe, yanked him across the kitchen, and tugged him into the hallway.

"Hey, that hurts."

But she kept her pincer hold on his ear, making him walk bent double to keep her from ripping it off. She led him down the hall and up one of the twin spiral staircases on the castle's north side.

"Where're we going?"

For answer, she gave his earlobe another sharp twist.

Okay, no more questions.

In several long, painful moments, they approached the Dominics' second floor study. She released him and rapped hard on the door.

Mrs. Dominic opened it. Her welcoming smile fled at the scowl on Mrs. Forest's face. "Ylana? Levi? What's the matter?"

"Might I speak to your husband, please, ma'am?" Mrs. Forest's words were clipped yet respectful.

"Certainly." Mrs. Dominic ushered them in and offered seats in front of the director's desk.

Mr. Dominic looked up from a large book with crinkled yellow pages. "Hello. Something I can help you with?" His eyes searched the little woman's face then Levi's. The twinkle in them told Levi the director pitied him for getting on the pixie's bad side.

"Caught him trying to open the cellar door, I did." Mrs. Forest glared at Levi as if he'd tried to steal one of her secret recipes.

Levi rubbed his sore ear. "I thought she'd locked herself down there. Or maybe Mr. Forest."

The director's gaze flicked from Levi to Mrs. Forest to Mrs. Dominic and back, the line between his brows deepening. "Why would you think that?"

"Because somebody's pounding on the door like the devil's after him."

Mr. Dominic stood so abruptly his chair banged into the wall and knocked the map of Terracaelum off kilter. "Pounding?" He raised an eyebrow at Mrs. Forest.

She nodded, her doll-size hands knotted in her apron.

"Did he get it open?"

Mrs. Forest shook her head. "I caught him in time." Color filled her cheeks. "Tried to argue with me though, the little upstart."

Little? Who was she to call him little? "Excuse me, will someone please explain to me why no one cares about the person locked in the cellar?"

Mr. Dominic ignored him, instead addressing his wife. "It's been a long time."

"Why now?" Her voice was the merest whisper. "First the trouble in the mountains and now this. You don't think . . ."

"Probably the storm down below earlier in the week—" Mrs. Forest began.

Mr. Dominic cocked his chin toward Levi then gave his head an almost imperceptible shake. He turned to Levi and said in a stern voice, "You must never open the cellar door, is that understood?"

Levi met his eyes, unblinking. No. It was not understood. Some poor person was trapped in a place that apparently terrified full-grown adults. Didn't Mr. Dominic care?

Mrs. Dominic laid a hand on her husband's arm. "Tobias, he doesn't understand. How can he?"

The director sighed, his expression gentler than before. "I'm sorry, son. Be assured that none of the campers or staff is down there."

Some of the tension left Levi's shoulders.

Mr. Dominic circled the desk, stood before him, and bent to meet his eyes. "I can't give you more information, but please, trust me and do as I say. Stay away from the cellar. It's a dangerous place."

His clenched jaw relaxed a little. He gave a single nod.

"Thank you." The director strode toward the door, patting Levi on the shoulder as he passed. "Now, I have a cellar to deal with."

Levi wanted to call after him, to demand that he tell him what was so dangerous, but he could only watch the man's retreating back.

Levi walked into his room and stared at the short set of steps beside his four-poster bed, so lost in wondering about the cellar he didn't even realize where he was. The confusion he thought he'd left behind when he'd entered Terracaelum came crowding back into his mind.

"Wouldn't they give you more sheets?"

He looked up. Steve waited beside Levi's bed, holding a bundle of dirty linens.

"Aargh." He stomped up the steps and plopped down on his bare mattress. "I forgot all about the stupid sheets."

Trevor glanced up from the card game he and Albert were playing. "How'd you manage that?"

"You'd forget too if some monster in the cellar freaked everybody out and you got in trouble for it."

Tommy's head popped out from behind his open wardrobe door. "Huh?"

"What monster?" Steve released the wad of wet sheets.

Trevor frowned. "What're you talking about?"

Levi fixed his attention on the only silent person in the room— Albert. At the mention of monsters in the cellar, the pixie had dropped his cards and now sat staring at his own bony bare feet.

"You know what's going on, don't you, Albert?"

The pixie's cheeks reddened, but he said nothing.

Levi hopped down from his bed and approached Trevor's, his focus on Albert's pimply face. "Out with it."

He shook his head, lips clamped shut.

"Come on," Levi wheedled. "You can tell us."

"Can't," Albert said from between clenched teeth. "Not supposed to tell."

"Why not?"

Albert shook his head hard, his face blood red and his eyes popping. Just when Levi thought he was going to spill the facts, the little man shot from the bed like he had a dragon after him. He shoved Levi aside, knocked Steve on his rump, and tore from the room without so much as an apology.

As soon as the door slammed shut behind Albert, Trevor rounded on Levi. "What in the world was that all about?"

"I don't know." Levi looked down at Steve flailing around in the pile of soggy linens. "But I'm gonna find out."

Chapter 5

In Plain Sight

The next day in Logic class, Mr. Dominic wouldn't meet his eyes. At least that's how it felt to Levi. After a brief review of the logical fallacies they'd studied in-depth the summer before, the director told them to break into groups of four. Levi, Trevor, Sara, and Monica pulled their desks together, leaving Tommy, Steve, and Lizzie with Gabrielle, a snotty ballerina-type who pranced around on tiptoes all the time.

Tommy rolled his eyes at Levi as she prattled on about her performance in *Swan Lake* that spring. Levi offered an apologetic shrug. Too bad Ashley hadn't come back. If there was one thing she never did, it was prattle.

Mr. Dominic gave Levi a sheet of paper. "Each group has been assigned a case study. Work together to figure out how more careful reasoning could've helped the person or persons involved to achieve a better outcome. Then appoint a spokesperson to report to the class." He pulled out a pocket watch and glanced at it. "You have ten minutes, starting now." He snapped the watch shut.

Levi peered from his group to the paper in front of him.

Monica rapped a knuckle on her desk. "Read."

"Okay, so it says, 'The giant Skrymir challenged Thor to perform several feats. Though a god, Thor could not finish the drink given him, lift a cat, or win a wrestling match against an old woman. Because of his failure, Thor thought he was a weakling. Skrymir then revealed that all had been an illusion. Thor had actually attempted to drink the ocean, to lift the world serpent, and to defeat old age.'"

Frowning, Levi looked up from the paper. The others stared blankly back at him.

"I thought these were case studies." Trevor jerked his chin toward Tommy's group, where Lizzie was reading something that sounded much more normal, something about a guy buying a house.

Levi shrugged. "That's what it says."

Monica glanced at her watch. "We have precisely eight minutes."

"Well," Sara said slowly, "it's a story from Norse mythology. The gist is that the giant king tricked Thor into thinking he was less powerful than he was—through these different illusions."

"Right. I got that much." Trevor twirled his hand in a get-on-with-it gesture.

"So this god was tricked?" Levi scrunched his face. "If he was a god, shouldn't he have seen what was going on?"

"Definitely," Monica said, "but only the one true God is omniscient. Pagan deities are not. Thor couldn't discern the truth until the giant revealed it to him. He was easy to delude, but—" Her tone grew tight with impatience. "—that's not the point of the story."

"Wait, maybe it is." Trevor scratched his head. "Sometimes things that seem true aren't really true at all? Is that what we're supposed to get?"

Sara's brow furrowed. "I think it goes beyond that. Look at it from Skrymir's perspective. If you want to hide something, put it in plain view."

Levi scratched his head. "Yeah, and then you let the other guy fill in the explanation for himself. In this case, Thor decided he was weak."

"Two minutes," Mr. Dominic called.

"I think we've got it." Trevor leaned back in his seat. "I vote Monica be our spokesperson."

She held up her index finger. "Just a moment. That wasn't the assignment. We're supposed to decide how better logic would have helped Thor in this situation."

"Isn't it obvious?" Trevor rolled his eyes. "If Thor hadn't made assumptions, he'd have seen the truth. All he had to do was use his brain for a few seconds, and he'd have figured out Skrymir was up to something devious. I mean, he's *Thor*. Wrestling and drinking and stuff would've been cake in any other situation. He should've known there was a trick."

Monica frowned thoughtfully for a few seconds. Finally, she nodded and began jotting notes on the back of the paper.

While they waited for the other groups to finish, Levi whispered to Sara, "What was the deal with the play yesterday? Did you ask your dad?"

She shook her head. "I didn't get a chance."

"Is somebody else acting as your go-between this summer? Since Miss Nydia's, you know . . ."

Again Sara shook her head, this time with misty eyes. "They decided it wasn't worth the risk. I'll just sneak into their room whenever I get the chance. It's safer that way."

Levi nodded. It had to be hard on Sara not getting to talk to her parents any time she wanted. To have to pretend all the time. "I was surprised you told your dad about Brock and Braden and their little trick on the drawbridge."

Her cheeks reddened. "I had to, didn't I? They couldn't get away with throwing that poor girl into the moat. Not to mention Steve."

Monica looked up from her notes. "Sara, why did they parade all those creatures before the entire camp? It doesn't seem necessary at all."

"You'd think they wanted everybody to know," Trevor said, twisting his pen between his fingers.

"It's like they want to attract every power-crazed maniac on the planet." Levi dropped his voice to a whisper. "I mean, dragons? Minotaurs? And what was that hooded thing? If all that got out . . ." He shook his head. "Talk about a media circus."

"There has to be a good reason. They wouldn't endanger their citizens." Sara looked down at her hands. "Or me."

Levi wanted to bite his tongue off. Of course Sara's parents wouldn't expose Terracaelum. They were good rulers, right? And they sure wouldn't set her up to get snatched. Because if Deceptor got hold of her again . . . He shuddered at the thought. He really had to stop criticizing Sara's dad. Which meant now wasn't the time to ask her what she knew about the cellar and why her dad would leave somebody trapped down there.

"Time's up," Mr. Dominic called. He looked at Levi's group. "Ready?"

Monica stood and assumed her teacher demeanor. She reported how Skrymir tricked Thor into believing what he wanted him to believe by making him see things as he wanted him to see them. "Sometimes," she concluded, "the best way to hide something is to put it in plain sight and let the person you want to deceive explain it to fit his or her worldview. A logical mind pays attention to such tricks so as to see past them to the truth."

At her words, Levi's jaw dropped. All of a sudden, he got it. Masks. Animatronics. Hollywood tricks. The campers didn't call CNN after yesterday's theatrics because they'd explained away all the weird creatures they'd seen to fit what they believed was possible. And now, since they'd made "trick" dragons and harpies fit their idea of Camp Classic, they wouldn't be bothered in the least if unusual creatures showed up around them.

Levi's astonished gaze slid to Mr. Dominic, who leaned against his desk watching Levi. The two exchanged knowing smiles.

Okay, so the director was pretty smart. But that still didn't explain the cellar.

The next morning during History, Levi's mind kept wandering to the person trapped beneath the castle. His roommates had grown tired of discussing whoever was pounding on the door, but he couldn't let it go. Why wouldn't Mr. Dominic rescue the poor guy? It didn't make sense.

Wait, what if he did? What if that's what Mr. Dominic meant when he said he had "a cellar to deal with"? That he needed to go help whoever was stuck down there?

Levi straightened in his seat. There was only one way to find out.

He'd slip down to the kitchen after class. If nobody was knocking, he'd know Mr. Dominic had handled the problem the right way.

Satisfied with his plan, he tuned in to Mrs. Dominic's lecture. "We'll be learning about the Norse people this summer, including Erik the Red, Leif Erickson, and even some lesser-knowns like Awilda the Pirate Princess."

A pirate princess? His sister would love learning about her.

"You'll study the Norse myths in Literature class, and we'll discuss how the Norse people's beliefs affected their culture and history. Oh, and Mr. Austin has a treat for you in Literature class this year." Her gaze suddenly landed on Levi. "But I'll let him tell you about that when he's ready."

He squirmed in his seat. Why did he suddenly feel uncomfortable? Like maybe he wasn't going to enjoy Mr. Austin's treat so much.

Levi and Sara walked down the hall together after lunch, speculating about the summer play.

"Don't you know?" He kept his voice to a whisper. "Since you live here year-round and all?"

She shook her head. "The staff kept it a secret so I'd be surprised along with everybody else."

"Hey, Levi," someone called.

He turned to see Morgan coming out of the dining room, Hunter at her side. What was she doing with that creep?

"Uh, hi." Levi shot her a brief smile and kept walking.

"You need to stay away from that jerk." Hunter's not-so-quiet words almost made Levi whirl around and say something ferocious.

Instead, he angled his head toward Sara and glanced back at Hunter and Morgan, using only his peripheral vision.

Hunter had his head close to Morgan's, his voice a low growl. "You know what I told you from the diary—"

"Yo, Hunter." Braden, the fox-faced twin, bumped fists with Hunter. "Hey, man, how's it going?"

Brock rushed up beside his brother and attempted a fist bump too, but he missed and smashed his knuckles into the stone wall. He let out a howl and started sucking on his bleeding knuckles. Morgan gasped in sympathy while Hunter gave his head a derisive shake.

Cheeks flushed, Braden snagged his twin's arm and dragged him away down the hall, his exasperated "How dumb can you get, Brick?" trailing behind.

Morgan frowned. "He shouldn't call his brother that."

"Why not?" Hunter shrugged. "Everybody does. Brick's so dense his own parents gave him that nickname."

Sara squeezed Levi's arm. "That's awful. The poor guy."

Levi nodded, though he didn't feel too sympathetic for the kid, not after his trick on the drawbridge yesterday. "Come on, let's go."

He and Sara continued to the great hall, not speaking again until they settled into deep chairs in a corner. Levi was preoccupied with thoughts of Hunter and Morgan. Why was she hanging around him? And what had he been about to tell her when the twins interrupted? It almost sounded like Hunter said *diary*, and the only diary Levi could think of was the purple one he'd found beneath Hunter's mattress the year before—the one belonging to a girl from the 1880s. But why would the bully be talking to Morgan about the journal of a girl who lived more than a hundred years ago?

Then again, maybe Hunter hadn't said *diary* at all. Maybe he'd said *diarrhea*, as in he and his creep friends put something in some poor sap's meatloaf so they'd get sick.

"Hunter's sure mean enough to do that," he mumbled to himself.

Sara frowned, obviously having heard him. "Hunter's not so bad, not always anyway."

He snorted. "How do you figure?"

"I mean, this summer he's been okay." Her face pinked. "The other day he helped me with some precalculus problems I didn't understand."

Levi glared across the room to where some kids played foosball. Sara had no business studying with Hunter. Maybe Levi had been wrong last summer when he'd believed Hunter was Deceptor. But he definitely wasn't wrong that Hunter was a bully and a jerk.

"Morgan seems to like you," Sara said softly.

Levi's ears heated. Morgan was too much like his little sister, following him around and pestering him for attention. "She's just being friendly." He shifted his gaze to Trevor and Monica's Ping-Pong game. "Probably homesick."

"Uh-huh."

He watched Trevor's next serve, which shot across the table. Monica whacked it back, and Trevor missed the return. "What I'd like to know is why a nice kid like Morgan is hanging out with a—" He stopped when Sara cleared her throat. "With, er, someone like Hunter."

"Jealous?"

"What are you *talking* about?" He made a how-weird-can-you-get face.

"Oh, never mind." She hopped up and rushed from the room.

Levi sighed. *Girls.* Why couldn't they just make sense?

Chapter 6

The Truth About the Cellar

The next night, Levi emerged from the bathroom into the middle of a battlefield. He could only duck as balled socks, wadded t-shirts, and bare pillows flew past. At a lull in the assault, he peeked from beneath the arms he'd thrown over his head. A pair of plaid boxer shorts smacked him in the face.

From various places around the room, Albert and his roommates stood frozen, red-faced and sweaty, waiting for his reaction. He could read the question in their faces: would he throw a fit like last year?

He forced down his eyebrows and tightened his lips as he gathered the pillows and articles of clothing. Then, before the others could react, he yelled, "Attack!" and fired ammunition into their stunned faces.

A half-hour later, he flopped in a giggling, sweat-soaked heap on his bed. Why had he gotten so mad at the others for horsing around like this last year? It was a blast.

But when Mr. Sylvester peered in the door for room check, Levi sat up in a hurry, glancing around the trashed room. The elf and his wife had treated the campers so differently this summer, with Mrs. Sylvester barely seeming to notice anything and Mr. Sylvester acting super-strict. After his recent run-in with Mrs. Forest, he sure didn't need another staff member mad at him.

Thankfully, Mr. Sylvester didn't snag earlobes or scream. He simply said, "Clean it up," and closed the door behind him.

Shoulders sagging in relief, Levi stood and scooped up the piles of underwear he hoped hadn't come from somebody's dirty clothes bag.

The next morning before Steve and Tommy were dressed, Levi and Trevor left the room, more than ready for breakfast. Trevor ran a hand over the suit of armor that stood guard outside their door, his expression wistful. "One day soon I'm gonna be tall enough to fit in that thing."

Levi laughed and shook his head. Still, Trevor was right. Give him another inch or two, and he'd fill out the armor perfectly. It'd be another decade before Levi could wear it . . . if ever.

"Maybe I'll try it on now." Trevor reached up with both hands and grasped the helmet.

"You're gonna get in trouble."

"Maybe, but it—"

The door three down from theirs opened with a squeak. Both boys whirled around as Mrs. Sylvester entered the corridor from her room.

With a noisy gulp, Trevor tucked both hands behind his back, but the hall chaperone didn't even glance their way. For a moment, she stared blankly through one of the floor-to-ceiling windows. Then she released a shuddering breath and turned toward them. As they caught her eye, she startled and her grayish face paled.

She didn't speak right away, but when she did, her voice trembled. "Breakfast time, boys." She headed for the stairs without another glance.

"Whew." Trevor swiped at his brow. "She about caught me."

"You were only touching it. How was she supposed to know you wanted to put it on?"

His roommate's cheeks glowed pink in the early sunlight. "Oh, yeah, right." He glanced up and down the corridor, reached out a tentative hand, and eased up the visor.

Levi gave his forearm a light slap. "Come on. Let's go eat."

Trevor dropped the visor with a clank.

"Oh, no, you don't." Levi cornered Albert after lunch. The pixie's eyes darted around the empty dorm room. He tried to make a break for the door, but Levi moved into his path. "I want to know about the cellar."

Albert shook his head.

"Come on. I already know about Terracaelum and Deceptor." He'd even fought the shape-shifting demon sorcerer the summer before, which was more than Albert could say. "It's not like you have to keep a secret from somebody who already knows most everything anyway."

Albert rolled his eyes. "Yeah, right, still full of yourself. You don't know near all of Terracaelum's secrets." His voice dropped. "I don't neither, for that matter."

Levi crossed his arms over his chest and waited.

The pixie perched on Steve's bed and let out a nasal sigh. "Fine. Guess it won't hurt nothin' to tell you about the cellar." He gave Levi a stern look. "So's you'll learn to leave it alone. Don't think I haven't seen you skulkin' around near the kitchen."

Though Levi opened his mouth to protest, he quickly snapped it shut again. He'd made lots of extra trips past the kitchen over the last two days, watching for a time when none of the workers were around so he could check out the cellar door again. But somebody was always there. He'd begun to suspect Mr. Dominic of posting guards. "Okay, you're right, but I'm just trying to understand what's going on."

Albert's mouth tightened like he'd been sucking limes. "What you heard the other night was most likely a sailor from down under."

"A sailor?" Levi jiggled a finger in his ear as he sank onto the steps beside Tommy's bed. "From Australia?"

"Australia?" Albert's face puckered. "What're you talkin' about?"

"What are *you* talking about? You said it was a sailor from Down Under. That's Australia."

"I don't know no Australia. Down under is—" He shook his head and pointed downward. "—*down under*. On the lake."

In a flash, Levi remembered Mr. Austin's explanation of Terracaelum as a sort of island that hovered over Lake Superior, the lake *down under* Terracaelum. "Oh. You mean a sailor from Lake Superior?"

Albert nodded as if he'd just made the most obvious statement in the world.

Levi scowled. As if anything about Terracaelum was obvious. Then the meaning of his own words sank in. "Wait, a sailor from Lake Superior is trapped in the castle cellar? Here in Terracaelum? How'd he get in there?" He leapt to his feet. "And why won't Mr. Dominic let him out?" Was the camp director so cruel he'd let a poor man wander in the darkness beneath the castle until something ate him or he starved to death?

"Whoa." The pixie held up a hand. "Sit. Let me explain."

Levi hesitated, trying to decide whether he should sit and listen or run down and open the cellar door—whether Mr. Dominic liked it or not. Albert's pleading eyes finally won out, and he sat, possibly because the pixie's expression reminded him of his dog begging to play ball. "All right, I'm listening."

Albert settled back on Steve's bed cross-legged, heedless of the dirt chunks his boots left on the red comforter. "Where do I start?" He tapped his chin with a stubby forefinger. "Sometimes when there's a storm on the lake down under," he said with a downward point, "the worlds sort of mash into each other, so's boats and sometimes them flying machines from your world end up in ours. See?"

Levi massaged his temples. "No, I don't see."

"Hmm." Albert squeezed his eyes shut as if such deep thought pained him. "You know what storms on the lake are like." He opened his eyes. "Wind's wild. Waves real high."

"Yeah, I know."

"So when a boat's out in a big whopper, the wind whips it around and the waves take it up real high then drop it real low in the troughs." He zoomed his hand up and down like Levi's little brothers Jer and Zeke playing airplanes. "Sometimes, when the weather's particular rough, a boat rides a wave up . . ." He raised his hand. "And it never goes back down."

Levi's mouth fell open. "You mean . . . ?" Last summer, Mr. Austin had told him about his Uncle Filbert, who'd fallen through the moat into Lake Superior during a storm on the lakes. Was Albert trying to tell him the same thing could happen in reverse?

The little man nodded, his hand still in the air. "Breaks through to Terracaelum in the tunnels under the mountains or maybe into the river. Sometimes into the cellar here. I'm not real clear on how it all works. Mrs. Austin's the expert on all that."

"Bizarre."

Albert picked at a hangnail. "Just the way o' things here."

"That may be, but you can't go leaving that poor person down there." His voice rose a couple of notches. "I'm going to let him out." He stood and took a step toward the door, half-expecting Albert to try and stop him again.

But he just gnawed at the nail, his expression serene. "You don't wanna do that."

The blood rushed to Levi's head. "Why not? That's just cruel."

"Nope, it's smart. See, you can't know it's a sailor down there. Could be one of them Dvergar."

"Them what?"

The pixie released a sigh so windy his nose whistled. "The dark dwarves."

Levi frowned. "You mean like Dr. Baldwin or the Austins?"

Albert snorted. "These guys ain't nothing like them."

"So they're a different color or something? What's the big deal about that?" His parents had taught him that prejudice was nothing but sinful. Mr. Dominic couldn't possibly hate these Dvergar creatures just because their skin was dark.

"This ain't got nothin' to do with their coloring." Fear hovered like fog behind Albert's gray-green eyes. "It's about their innards."

"Huh?" Their guts? *Gross.*

"They're black-hearted." Albert clutched the shirt over his own small chest. "Evil through and through."

Chapter 7

A Bride Named Thor

"You're so good at this," Morgan told Levi a few days later in archery class, right after he shot an arrow into the white outer rim of his target. As soon as they'd arrived at the archery mound, she'd darted into the spot next to his—the one he'd been saving for Sara—and had been talking to him non-stop since the lesson began, earning him more than one dirty look from the instructor, Mr. Sylvester. Levi wished the staff had separated the younger kids out for archery and the other activities, like they had for the academic subjects.

But they hadn't, and for the last several minutes, instead of shooting arrows toward her own target, Morgan had done nothing but toss compliments his way while he tried to focus. He smiled and said thanks, but it was getting old. Distracting, too, because he wasn't great, despite the fact that this was the third week of camp already. But then he'd had no chance to practice during the school year. When he'd asked about getting a bow and arrow, his mom had looked horrified. Instead, she'd gotten him a plastic bow and rubber-tipped arrows, which all broke within days.

And the fencing lessons he'd begged his dad for . . . there was no way they could afford them on a pastor's salary, especially with four kids to feed. Even with Levi shoveling snow and doing odd jobs for people from church, the cost was way too high. Worse, it was clear Hunter hadn't had to practice against a nine-year-old with a plastic sword. During fencing lessons the day before, he'd beaten Levi in five seconds flat. That was after Levi dropped the sword and nearly chopped off his own foot, despite the lightweight protective sheath intended to make it impossible for the kids to hurt themselves. Or each other—unless, of course, they managed to dislodge the sheath during the fight as Hunter had done against Levi in the Camp Classic Olympics the year before.

"You're a natural archer." Morgan's words almost made Levi laugh out loud as his arrow soared well above the mound and into the trees beyond. He hoped none of Albert's brothers were doing any groundskeeping back there. Nobody yelped or screamed in agony, which was a good sign.

He turned a frown on Morgan. "Are you messing with me?"

A blush darkened her cheeks. "Of course not."

"Why do you keep saying I'm so good at stuff when I'm not even half-way decent?" He didn't want to sound rude, but enough was enough. He enjoyed compliments like the next guy, but only the ones he deserved.

"I'm just trying to be nice. I want to be your friend." She ground a dandelion beneath the toe of her shoe. "It's hard to find friends here."

Levi bit his lip. He'd noticed Morgan off by herself most of the time. Except when she was following him around. "Listen, you don't have to compliment me all the time. I'll be your friend without all that." He hoped he didn't regret the offer.

"Really?" Her pale blue eyes lit up like marbles in sunshine.

He gave her a crooked smile. "Really."

Literature class the next morning brought answers to two of Levi's questions: what the summer play would be and why he wouldn't like Mr. Austin's "treat." The moment he stepped into class, the short, stumpy dwarf fixed his beady eyes on him. A grim smile twisted his lips. "Here's my star," he said in a way that made Levi's blood run cold.

He sank into his seat. *Star*? Why did that sound so horrifying?

Once everyone was seated, Mr. Austin began his lecture. "This summer, we'll study the Norse myths. Since last summer's play was such a success . . ." The dwarf paused in apparent expectation. A few people clapped.

Levi smacked his palms together a few times, though he wasn't so sure he'd call *The Trojan Horse* a success. There wasn't anything wrong with the play itself, but considering that Nydia Sylvester had used the horse prop to smuggle Sara to Deceptor and that the elf herself ended up dying in a fight that still gave Levi nightmares . . . well, he'd pretty much decided he wouldn't help build props for this summer's play, no matter how cool they were.

Oblivious to the weak reaction, Mr. Austin gave a grandiose nod. "This year's play is based on a favorite figure from Norse mythology and is comedic rather than tragic. It's built around Thor, the god of thunder. In our story, the giant king, Thrymr, steals Mjolnir, Thor's famed hammer, and buries it eight leagues under the earth in an effort to compel the beautiful goddess Freyja to marry him. Instead, the mighty Thor arrays himself in bridal finery and tricks the giant into thinking he's Freyja. When Thrymr returns Mjolnir in exchange for his 'bride,' Thor reveals himself and slays all of the giants."

The teacher rocked back on his heels as if pleased with himself. "We'll have tryouts for all but one of the parts. Since Thor is known for his flame-red hair, our star actor is already set." The teacher's eyes pinned Levi to his desk.

Heat flooded up Levi's neck, across his face, and into his flame-red curls. "Me?" His voice came out a squeak reminiscent of Trevor's the summer before.

Mr. Austin's triumphant smile soured slightly. "Of course. Who else?"

A loud snort erupted from the back of the classroom where Hunter sat with Martin. Tittering and giggles sounded all around Levi.

"But . . ." He glanced wildly around the room. Surely there was someone else with red hair. "But . . ." He didn't see anybody. "I can't . . . because . . . um, I can't act." He gave the teacher a look of desperation. "Maybe you could use a wig?"

Mr. Austin scowled at him. "You're Thor, boy. Get used to it."

He sank back against his chair. "What's the play?"

"I've titled it *A Bride Named Thor.*"

A low groan escaped Levi's numb lips. He was doomed.

Levi walked around in a stupor the rest of the day, shoulders slumped, head hung low. He did his best to ignore both his friends' congratulations on winning the part (as if he'd wanted it) and Hunter's jeers about how his scrawny legs would look in a dress (so much for a stress-free summer). He had to think of some way to get out of the stupid play.

He considered coloring his hair, but he didn't have a way to get the dye. He could shave his head, but he didn't have a razor and it would just grow back anyway. Maybe if he just flat-out refused, didn't learn his lines or something. Or what if he threw himself down the spiral staircase and broke a leg? Then he certainly couldn't be made to play Thor running around in some ridiculous wedding dress.

He heaved a massive sigh. No way he'd do any of that. He'd just have to pray he survived the embarrassment. At least there was one good thing in this whole mess—Deceptor couldn't use this play as a way to kidnap Sara. No horses to hide her in this time.

He smiled grimly at the thought as he walked past the open kitchen door. And stopped cold. For the first time all week, the room was devoid of workers. He shot a quick glance up and down the empty hallway. Since it was mid-afternoon, all the kids must've gone outside to enjoy the sunshine, and the staff must not have been ready to start supper preparations yet.

Levi slipped into the kitchen and peered around. When he didn't see anyone hidden behind the cabinets, he slunk over to the cellar door. He pressed his ear to the old wood, careful not to wiggle around and get a splinter in his cheek.

Although he listened for a long time, he heard nothing. Whoever had banged so loudly before must have been gone. Or maybe they didn't have the energy to pound anymore. The thought made his heart twinge. What if a sailor really was trapped down there, lying on the stone steps beyond the thin panel? Just beyond the bright kitchen that smelled of cherry pie, breathing in his last puffs of moldy air, starving and desperate for some hint of help, of humanity?

Levi clenched his jaw. He couldn't leave the poor guy to die. No rule was worth that. His fingers trembled as they inched toward the knob. Dare he defy Mr. Dominic? *Yes.* Somebody had to behave like a decent human being around here. He'd open the door, whether Mr. Dominic liked it or not.

Wrenching the handle hard to the right, Levi yanked. The door popped open. At the same moment, a strong breeze from behind slammed it shut. Blinking in confusion, he peered around the now-still kitchen. Where had the wind come from?

The windows along the back wall were shut. Only the door to the hallway stood open. Maybe it was some sort of backdraft from the cellar? *Strange.* With a shrug, he pulled the door open once more. This time he wedged his hip against it to make sure it didn't slam.

Before him, a yawning cavern of blackness devoured the light. Stale air seeped into the kitchen, souring the sweetness. He covered his nose with his sleeve and crept forward a few millimeters. As he peered down into the darkness, his entire body quaked with the cold damp slithering around his ankles. And something more sinister he couldn't identify.

"Hello?" His voice came out the tiniest whisper. He needed to speak up. If the sailor was unconscious, he wouldn't be able to hear his pitiful mewling.

"Hello?" Levi moved into the darkness, edging one foot in front of the other, trying to find the first step down. Why was the blackness so complete? Why didn't the sunlight streaming through the kitchen windows penetrate it?

"Is anybody down there?" His voice came out louder this time, but it echoed indistinctly as though slogging through a vast, soggy cave.

When no answer came, Levi knew he had to make a decision: slam the door and run, or go down those steps.

He inched forward, eyes straining, feeling with his feet for the step while half-expecting to find the body of some pathetic sailor. Would it be warm and alive? Or cold and stiff, like Miss Nydia's?

The stone floor ended beneath the toe of his right shoe. Before he could stoop down and check the steps, something caught his ankle and yanked. Though Levi opened his mouth to scream, no sound came.

A slamming sound echoed in his ears.

Utter darkness pressed against his wide-open eyes.

His body dropped, weightless but for the heavy clamp on his right ankle.

Chapter 8

In the Cellar

Levi landed on his feet. His knees buckled and he sat down hard. The darkness was so complete he couldn't make out any light from beneath the kitchen door. He squeezed his eyes shut tight until stars appeared behind his lids. He rubbed his aching knees. How far had he dropped? Why hadn't he hit the cellar steps as he fell? And—his eyes flew open at the thought—where was the thing that yanked him into this black pit?

Levi peered around blindly. The blackness seemed somehow darker after the shooting stars behind his lids. Panic gripped his throat. His breathing grew raspy and shallow. Little blue lights popped in his peripheral vision. He was suffocating under the weight of the moist darkness.

Why had he disobeyed Mr. Dominic's rule? Why had he ignored the wind that slammed the door in his face? After last summer, he should've known better than to ignore the warning.

Levi forced himself to breathe out, willed his wildly pounding heart to steady. He rubbed his sore knees in rhythmic circles until the little lights stopped popping and the sound of his breathing evened in his ears. The dankness pressed in until his skin grew cold and clammy, slowly raising goose bumps.

As his heartbeat settled into a more normal rhythm, he forced himself to think. How was he going to get out of here? He couldn't see a thing, so he'd have to depend on his other senses to find an exit.

He sniffed the air. The stench of rancid water filled his nostrils, and his stomach churned. He gagged then made himself swallow back the hot bile. Throat burning, Levi scrabbled with his hands across the floor. Cold stone, gritty and damp, scratched the pads of his fingers. He reached farther and scraped his knuckles against a jagged edge. He stuck his stinging knuckles in his mouth, and a metallic taste coated his tongue.

Blood.

His heart rate kicked into a higher gear. What else was down here with him? Would it smell his blood? His breathing shallowed, and he had to go through his calming routine once more.

After a moment, he heard something. A faint dripping then a light splash. A harsh, low rhythmic swooshing like the bellows being worked on the blacksmith's fire at Greenfield Village.

He hunched inward, listening, trying to understand what he was hearing.

Then he figured it out: breathing.

Not his own, but that of something nearby. Something not at all like a poor sailor from Lake Superior. More like that hooded monster from the staff play.

Trying not to breathe, he held his bleeding fingers in his mouth so that maybe, just maybe, the creature wouldn't smell his blood and come after him.

A loud shuffling sound forced a gasp from between his lips. Light blinded him.

Levi blinked furiously, shielding his eyes with his hands. When his vision finally adjusted, he wished it hadn't. A creature with a blazing torch stood barely two feet from him. Bare except for a loincloth, the creature—obviously masculine—was purest white, including long, sleek hair. His eyes were pinkish-white, except for the pupils, which were dilated to a pinpoint. Muscles bulged over his entire body.

Levi wanted to run, but he didn't dare look away from the creature studying him with those freaky albino eyes.

"Who are you?"

"Levi," he croaked out.

"Why have you come to my domain?"

"Your domain?" Despite his terror, a part of Levi's mind wondered if this thing had assumed the color of his surroundings, a natural camouflage against the pale sandstone walls of what clearly wasn't a normal cellar. It looked more like an underground cavern.

"Yes." He took a menacing step forward. "My domain."

Levi scooted backward on his rear. *No problem. Your domain.* A knife-sharp stone bit into his back—the bottom step? Would this creature let him escape? "I, um . . . I thought a sailor was down here and so I came to help him."

The massive head angled to one side. "A sailor? Those pasty creatures that wash up from down under?"

Pasty? Levi had never seen skin pastier than this guy's, but he didn't think it would be wise to say so.

"They come here every so often, and I take care of them." The creature dug a long nail between pointed fangs.

Levi wished there were a bathroom nearby because suddenly he really had to go. "What . . . what do you do with them?"

Grinning, he bared an entire mouth full of the sharp white teeth. "Same thing I'll do with you."

Chapter 9

Regin of the Dvergar

"Take you to my master."

Levi shrank into the stone step, feeling the skin shred from his back. "Your master?"

The creature lifted hands like big white spiders, giving Levi a view of the silver shackles on his wrists, so thin he hadn't seen them at first against the white skin. The bands looked tight—too tight to be slipped off. And strong.

"Deceptor is my master." The creature's shoulders slumped slightly.

"Deceptor?" *Oh, God, get me out of this!*

An irritable grunt, then, "Are you a parrot, boy?"

Levi blinked. "You know about parrots?"

"Of course. Do you think I've lived here always?" He shot a derisive glance around the dark, smelly chamber.

Levi half-shrugged.

"I have not." The pale eyes fixed on him again. "Now rise. We've a long way to go."

"But," Levi said as he slowly stood, "can't you just let me go back upstairs?" He darted a glance behind him, just long enough to glimpse jagged gray steps. After his obsession with getting back to Terracaelum and with finding out what was in the cellar, now all he wanted was to go home to his parents. "You could pretend you never saw me." He turned pleading eyes on the creature. "No need for Deceptor to know anything about it, and I'll never try to come back, I promise."

His captor seemed to waver for an instant, sending a shot of hope through Levi's heart.

"No." He paused. "No, I cannot. He would surely find out."

"Please?" Levi sent another glance back, but he couldn't see even a sliver of light in the hovering darkness, much less the outline of the kitchen door. How far had he fallen? And how had he managed not to break his neck?

A cold, brittle grip to his wrist drove all other thoughts from his mind. He whipped around to find the creature's pinpoint black pupils inches from his face. He gasped and inhaled putrid, icy breath.

"Come."

Levi had no choice but to obey, but his eyes searched the walls, dim in the flickering torchlight. He had to get out of this mess. But how?

Maybe if he could convince the creature to pity him, to see him as human. But what if *human* meant *supper*? Ugh. Still, he had to try. Deceptor sure wouldn't show any compassion. "What's your name?"

"Regin of the Dvergar."

The Dvergar? So this was one of the dark dwarves Albert had warned him about an eon ago, before he'd so foolishly opened the cellar door. Why was he called a dark dwarf when he was so very pale?

His heart. Albert had called the Dvergar black-hearted. Evil through and through.

Then there was no hope.

But he couldn't just give up. "My name's Levi Prince."

Regin lifted his smooth white eyebrows in a look that plainly said he didn't care.

"I'm just a kid, you know. I'm not a threat to your master." He chose not to think of the battle he'd fought with Deceptor the summer before. After all, he hadn't been the one to stab the shape-shifter.

Regin gave his wrist a sharp twist.

"Ouch!"

"Do not attempt persuading me to release you." A tortured look flashed across the dwarf's face. "I cannot do it."

Maybe he wasn't so black-hearted after all. "Why not?" Levi tried to rub his wrist and ended up stumbling on the slick rock floor.

Regin steadied him. "There is more at stake than myself alone."

Did that mean Regin had a family? Maybe kids? Levi opened his mouth to ask but shut it at the dwarf's glare, harsh and determined. Levi sighed. Regin would never release him as long as he thought Deceptor would harm those he cared about more than some scrawny redheaded kid idiotic enough to disobey the Prince of Terracaelum.

God, please. I'll never disobey again. Just show me a way out. I know I don't deserve help, but please . . .

He straggled along behind his captor in silence, the prayer chasing around his mind over and over. He had no weapons and no friends. He had no idea where they were going, and his strength was seeping away.

If God didn't rescue him, he'd be dead.

Because there was no way he could defeat Deceptor on his own.

No way at all.

After what felt like hours, Levi heard a trickling sound. He strained both ears and eyes, but it wasn't until later that the sound increased to a rushing. A stream? A river? Could it be an underground feed to the river that flowed east-west across Terracaelum?

His shoulders straightened. What if he somehow managed to dive into the water? Then he could swim with the current until it broke free of the caverns and . . . He shot a glance at Regin, trying to blank his features so the dwarf wouldn't notice his sudden excitement. If he could swim out, he knew he could find his way back to the castle. He'd be saved. *Thank You, God.*

"Come. The bridge is this way." Regin jerked his wrist toward the left.

The dwarf's grip hadn't loosened the entire time they'd walked, but maybe—

"Once we cross, you mustn't look into any side passages or tunnels. In fact, 'tis safest to keep your eyes tightly shut."

"Why?"

"Basilisks. They will not approach the bridge."

Levi stared at Regin, his jaw hanging wide. "You mean those monsters that kill you if you look at them?"

The dwarf's nod was matter-of-fact.

"How am I supposed to tell where I'm going?" Panic made his voice shrill.

"Trust me to guide you."

Yeah, right. He was definitely jumping into the water. Basilisks and Regin were too much to deal with. Especially with Deceptor to face . . . if he survived that long.

The torchlight illumined a stone bridge that crossed a fast-flowing current at least ten feet wide. The light striking the water threw glittering shafts upward into the shadows. Levi stepped onto the slippery arch. Regin marched him along, apparently not bothered by the waters racing away below. Thankfully, no rails lined the bridge. Levi eased toward the edge, keeping his motions casual.

When they were more than halfway across, his heart slammed into double-time at the sight of the yawning blackness that was their destination. If he didn't make his move now, he might never get free. Sucking in a deep breath, he threw all his weight to the right while jerking his arm upward as hard as he could. His wrist slipped free. Regin bellowed.

Without a backward glance, Levi used his momentum to propel himself over the side. He splashed into the icy water, and his breath left him in a whoosh.

He fought to the surface, fending off the shock waves the frigid river sent through his body. He slurped in a huge breath and blinked the water from his eyes. He caught a glimpse of Regin standing on the bridge with his arms folded over his chest and a look of near-satisfaction on his face. Then the current yanked Levi out of the circle of torchlight.

For a long time, he struggled to keep his head above water, unable to maneuver anywhere but where the current shoved him. Not that he wanted to swim to shore in the black cavernous depths. Or that he could even see the shore. Completely blind, he could only gasp the tiniest breaths and pray the river would carry him from the darkness.

Just as he began to tire in the ice-cold water, the darkness around him changed. Something jagged sliced into the top of his head, then he saw tiny pricks of light overhead. Several seconds later, his sluggish brain registered that he'd flowed out from underground, and the lights were stars. How many hours had he been underground? How many days? He no longer knew and barely cared. Fatigue crept through his mind like a slow-acting poison, drugging him so he forgot he needed to swim to shore. Soon he closed his eyes, needing a short rest.

Before his head went underwater, a gust of hot wind blew into his face, warming his frozen nose until it burned. His eyes burst open. Dark blots passed in a dizzying stream. Nausea gripped his belly. Was he carsick?

No. Those were trees, and he was the one whipping past, dragged by the racing water. He had to get to shore, had to find the strength to swim. He flailed his arms and legs, but nothing happened. Did he still have arms and legs? *Help, God!* Panic clouded his vision.

Fight, a voice murmured in his ear. *Battle the current.*

He forced his arms and legs to move, forced himself to try to get out of the rapid stream. Gradually, he moved toward the right-hand bank.

But the water grew rougher. Swirling bubbles popped and splashed in his face as the current sucked him along. His willpower waned, and exhaustion weighed him down.

Thunder filled his ears—louder than the rushing river. He glanced around, sputtering and spitting as the rough waves forced their way into his gaping mouth.

Down he went, into a chute of wild wetness, like a giant water slide. The meager contents of his stomach shot into his mouth but his teeth clenched too tightly to allow them escape.

His freefall propelled him underwater then outward on a tidal wave. The icy spray bulleted his face.

Suddenly his immediate surroundings calmed. He blinked at the water falling from the sky a dozen yards to his right, its noise still thunderous in his ears. Bobbing in the gentler swells away from the waterfall, he sucked in much-needed oxygen. Overhead a half-moon shone its sickly rays. To his left spread an endless expanse of light and shadow.

Glistening colors surrounded him for the merest instant. The northern lights?

Then came silence.

Had he gone deaf? No, he could hear the water gurgling and bubbling as his arms arced feebly beneath the surface.

The waterfall. It was gone. Vanished. And he was in the middle of nowhere, tired and frozen. He had to swim, but to where? His mind clouded again until he felt detached from himself, as if he were merely reading about the effects the freezing water had on someone else.

Slowly, his eyelids drooped. His feet and hands stopped moving. He began to sink beneath the black surface, knowing his lungs would fill with liquid, and he would drown. His family and friends would never find out what had happened to him. He'd never get the chance to make amends with his parents. All because of his stupidity.

A mild, foggy sadness filled him. *I'm sorry.*

Suddenly, with a sucking sound, water frothed into a whirlpool beside him. A large dark monster emerged from the deep. The fog left Levi's brain. His arms and legs flailed under the powerful stimulant of terror.

The thing rose until it towered a good ten feet above. It bent its massive horse-shaped head toward him. Brilliant green eyes and long teeth reflected the moonlight. Jaws wide, it swooped down on him, dribbling hot saliva on his upturned face.

His mouth opened in a silent scream.

Chapter 10

The Lake Monster

Levi woke to something rough chafing his cheek. Eyes closed, he took mental stock—pain, plenty of pain, told him he was still alive. *That creature* . . . His mind sharpened to full alert. Was he inside its belly? Couldn't be. The redness behind his swollen eyelids told him it was light, and he heard water splashing somewhere nearby. Opening his eyes to slits, he saw sand.

Where was he?

More importantly, where was the creature?

Keeping his movements slow, he lifted his head and peered around. He was lying on the beach, and the sun was either rising or setting, he couldn't tell which. He didn't much care. All that mattered was the monster had gone.

He eased into a sitting position, legs outstretched, too stiff and sore to bend. He worked his aching jaw, and sand crunched between his teeth. *Water.* He forced himself to stand, and when his swirling vision settled, staggered past a weathered pier until he came to a natural stairway. He stared at it a moment, at the way the sandstone steps snaked upward to brown buildings on a ridge, buildings almost hidden by oaks and pines, and it dawned on him where he was.

Castle Island. But how had he ended up here?

Levi gingerly began the climb. When he reached the camp cabins, he searched for an open door or window. After a fruitless hunt, he discovered a spigot behind the dining hall. He curled his swollen fingers around the handle and worked it until water trickled out. He fell to his knees and drank like a dog lapping water from a hose.

Thirst quenched, he pushed himself upright and stumbled up the path toward the castle. He arrived when the sun was halfway up the eastern sky and settled against a tree trunk, face toward the empty horizon. He fell asleep waiting for the castle to appear.

Levi's eyes flew open as two rough hands gripped his arms and yanked him to his feet, smacking his head against the tree trunk.

"What—?" The toes of his shoes scrabbled for purchase on the grass. His mind whirled in dizzying circles as he tried to understand what was happening.

"Do you think this is funny?" a harsh voice demanded.

Levi somehow managed to plant his feet, blinking repeatedly at the hot pink flower inches from his crossed eyes. With a slow, painful shake of his head, he looked up to meet the fiery green blaze of Mr. Dominic's glare.

"What are you doing out here?" Mr. Dominic gave him a little shake.

Levi swallowed, trying not to puke.

"We've been searching for thirteen hours." The director's strong fingers bit into Levi's upper arms. "Thirteen hours. And you're here? Taking a nap under a tree."

"Tobias, stop." Mrs. Dominic put a restraining hand on her husband's forearm. "Can't you see something's happened to him?" She placed cool fingertips to Levi's brow. When she pulled them away, blood dripped onto the grass.

Levi frowned at the crimson drops. Had she cut herself? She should get a bandage.

The director's grip loosened as he bent and studied Levi's face. The fire in his eyes still smoldered, but his voice gentled. "What happened to you?"

"I—" Levi tried to make his mouth form words, to explain that his stupidity was what happened, but his tongue wouldn't do what he wanted it to. The ground tilted upward, his knees gave way, and he sank into unconsciousness.

"What happened to the boy?"

Levi felt like he'd been strapped down under a tarp. He couldn't move, couldn't even open his eyes. Yet he knew that deep voice, currently hoarse with anxiety. It was Dr. Baldwin's.

Did that mean he was in the castle? In the infirmary?

Safe?

"We don't know." Mr. Dominic's words were quiet, no longer harsh, though he had every right to be angry. "Will he be okay? Do I need to contact his parents?"

"I won't know for certain until he wakes up," Dr. Baldwin replied. "However, I think he's simply exhausted. He has multiple bruises and cuts, and it appears he hit his head a few times, so we'll have to watch for a concussion." A long sigh filtered through the air. "We'll just have to wait and see."

I'm okay. Levi tried to move, to open his eyes, to speak, because they sounded so worried. And Mr. Dominic sounded so guilt-ridden. *It's my fault. I was such an idiot, going down into that cellar.* He managed to push a grunt from his sore throat.

"Did he make a noise?"

There was a shuffling sound, followed by heavy breathing in his face. Horrible breath.

He groaned this time and tried to turn away. Had to escape that stench.

"He's coming around." Dr. Baldwin's excited words exhaled more of the rancid fumes.

Levi wrenched his head to the side, his eyes popping open. "Ugh. Brush your teeth, will you?" His voice came out a raspy whisper.

The dwarf's hairy face pulled back a few inches. First his mouth dropped open, then he grinned. "Guess you're feeling better."

"I was." His nose wrinkled, and even that small movement hurt.

Dr. Baldwin puckered his lips and blew out a narrow stream of air. "Better than smelling salts."

Mr. Dominic released a short bark of laughter. "I'm just glad it worked."

When Levi attempted a smile, his bottom lip split. He licked at it, but his parched tongue only scratched the spot. "Can I have water?"

Dr. Baldwin adjusted his pillows and held a cup to his mouth.

The tepid liquid burned as it went down. He choked but kept drinking until the doctor pulled the cup away. "Thanks."

The doctor nodded and moved to the sink.

Mr. Dominic sat on the edge of the bed. "I need to apologize."

"Why?" Levi's voice still croaked, but not as much as before.

"I was too rough with you earlier." The director looked down at his big hands gripped in his lap. "You had me scared, disappearing like that. I was afraid you'd broken one of the rules and gotten yourself into a dangerous situation." He shook his head. "I thought we'd lost you for good."

"I did."

Mr. Dominic cocked his head to the left. "How's that?"

"I opened the cellar door. I disobeyed you and went down." A shudder coursed through him, and a slow ache began in his temples. "I barely made it out alive."

The director's face paled. "What happened?"

"How did you end up south of the castle?" Dr. Baldwin asked sharply at the same time.

"Um . . ."

Mr. Dominic made a calming gesture with his hand. "Start at the beginning, son. Tell us everything."

Levi took a deep breath and told them what happened, all but the part about the hideous creature on the lake. He wasn't sure exactly why the monster bothered him so much, more even than Regin and Deceptor. Maybe he'd hallucinated it.

Dr. Baldwin gripped the cup so tightly his hand shone white through the glass. "You washed down the waterfall into the lake?"

"How did he survive the drop?" Mr. Dominic's voice was a breathy whisper. He was looking at the doctor, so Levi didn't try to come up with an answer.

Dr. Baldwin shook his head. "The cold water is all I can figure. It must've . . . drugged him until his muscles were relaxed, so he didn't shatter . . ." He turned to Levi. "How long were you in the river before you fell?"

"I'm not sure."

"It must've been close to an hour, I'd guess. But how did you not drown?"

Levi shrugged as a numbing fear crept into his heart.

"Lake Superior is much colder than the river." The doctor touched Levi's forehead. "I don't know how you survived, much less how you made it to back to the castle."

Mr. Dominic released a long, shuddering breath. "The Great Emperor of the Universe spared him, that's all we know for certain." He patted Levi's arm. "We'll praise Him for saving your life, and you'll show your gratitude by obeying the rules." He fixed him in a stern glare. "Or else."

Levi gulped. He hadn't considered punishment—not that he didn't deserve it.

"Stay away from the cellar from here on out. Am I making myself perfectly clear?" Mr. Dominic raised both eyebrows and waited.

"Yes, sir, I'll stay away. I promise."

"Okay, then." The director rose and moved toward the door.

"Da—" Levi stopped himself just before he called the camp director *Dad*. Must still have a foggy brain. "Mr. Dominic?" He waited for him to look back, then said, "I really am sorry."

The director offered a small smile. "You're forgiven."

Levi returned the smile and snuggled deeper under the covers.

Chapter 11

Nightmares

Levi startled awake. Darkness pressed in on him. His heart pounded, his chest heaved, and his eyes darted back and forth. Was he underground or in the water? Was that hideous sea creature hovering in the night, ready to pounce?

At a loud snort, he flinched. The pale moonlight seeping through a crack in the drapes revealed Dr. Baldwin asleep in the chair beside Levi's bed. The infirmary. He relaxed against his pillow as he remembered the dwarf rousing him several times throughout the afternoon and evening as a precaution against concussion.

Gradually, his heart rate settled, and he tried to calm his mind as well. He should be asleep; it was the middle of the night after all. But each time he closed his eyes, nightmarish visions filled his mind . . . first Regin's albino eyes, then Deceptor's silvery-blue ones, and finally the sea monster's poison green glare.

Not wanting to face his tormentors again, he eased to a sitting position and stretched his sore limbs. His neck and back popped, and his head throbbed. He scooted to the edge of the mattress, silent so he wouldn't wake the doctor, and tried to decide what to do. He wasn't about to leave the room, not even to visit the library. He'd learned his lesson about going off on his own, scaring the staff half to death. Besides, his nerves were too raw to wander the dark castle right then.

Levi stood and gripped the nightstand until the room stopped swaying.

He crept to the window, pulled back the edge of the curtain, and peered out. Was the monster out there somewhere? Had he imagined it?

Something swooped at the glass. His heart skittered into double-time. Then he realized it was only the trees swaying in the breeze. Clouds flitted across the moon, making shadows creep across the lawn and up the stone castle wall.

Gooseflesh broke out on his skin, more from the darkness than the chill. He pulled the blanket from his bed and wrapped himself in it, pretending the warm cover was his mom's arms embracing him, sheltering him from the nightmares as she'd so often done when he was little.

Twin tears spilled from his lashes. Since no one was around to see, he let them trace a path down his cheeks. He felt so confused, so guilty, and the residual horror from the night before wouldn't leave him alone. But his mom would make it go away. She always did.

A ragged sigh seeped from between his lips. He hadn't been very nice to his mom the past few months. After last summer, it was hard to take his mom's rules when he no longer felt like a child in need of them.

And his dad . . . He'd wanted so many times to tell him about Terracaelum, that Papa Levi's stories were true. But he'd never been able to muster the courage. Instead, he'd kept silent, the confusion eating away at him until he snapped at his mom, said he didn't have to obey her, didn't have to do his chores and schoolwork, didn't have to speak with respect. That he didn't need a mommy anymore . . .

He shivered. He was wrong. He needed his mommy. Because being back in Terracaelum hadn't taken away any of the bad feelings. And yesterday he'd added new nightmares to his mix of torments.

"Can't sleep?"

At the deep voice just behind him, he whirled around, catching his feet in the blanket. He stumbled, wrenching his achy body.

"I'm sorry." Dr. Baldwin hurried to steady him. "I didn't mean to scare you."

With the blanket, he swiped the dampness from his cheeks. "No problem."

The dwarf's eyes glinted in the pale light as he studied Levi's face. After a moment, he crossed to the nightstand and flipped on the battery-powered lantern. "There. That'll brighten things up some." He settled into his chair. "I should've left the nightlight on."

Levi's face burned. "It's no big deal."

"Still, I should've thought. I'd imagine you're pretty sick of the dark after the night you just lived through."

Levi shrugged and turned away, feeling the weight of the doctor's scrutiny. He braced himself for questions he didn't want to answer.

"How about a game of chess?"

A reprieve. "Yeah, sounds good."

Dr. Baldwin kept him in the infirmary the entire next day, wanting him to have extra recovery time from his hypothermia and exhaustion. Levi didn't mind. Trevor stopped in with clean clothes, and Sara brought him a couple library books. Even Morgan came by and chattered for a solid half-hour before the doctor sent her on her way.

As evening fell, Levi felt the doctor's eyes on him. He glanced up as the man averted his gaze. Levi returned to his book. A few moments later, he felt Dr. Baldwin's gaze fixed on him again and snapped the volume shut. "What's wrong?"

"What do you mean?"

"You keep staring at me."

The doctor's rough cheeks reddened. "Sorry." He cleared his throat and shifted. "I just wondered how tonight would affect you after last night . . ."

This time it was Levi's cheeks that flamed. "Oh, um . . . I'm okay."

"Are you sure? Because I'd like to send you back to your room." The dwarf shook his head. "Not that I'm trying to get rid of you, but you might sleep better in a familiar environment, with your roommates nearby."

He thought of Trevor and Steve's nightly snore fest. At least with all that racket he wouldn't dream he was underground. Unless, of course, he thought a snorting minotaur was chasing him through the tunnels . . . He finally shrugged. "Yeah, okay, it'd be good to sleep in my own bed."

"Off you go then. Just mind you keep plenty warm."

Levi headed for his room. Only the occasional torch relieved the gloom in the corridors and staircases. Passing the windows with black shadows moving outside made him shiver and scurry along. By the time he reached his door, he was panting and wishing he'd spent the night in the infirmary. But being back in his own welcoming room was worth the scary trek across the castle.

Sighing, he opened the door to a loud, long belch.

"Levi!" Tommy jumped up from his bed, grinning, soda can in hand.

Steve swallowed a huge mouthful of soda. "You look terrible." The last word came out a three-syllable burp.

"Nice, Steve." Trevor smacked Steve lightly on the back of the head. "You're not supposed to tell him that." He turned to Levi and flashed a cheesy smile. "You look great, dude. Really."

"Thanks, I think." Levi shut the door, crossed to his bed on wobbly legs, and eased onto his bed.

"Want one?" Trevor held out a Coke can, releasing a belch that lasted a solid minute.

Tommy cackled. "Good one."

Something that sounded half-snort and half-hiccup erupted from Steve.

Levi rolled his eyes. "No thanks. So, what've you guys been up to?" He waved a hand toward the sodas. "I mean besides this."

"Uh-uh. No way." Trevor flattened an empty can on his side table. "You're gonna tell us exactly what happened to you."

Tommy plopped down on the end of Trevor's bed, facing Levi. "Yeah, we've been dying here, trying to figure out where you disappeared to."

"You scared us half to death." A sprinkling of brown freckles stood out on Steve's pale cheeks. His voice dropped to a dramatic whisper. "We thought you were dead."

"Or that Deceptor'd got hold of you." Trevor flopped down beside him. "With all the worry you've caused, you'd better tell us everything. You owe it to us." He pursed his lips in a look that reminded Levi of his great-aunt Miranda.

"I'll tell you all about it, but give me a minute to catch my breath. I'm kinda worn out."

They waited, tapping their toes, heaving sighs, and shifting around, all while staring fixedly at him.

His lips bent into a wry grin. "Guess that's all the rest I get." He told them everything—all but the part about the water monster. He couldn't bring himself to do more than give the creature a passing thought, much less talk about it. Still, the parts he did tell got plenty of oohs and aahs from the boys. By the end, Steve's face had lost all color, but Trevor was bouncing up and down on his bed.

"You rode a waterfall?" Trevor looked completely awestruck. "That is so cool! I wish I could do that."

Tommy shook his head. "No, you don't. That must've been, what, a hundred-foot drop?" He cocked a brow at Levi, who responded with a small nod. "You should've died on impact. How'd you survive?"

Trevor stopped bouncing, his mouth open wide.

"Dr. Baldwin says hypothermia saved me."

"Huh?" Trevor scratched his head. "How?"

"I was completely numb, so I didn't tense up before I hit the water." His throat tightened as the horror of what might've happened crept in once again.

"Wow."

"Yeah, wow," Steve said softly.

Sobered, the boys brushed their teeth and put on their pajamas in silence. Levi was the last one to climb into bed. He hesitated before turning off the battery-powered lantern on his nightstand, dreading the darkness that was sure to bring nightmares. But Trevor popped up from his pillow and sent Levi a look that said *Get on with it, already.* So Levi flicked the switch.

Darkness pressed in on him. He closed his eyes, willing himself to sleep. Instantly, a pair of vivid green eyes filled his mind. He opened his eyes, but the image didn't go away. *God, please* . . . Why did the lake monster scare him so much? Regin and Deceptor and his trip down the waterfall were plenty freaky. But that monster . . .

Then the reason hit him: such creatures might belong in Terra-caelum, but they did not belong in Lake Superior. That was his world, his territory.

How was he supposed to handle a monster invading his home?

Chapter 12

Overcoming Fear

Sunday after chapel, Levi stayed seated in the quiet room long after the others left. Mr. Dominic had preached about the reality of hell and the need for each individual to repent of his sins and run to Christ as his only hope of salvation. Jesus had saved Levi when he was eight, but he hadn't been acting much like a Christian the last few months. Disrespecting his parents, disobeying Mr. Dominic, acting like he knew better than those in authority over him . . . all those things sure made him look more like a rebel than anything else.

He squeezed his eyes shut tight, blocking out the soothing muted light filtered through the stained-glass windows. In his mind, he fell hard into the cellar again. Darkness. Bleak emptiness. Cold loneliness.

If the cellar he'd been forbidden to enter was even a small taste of an eternal hell, he wanted nothing to do with it. "God, forgive me. Please. I've been so self-centered. Help me obey."

That afternoon, Levi waited his turn in the musty, overcrowded telephone room. He'd made up his mind on the hike down that he needed to tell his parents everything about Camp Classic—regardless of the consequences. He was sick of being trapped in his guilt.

When Martin slapped down the receiver of the black rotary phone after only seconds, Levi jumped. The hulking boy narrowed his tiny eyes and snarled, making his round, reddish-orange face look more like a badly carved pumpkin than ever. Growling something indiscernible, Martin shoved Levi into the wall, stomped past, and stormed out the door.

Levi muttered, "Cranky, cranky," rubbed his banged hip, and picked up the receiver. He dialed his home number, drumming his fingers as the rotary slowly spun after each digit. He understood that electronic devices weren't allowed at camp, which wasn't a big deal since there were no cell towers out here anyway, but why couldn't the director at least get new phones? Ones with buttons.

Finally, an obnoxious ring sounded in his ear. His stomach clenched as he waited for someone to answer.

"Hello?"

Dad. Good. He wasn't as likely to freak out as Mom. "Hi, Dad. How's it going?"

"Levi! It's going great now that I'm talking to you."

The unbridled joy in his dad's voice made his eyes sting. "So what's going on there?"

"Oh, I'm batching it this weekend." Dad's voice was quieter, more subdued. "Your mom and brothers are at Grandpa's helping out this weekend, and Abby's spending the night at Molly's so Mrs. Maguire can take the girls to choral practice in the morning."

So his family was still way too busy—just like every other Sunday he'd called. They hadn't even driven him to camp this year. His dad had planned to, but one of the old lady Sunday School teachers died so he had to do her funeral. Instead he dropped Levi at Trevor's house, two hours from home, and the boys had ridden up with Trevor's dad. It should've been fun, driving all that way with his best friend, but Trevor's dad had been so snarly . . . Not to mention Levi felt somehow abandoned by his family. He knew it was a ridiculous way to feel, but he couldn't help himself.

He shook himself out of his pity party. That wasn't why he'd called. "Is Grandpa feeling bad again?"

"He is." Dad sighed. "He's still having those fainting spells. I wish the doctors could figure out what's wrong. It's getting to your grandma and your mom."

Sounded like it was getting to his dad, too. "What about Cerberus?" Levi missed the overgrown mutt he'd gotten for Christmas. He'd named the puppy Cerberus after the three-headed dog from Greek mythology because his puppy seemed to have three tongues, all for licking Levi's face.

Dad chuckled. "Had to send him with your mom and the boys. Zeke's taking care of him."

Would Cerberus think he was Zeke's dog by the time Levi got home? He swallowed the clump from his throat. "So you're home by yourself tonight?"

"Not for long. I have a deacon's meeting in—" A pause followed by a groan. "—less than five minutes. I'm sorry, son. We have to talk fast."

"Oh, okay." That didn't leave much time to spill his guts.

"So tell me everything. What's happening at camp?" Again the upbeat tone, which sounded forced to Levi's ears.

"Um, well . . ." *I almost died.* "Let's see . . ." *I'm sorry I've been such a creep to you and Mom.* "What's new here . . . ?" *Five minutes.* His shoulders slumped; he couldn't do it, couldn't add to his parents' problems. "Mr. Austin's making me be the lead in the summer play," he finally blurted out.

"Yeah? You've never been too fond of getting up in front of people." Dad sounded distracted, like he was putting on his shoes or looking for his car keys. "What's the play?"

"*A Bride Named Thor.* I'm Thor." Levi's face burned. "Because of my hair."

"So does that mean you have to wear . . . ?" Dad sounded totally focused now. And totally amused.

He rolled his eyes. "A wedding dress, yeah. Wonderful, huh?"

Dad's deep, full-bellied laugh rumbled across the line. "Are you serious?"

Levi's entire body burned now. "Yeah, I'm serious." He knew he sounded as mopey as Eeyore, but he couldn't help it. His own dad was laughing at him, for crying out loud.

"I'm sorry, Levi." The laughter faded. "I know this must be torture for you."

"You got that right."

"But, son," Dad said gently, "it would be so much easier if you could see the humor in it yourself."

Levi released a heavy sigh. This conversation wasn't going the way he'd planned.

"Listen, I have to run." Now Dad sounded sad. "I wish I could talk longer." He hesitated. "I miss you. You know that, don't you?"

He hated the uncertainty in his dad's voice. They'd always been so close, before Levi let Terracaelum come between them. "Yeah, I know. It's . . . hard, you know?"

"I know," Dad said softly, then his tone turned brisk. "About this play business, I'm afraid it's just one of those times when you have to suck it up and do what needs doing. That's part of becoming a man."

Easy for you to say. You don't have to stand on stage in a dress. "Yes, sir."

Dad's voice gentled again. "I love you, son."

His head drooped as sorrow replaced his irritation. "I love you, too."

He set the receiver in its cradle with a dull thud, the sound of his heart falling into his shoes. Without a word to any of the chattering campers waiting in line for the phones, he headed for the door.

Once outside, he turned away from the grassy central area where Trevor and Tommy wrestled while they waited for Levi and the girls to finish their phone calls, and slipped into the wooded area behind the building. Hoping to gain control of his emotions before the others were ready to go, he sat on a stump and drew in several deep breaths. He'd really hoped to confess everything to his dad, to get that weight off his chest, but now—

Loud, nasty-sounding giggles came from the trail that led to the castle. He peeked through the trees. Morgan stood at the base of the trail, her face as forlorn as Cerberus's when Levi left for camp. Three girls headed up the path without her, sending sneering looks back at her. Levi frowned. Weren't those Morgan's roommates?

A dandelion spore tickled Levi's nose, and he sneezed.

"Bless you." Miss Althea stood beside him, her back ramrod straight and her gaze vigilant as she scanned the river for any sign of danger to her charges.

It was more than a week after Levi's underground adventure, and he and his friends were canoeing. They'd decided to do the same events in the Camp Classic Olympics as they'd done the previous year, but without Ashley, they were an odd number. For the moment, he was the odd man out. He was fine with that. The idea of getting into a flimsy canoe on the river . . .

Shaking away his anxiety, Levi watched his friends try to regain the paddling rhythms they'd achieved the summer before.

When Steve dumped the canoe he and Lizzie shared, she came up sputtering. "You messed me up," she shrieked as she climbed out onto the grass. "Now I have to redo my hair and makeup."

Steve clambered out beside her. "What about me?" He shook his head like a St. Bernard puppy, spraying more water into her furious face.

She glared at him through mascara-ringed eyes. "You're hopeless." She shoved him backward into the river.

Levi snorted out a laugh that quickly died under Miss Althea's cocked left brow. Lips puckered, she returned her scrutiny to the water. He watched her from the corner of his eye. Albert's second cousin, twice removed, wasn't the same as she'd been last summer. Sadness lurked beneath the surface, stealing her smile and her fire. It wasn't like she'd ever been overly talkative before, but now she stayed silent almost all the time. And obsessively vigilant over her charges.

This year, she was acting as hall chaperone for Sara, Lizzie, and Monica. Along with teaching art, assisting Mr. Drake with canoeing classes, and helping Dr. Baldwin in the infirmary as needed. She was diligent, almost militant, in her duties, but it was clear her joy was gone. Levi couldn't figure out why. From all he'd seen, Miss Althea and Nydia Sylvester had been more rivals than friends, so why would the elf's death bother the pixie so much?

"You're up, Levi," Tommy called as Sara exited their canoe.

"Oh, uh, yeah." Levi strode to the water's edge. He did not want to do this. Still, he lifted a foot to climb in beside Tommy. And froze like a popsicle in the deep freeze.

He watched the water toss *My Little Pony* sparkles and rainbow bubbles into the air and was completely freaked out. He was such a wuss.

It's not like the other night. You'll be in a boat. Still, he couldn't move. With a deep inhalation through his nose, he squeezed his eyes shut. He opened them and tried again.

He couldn't do it.

"What's the matter?" Tommy's voice broke into his internal struggle. He didn't answer.

"What's up?" Trevor called, steering toward them in the craft he and Monica shared. Lifting one shoulder in a shrug, Tommy jutted his chin toward Levi.

Sara touched his arm. "Something wrong?"

He had to tell the others to do this event without him. They'd be better off anyway, then there'd be an even number. He'd just sign up for boxing and let Martin pound on him. That'd be easier than facing the river. And possibly the waterfall. And the lake monster. His knees went weak.

Levi opened his mouth to confess what a chicken he was, but Sara tugged his hand. As he met her gentle gaze, she gave her head the tiniest shake. He closed his mouth and waited.

"I'd like to canoe with Levi this time, Tommy," she said.

"Whatever." Tommy climbed out of the boat, crossed to where Miss Althea stood watching Steve and Lizzie paddle in circles, and flopped onto the grass, arms across his chest.

"Don't worry about him," Monica told Levi and Sara. "He'll get over it."

Trevor shot them a questioning glance. "You guys okay?"

Sara nodded, her expression confident. Levi wished he felt so sure.

When the others paddled out of earshot, she faced him. "It's normal."

"What do you mean?" He knew exactly what she meant. He fixed his gaze on the place near his dirty Nikes where the black earth and thick green grass dropped away into the rushing water.

"You don't have to pretend with me, Levi. I know how you feel. I've been there, remember?" Her smile was soft, sad. "Trust me, it's easier to deal with the bad stuff if you have somebody to help you." She gently touched a brownish-yellow bruise still visible on his forearm. "It took me weeks to go into the woods again after what happened last year." Unshed tears shimmered in her blue-green eyes.

"How'd you get past it?"

"My dad went with me every day, coaxing me, encouraging me, until finally I did it." She sighed. "And you know what I found out?"

"What?" he whispered.

"The woods aren't scary in and of themselves. I actually enjoy exploring them. It's the bad stuff others did in the woods that made me afraid."

Regin and the lake monster filled Levi's thoughts, along with his near-fatal trip down the river and falls. Maybe if he'd been able to talk to his dad about all the junk he was feeling, he wouldn't still be so panicky.

But he had to wait. Next Sunday's phone call was an eternity away.

And yet, would it really be right to spring Terracaelum on his dad in a hurried phone conversation? Especially when his family already had so much on their plate—with Grandpa's poor health and all. He didn't know, and he couldn't think about it right now. He had a monster to face, and he wasn't up to the task. "I don't know, Sara." He backed a couple steps away from the river's edge. "I don't think I can. Not yet."

"Well, we won't then. Not today anyway." She smiled at his frown. "But we'll come back every day until you're ready. Deal?"

He started to refuse, to give up and stay away from any body of water larger than a bath tub for all eternity. In fact, he'd probably stick to showers from here on out. Quick ones. But at the look of expectation, of hope, in her face, he blew out a breath. "Oh, all right, it's a deal. But don't expect too much too soon."

Chapter 13

Combustible Commodes

Levi opened his bedroom door. Something clattered behind him, followed by somebody grumbling. Steve shoved past him.

"What's your problem?" Trevor disentangled himself from the suit of armor Steve had apparently rammed him into. With reverent motions, he straightened the knight's visor and shield.

Tommy stood behind him snickering.

Levi looked back into the room as Steve sprinted into the bathroom and slammed the door. "Guess he had to go." He couldn't stifle a snicker. "Bad."

The other boys entered the room, Trevor shaking his head with a look of disgust. "He didn't have to push me. He could've messed up my man."

Tommy rolled his eyes. "It's a suit of armor, goober. Get over it."

Trevor grabbed his pillow and reared back to throw it at Tommy but froze when a boom and a shriek echoed from the bathroom.

"What in the wor—"

Levi called through the bathroom door, "Steve? Are you okay?"

A weak "help" reached his ears. He wrenched open the door and halted, mouth hanging wide, as Trevor and Tommy crowded in beside him.

Water flooded the mosaic tile floor. Droplets streaked the mirror, windows, and bathing partition. Bits of soggy toilet paper hung from the stone ceiling like streamers at a rained-out birthday party. A strong stench—vinegar?—filled the air. The sounds of dripping water and muffled moaning came from one of the stalls.

"Uh, Steve . . . you in there?" Levi took hesitant steps toward it, thankful he still had his shoes on.

Trevor splashed to his side and knocked on the stall door. "Steve?"

"I . . . I'm okay." Steve's voice quavered.

A faint smoky mist crept over and under the door. "What's that?"

Trevor shrugged. "Open the door, man."

"It's gross." Steve started blubbering.

"What's gross?" Tommy asked from Levi's other side.

"The . . . the toilet." Steve made a loud sniffling sound." "It . . . it threw up on me."

Trevor's eyes bugged out. A look of disbelief crossed his face, then his cheeks reddened and his lips twitched. A tiny bubble of laughter burst from him.

Levi looked away fast, barely containing the giggles fighting for escape. "What do you mean 'threw up'? Like when you were . . ."

By then both Trevor and Tommy were bright red with stifled laughter. Trevor stuffed his fist between his teeth. Tears ran down Tommy's cheeks. The occasional snort made its way past the hand he'd clapped over his mouth.

"I was just . . . you know . . . and there was this hissing and bubbling sound, and so I jumped up and . . . it just . . . went off."

At this, all three boys doubled over, cackling.

"It's not funny!" Steve snuffled some more.

"No, it isn't funny at all." The low voice from the bathroom doorway brought an immediate end to their laughter.

Levi turned to see Mr. Sylvester standing in a puddle of toilet water with his arms folded across his chest.

"Who is responsible for this mess?" The hall chaperone crossed to them in two long strides.

"Not me," Tommy said in a tiny voice, and Trevor shook his head.

"Steve—" Levi began.

"It's not my fault," Steve said with a whimper. "The toilet just sort of puked all over the place."

A wad of soggy toilet paper unstuck from the ceiling and plopped onto Mr. Sylvester's white-blond hair. He didn't look at all amused. Even Trevor didn't dare snigger.

The elf plucked the wad from his head as he turned stern eyes on each of them. "Did you do something to that toilet?"

"Uh-uh."

"No, sir."

"No way."

Mr. Sylvester crossed to the empty stall opposite. He yanked open the door and went inside, the top of his head visible above the high walls. His head disappeared, and Levi heard the clatter of the toilet top being lifted.

Steve's sniffling stopped.

After a few seconds, Mr. Sylvester came out, his gray eyes more serious than before. He held up several small packets of something white. "It's been sabotaged."

"Excuse me?" Levi frowned.

Trevor surged toward the stall. "You mean like a bomb?"

Mr. Sylvester nodded grimly then shook his head. "Not a real bomb, more like a bad prank." He strode to Steve's cubicle. "Are you, er . . . injured, boy?"

"No, sir, just covered in . . . stuff."

Levi didn't feel the slightest urge to giggle this time. An exploding toilet? That could've hurt Steve.

Levi stood outside the Dominics' study door. He'd delivered Mr. Sylvester's note about the exploding toilets. Only the smallest twinkle of amusement had crept through Mr. Dominic's eyes before the possible seriousness of the situation must've hit him. At that point, he'd darted off to warn the staff to check for other "combustible commodes," as he'd put it. Thankfully, most of the campers were still outside enjoying the nice weather. Maybe the staff could prevent further explosions.

Levi took his time climbing the stairs, not in a hurry to get back to his room. He'd left Trevor scrounging through Steve's wardrobe for clean clothes and Tommy heading to the kitchen for one of the Forests to help restore the bathroom. Mr. Sylvester had stayed to help Steve out of the stall so he could shower the toilet scum from his body. Levi sure didn't want to be around for that.

He decided to spend a few minutes in the chapel instead. On the fourth-floor landing, he pushed open the door to the north corridor and slipped inside. The faint scent of flowers and the soothing quiet enveloped him with peace. He sank into a pew and rested the back of his head against the wood, staring at the high stone ceiling over which occasional shafts of colored light played.

Who had rigged the toilets? Was it somebody's idea of a joke? Could Trevor have done such a thing? He did love practical jokes; he'd tried the rubber-roaches-in-the-underwear-drawer trick on Tommy only the day before. Plus, Trevor had been the first to laugh in the bathroom.

But Steve could've gotten hurt. Trevor would never do something that might injure someone. Would he? No, of course not. His mischief wasn't malicious.

But Levi knew a few people whose mischief went beyond malicious. Hunter and his twin thugs. If anybody would think rigging toilets was funny, it'd be them. Levi hadn't heard of any other mean pranks—at least not major ones—since the drawbridge thing, but Braden and Brock seemed the type who could only behave for so long.

He popped up and headed out the door, intending to tell Trevor and the others what he'd figured out. But in the corridor, he hesitated, his focus on the door opposite the one leading to his room—Hunter's hall. He'd only been in his enemy's room once, and that time he'd almost gotten himself pitched out the fourth-floor window. Did he dare go there now? Would Hunter and his minions be cackling about the toilets blowing up all over the castle? Or maybe they'd only rigged the ones in Levi's bathroom.

With his jaw clenched so tight it hurt, he marched to Hunter's corridor then paused to listen. Laughter rang from behind Room Two. Not

Hunter's, unless he'd changed rooms since last summer. Frowning, Levi knelt and pressed his ear to the dark wood.

"How'd he do it?" Cackles followed the deep-voiced question.

"He's a genius," said a voice Levi recognized as Hunter's.

"His brother's sure not." The deep voice sounded like Martin's.

A snort then Hunter again: "Nah, Brick's dumb as they come."

"Dumber than a brick." A harsh guffaw. "So when did they set it up?"

"While everybody was outside."

"What'd they use?"

Hunter laughed. "They just added a little extra something to an old recipe. Braden wouldn't want me to give away his secrets."

"Won't somebody wonder why ours are the only ones that work?"

Another snort. "They don't, stupid."

Martin's short laugh didn't sound amused. "But what about when we have to—"

Someone gripped the hair at the top of Levi's head and yanked until he thought his neck would break. Eyes watering, he let out a yelp.

Braden's face loomed over him. "It's not polite to eavesdrop on other people's conversations."

Chapter 14

A Serious Infraction

Braden gave his hair another hard yank. Levi's neck popped. He groaned.

Brock's face entered his line of sight, wearing a half-dim, half-nervous expression. "Hey, Braden, I think you better stop, or you're gonna hurt him."

"You ought to know better than trying to think, Brick." Braden glared at his twin. "Leave that to the smart people."

The door sprang open and Hunter appeared. A look of surprise preceded his usual smirk. "Catch something, Braden?"

Braden's gold chains jingled as he released an ugly laugh.

"Well, bring him inside." Hunter spread his arms wide in an exaggerated gesture of welcome.

As Hunter stepped back, Martin howled, "That's my foot!"

Braden's grip slackened just slightly.

Levi didn't waste the opportunity. He shot upright, ramming the top of his head into Braden's chin, and sprinted down the hall. There was a squeal of pain followed by thudding footfalls. He ran faster. He reached the door, ripped it open, tore through it, and slammed it shut—right on somebody's pale, freckled fingers.

A shrieked curse word chased Levi across the landing. He galloped down the chapel corridor, skidded into his own hallway, and scrambled through the door to his room. He didn't stop until he'd closed it behind him.

He leaned against the cool wood, gasping for breath, eyes squeezed shut.

"Uh, Levi?"

He opened his eyes to his gaping roommates. Mr. Sylvester, mop in hand, stared at him from the bathroom doorway.

"Hi." Levi wiggled his fingers in a pathetic attempt at nonchalance.

"What's the deal?" Tommy asked. "Why were you running?"

"Oh, um . . ." Levi's gaze skipped from his friends to Mr. Sylvester, who looked both suspicious and confused. Should he tell the hall chaperone what he'd overheard? He chewed the inside of his cheek. *Think.* What exactly had Hunter and Martin said? Had they ever actually mentioned explosives or toilets or anything of the sort?

No.

It didn't matter that Levi was absolutely certain Braden had rigged the toilets. He had no proof.

His scalp tingled where Braden had probably left a bald spot, which wasn't proof either. He'd gotten caught eavesdropping. Tattling that Braden pulled his hair would just make him sound like a big baby.

"Uh, Levi?" Trevor said. "You still with us?"

Lips puckered, Levi cut his eyes toward Mr. Sylvester. "I'm fine. Just . . . in a hurry to get back here." He focused on Steve. "You okay?"

As Steve shrugged, pink-cheeked, Levi flicked a glance at Mr. Sylvester.

The hall chaperone still looked suspicious, but Alexander Forest, one of Albert's many brothers, poked his head out of the bathroom at that moment. Alexander was almost identical to Albert except for the thin curly-tipped mustache making him resemble a dastardly villain in some old cartoon.

"Somethin' the matter?" He leaned against the doorframe and twisted his mustache. Clearly, he had no intention of cleaning up the mess by himself.

Mr. Sylvester released a heavy sigh. "No, no, I'm coming." His eyes searched Levi's once more before he headed back into the bathroom.

As soon as he was out of earshot, Trevor whispered, "What happened?"

The four huddled up. Levi told them, as close to word-for-word as he could, what he'd overheard.

Steve's face reddened. "That . . . that . . . that snake! He deserves to get expelled."

"Yeah, but what could I do?"

"He's right, you know," Tommy told Steve. "What they said was too vague to be proof they rigged the toilets."

Trevor fingered the half-dozen hairs on his chin. "But maybe we can prove they did it."

Steve's eyes brightened a little. "How?"

"Well . . ." Trevor shot a glance toward the bathroom door and lowered his voice. "What if we take a look in their room? There's got to be some evidence of what they did."

"Whoa, wait a minute." Levi held up a hand. "I scrounged through Hunter's room last year and almost died for it. And just today . . ." He fingered his sore scalp.

"I didn't mean you. They'll be on the watch for you hanging around their room, but not me." His best friend flashed a reckless grin.

Levi's nerves zinged. "What do you mean? Why wouldn't they be on the watch for you?"

Trevor's grin widened, and a slightly insane look entered his eyes. "Don't worry about it. They won't even recognize me."

"What's that supposed to mean?" Tommy sounded as anxious as Levi.

Trevor only shook his head. "I got this. When the right time comes, you guys just have to keep 'em occupied."

"Occupied?" The word broke from Steve's lips like a yelp. "How're we supposed to do that?"

After supper, Mr. Dominic lectured the campers for ten solid minutes. "Sometimes pranks get out of hand and somebody gets injured. That could've happened today. If you are the guilty party, I advise you to turn yourself in immediately." His piercing green gaze landed on each camper's face, lingering the longest on Brock's and Braden's.

No one spoke or moved.

"Supplies were stolen from the kitchen as well. That means your infraction also extends to theft." Vinegar? And whatever that white stuff was? Maybe baking soda, but what about the "special" ingredient Hunter mentioned?

Still no one said anything. Levi's ears burned even though he knew he hadn't set the explosions. Yes, he was pretty sure he knew who had, but what could he do about it? He sneaked a peek at Trevor, who mouthed *I got this*, then returned his gaze to the director.

Mr. Dominic waited another moment. "Yes, well, you would do well to keep this in mind: such behavior is unacceptable, and I will not tolerate it. You will refrain from any such practical jokes from here on out or risk expulsion, is that clear?"

Levi murmured, "Yes, sir," along with the rest of the campers.

"I trust there will be no further need to address this issue."

Again the kids chorused, "Yes, sir."

The director nodded. "Now then, on a much pleasanter note, tomorrow after chapel and telephone time, we will take any interested persons to the beach for a swim."

"Yes!" Trevor pumped his fist in the air.

Most of the kids laughed and exchanged excited chatter with their friends. Mr. Dominic smiled. "I quite agree, young man. I quite agree."

But Levi didn't agree. In fact, his stomach, grumbling with hunger seconds earlier, now felt queasy with dread.

"Last one in's a rotten egg!" Trevor thundered past Levi and splashed into the lake, Tommy at his heels. Steve jogged after them, his belly fat jiggling. Levi walked slowly toward the water. He'd called home that afternoon, like everybody else, but no one had answered. Between discouragement with his family and memories of that lake creature, he didn't think he could deal with beach time today. Not that any of his friends so much as noticed how he felt.

Even Sara raced full-throttle into the crashing waves, while Monica let out an uncharacteristic giggle as she jumped into the surf. In seconds, the five of them were engaged in an all-out water battle.

To Levi's left, Lizzie touched a hand to the hair piled just so on top of her head. "Don't y'all splash me now." She tiptoed to the edge and dipped a coral-nailed toe—the exact shade as her swimsuit—into the water. She shivered. "It's so cold!"

Trevor barreled toward her and splashed as hard as he could for sixty long seconds. When he stopped, she stood sputtering, her hair a soggy wad. Levi laughed out loud at the mascara streaming down her face.

"Ooh, I'm gonna get you now, honey." She tore off after Trevor, splashing madly.

Levi took a couple more steps toward the water.

"C'mon, Levi," Steve called. He did a huge belly-flop right next to Monica and came up cackling.

Levi waved, but he didn't step near enough to touch the water.

He peered around. The staff had set up buoys to mark off the safe swim zone, and the lake was calmer than usual. The Drakes and Mr. Sylvester had spaced themselves out along the beach, their eyes constantly scanning the water. Their height made them the ideal lifeguards for the thirty or so kids who had come to the beach. Mr. Dominic stood watch also, dressed in powder blue board shorts that brushed his knobby kneecaps. His face wore a broad smile, and his eyes danced. His bare feet shuffled in the sand as though he'd love to splash down in the water with the campers.

Levi stuck a tentative toe in the chilly water. Surely it was safe. Surely the monster wouldn't come in the swim area. He turned around and scanned the beach one more time. Okay, he could do this. He wouldn't spend the whole summer scared of water.

"Cowabunga!"

The screech blasted his eardrums. Something grabbed him around the waist and yanked him backward into the lake. He opened his mouth to scream for help. He swallowed sandy water, choking and gasping. When whatever-it-was released him, he pushed to his feet and wheeled around, half-expecting to see a scaly creature with fangs bearing down on him.

Instead he found Trevor, doubled over with laughter. For a second, anger burned through him. Then he looked down at his sand-encrusted chest and back up at Trevor, whose hair stuck straight up all over his head. His anger drained away in laughter.

"You nerd!" He tackled Trevor, pushing him under.

Trevor came up spluttering. "Nerd? I'll show you nerd." And he chased Levi, splashing like a water fiend.

"What do you know about the Loch Ness monster?" Levi asked Trevor that night as he settled against the pillow he'd carried up to cushion the stone tower roof.

Trevor shot him a puzzled look. "Where'd that come from?"

His face heated, and he was glad for the clouds blocking the light of the three-quarter moon. "I was just thinking. We're in a place with all kinds of bizarre stuff. Makes you wonder about those legends and tall tales people tell. How many of them are real?"

"Yeah, I've thought about that too." Trevor lay back on his pillow. "I mean, some things are too weird to be true, like vampires and Paul Bunyan and stuff."

He snickered. "Vampires and Paul Bunyan? Not exactly in the same class."

Trevor elbowed him in the ribs. "You know what I mean." He sobered. "But I know lake monsters are real. I've seen one."

Levi popped upright. "Where?" Could it be the same one he'd seen?

"When I was a kid, we had a boat we'd go out in. Sometimes for the whole day. We'd fish and swim and stuff." The moon peeked from behind the clouds and illuminated the far-off expression in his eyes. "One day we stayed out later than usual, and just as the sun was sinking into the water, I saw this huge hulk a good hundred feet away. It hovered there a minute and sort of stared at me, then it disappeared." He shrugged. "Nobody else saw it, but Dad told me it had to be Bessie. That's Lake Erie's monster."

"Your dad believed you?" He had trouble imagining his best friend's dad spending entire days on a boat with him, much less believing him when he claimed to see a mythical creature.

"Yeah, well, that was before Mom died."

Levi squirmed. He allowed a few seconds of uncomfortable silence before he asked, "What did this . . . Bessie look like?"

Trevor sighed, but his voice came out stronger. "It was kinda hard to see with the sun behind it, but it had sort of a horse head. Not with a mane or anything, but with that shape. Its skin was kind of rubbery-looking and dark, maybe gray or black. Kinda like a seal's. That's about all I remember, that and its size. Even from a distance, I could tell the thing was tall. Real tall."

"Oh." His own lake creature reared in his mind, its vast shape, dark horse head, and sharp teeth making him shudder.

Trevor squinted at him. "What's wrong?"

"Nothing." He cleared his throat. "I was just imagining the thing." He lay back on his pillow and tried to make his voice sound casual. "So, have these lake monsters, Bessie or Nessie or whatever you call them, ever attacked anybody?"

"Don't know, but I guess it's possible." Trevor yawned and stretched. "There're lake monsters all over the world. Ogopogo in Canada and Brosnya in Russia. And a whole bunch more."

"What about Lake Superior? Does it have a monster?" He peeked at Trevor from the corner of his eye.

"Sure. Name's Pressie. I was hoping to see her since we're in the middle of the lake." He grinned. "Well, I guess you'd say we're over the middle of the lake."

Levi forced a chuckle. "Pressie?"

"Yep. She's a shy one. Not seen very often." Trevor yawned again. "Probably because the lake's so huge, she has plenty of places to hide. Nobody knows where her lair is, but I bet it's around here. Since we're smack in the middle. It would be so cool to find her."

Levi tried to control his frantic breathing. "Yeah, um, cool."

Chapter 15

The Lead in a Skirt

"You will too." Steely-eyed, Mr. Austin thrust the lacy white dress into Levi's stomach on Monday afternoon.

"Oof." He clenched his fists and shook his head hard. "Uh-uh. I'm not wearing that thing."

"You're Thor." The literature teacher advanced until the oily smell of his hair filled Levi's nostrils. "You will wear the gown. Now try it on so we know whether it needs to be altered."

Giggles and catcalls came from the pack of kids waiting to hear which parts they'd won. Hunter and Martin were both pointing at him and cackling loudly.

He lowered his voice, hoping he sounded mature, reasonable, respectful. Because he wasn't about to parade around in a dress, especially in front of the entire camp. "I'm sorry, sir. I'm just not an actor. You'll have to find somebody else. Maybe Braden or Brick . . . er, Brock . . . they're both redheads." He wedged his fingers between his stomach and the silky fabric and shoved.

Mr. Austin didn't back down an inch. "The twins' hair is not true red like yours. You are Thor." His jaw set hard enough to break rock as he dropped the dress on the desk in front of Levi and stalked off to speak to Yasmin.

"It'll be okay," a soft voice said in his left ear.

He turned to see Morgan standing at his elbow, a gentle smile on her lips. "Really, it's not a big deal. It's just a play."

Levi only grunted, steeling himself against Hunter and Martin's current batch of comments about how his scrawny legs would look in the dress and how he probably wouldn't even need to shave them. This was not how his summer was supposed to go. Morgan . . . Sara too, for all he knew . . . probably found Hunter's comments cute. As much as he'd seen both girls hanging around his nemesis, they must be his buddies.

Yet nothing in Morgan's expression indicated scorn as she fingered the silk dress. "Don't worry about them. They're probably jealous you got the lead instead of them."

"I'm sure." Sarcasm laced Levi's words, but he offered her a begrudging smile.

Whether this whole thing earned him sympathy points or not didn't really matter. How could Mr. Austin get away with casting him as Thor against his will? It was insane. He didn't want to be in any play. He sure didn't want to be the lead. Much less the lead in a skirt.

That evening, Levi and his six friends settled around a long table in the library to work on their group science report.

"All right, everyone, let's begin." Monica sat at the head of the table and opened a large book. Levi didn't even consider questioning her right to lead. She was the smartest among them, hands down. "We'll divide up like this: Steve, check for Superior's tributaries. Tommy, look up outlets. Trevor, you do tides. Levi, you do hydrography. Lizzie, take marine biology. Sara, you do waterfowl, and I'll take the islands."

He was still trying to figure out what hydrography was when Lizzie snapped shut the compact she was using to check her lip gloss. "Excuse me, honey," she said with an icy glace, "but who put you in charge of our little project?"

Monica's face turned a deep shade of purple, but Sara placed a hand on each of their arms. "That's fine, Monica." She widened her eyes at Lizzie. "Let's get busy, everybody. This thing's due tomorrow."

Levi pushed back from the table. "C'mon, Lizzie. Let's go do some research."

She followed him, muttering that know-it-alls were a pain in the rear.

Once the two roommates were separated, the group worked in relative quiet, the only sounds an occasional whispered conversation about their project and the rain pattering on the windows.

Levi was jotting a note about the different kinds of lake plankton when the door creaked open. Morgan poked her head in, her expression uncertain until she met his gaze. Then her eyes lit up, and a smile curved her lips. She walked straight to him. Just like his little sister, Morgan could find him anywhere.

"Hey, Levi, can I study with you?" She put a textbook on the table and sat in the seat Lizzie had temporarily vacated. "I could use a little help with my Latin homework."

"Well, actually . . ." He waved a hand at the science materials covering every inch of the table and darted help-me glances at his friends. Couldn't she see they were busy?

No one spoke up until Lizzie emerged from between bookshelves lugging several large volumes. She halted beside her seat. The look on her face told him a volcano was about to erupt—all over pesky, unsuspecting Morgan. He couldn't let that happen.

"Uh, Morgan . . ." He leapt to his feet and snagged her arm. "Come on over here, okay?"

Though she looked confused, she rose with her Latin book and followed him to a table on the far side of the room.

"Listen," he said quietly, "we're sort of in the middle of a science project that's due tomorrow, but I can help you out a little." He tapped a finger on the table. "Over here."

"Oh." She glanced at the others for the first time. Pink colored her cheeks. "That's okay. You're busy." A fine layer of tears misted her eyes.

He heaved a sigh and sank into a chair. "Really, it's not a problem."

She let out a breathy "thanks" and sat beside him, scooting her chair a little closer than necessary.

Across the room, Trevor caught his eye and pretended to smooch the air. Levi wanted to throttle him.

"This weekend will begin a new era in our campout routines," Mr. Dominic announced from the head table after breakfast and devotions the next morning. "We've decided to change up your groups to give you an opportunity to get to know other campers, maybe make new friends." The director grinned like this was the best idea he'd ever had. Levi barely suppressed a groan. There were a few "friends" he had no desire to camp with.

"The new groups will take turns hiking to the Medicollis, the midland mountains, for an extended campout. With their longer hikes, those campers won't return to the castle until late Sunday afternoon. On other weekends your group will camp in the usual spots north and south of the castle, returning, as is our custom, on Sunday morning in time for chapel." He looked around, eyebrows raised, as if waiting for questions.

When no one spoke, he went on. "You'll find postings in the great hall assigning you to a group and telling you which weekend you'll camp where." He clapped once. "Now, off to class."

Levi and his friends rose from their seats and carried their trays to the pass-through.

"Do you think they split us up?" Panic hovered behind Steve's eyes.

Trevor shrugged. "Only one way to find out."

Monica gave him a stern frown. "Not now. Latin begins in three minutes. It'll take that long to get there."

Levi sighed. "She's right. We'll have to wait for break."

As soon as the bell rang at the end of class, Levi and his friends shot to their feet, snagged their backpacks, and surged toward the door. They shoved into the hall with the rest of the class and joined the swarm of campers headed for the stairs, everyone talking about the new camping plans.

"Think they put us in separate groups?"

The question came from Jacqueline, a beefy girl he'd sat next to in art class the year before. It hadn't been a pleasant experience. Now, with her purple-shirted bulk filling three-fourths the width of the corridor, she stomped along talking to Suzanne, who was so skinny she didn't even fill the one-fourth left to her.

"I hope not." Suzanne's voice was loud and petulant. "I'll die if I have to spend a weekend with *them*." She pointed at Sara, Lizzie, and Monica, who walked together a few steps ahead of her.

Levi ground his teeth. He really hoped he didn't end up in a group with either of Hunter's annoying friends.

Trevor grabbed his elbow and whispered, "I'm doing it now."

"What are you talking about?"

The boy widened his eyes and nodded toward Hunter and Martin, who had just reached the stairwell in front of Sara, Lizzie, and Monica. "It's the perfect opportunity. Everybody's going downstairs."

When his meaning sank in, Levi released a tiny gasp. He'd forgotten all about Trevor's mysterious plan to find toilet explosion evidence in Hunter's room. "You can't. There's not enough time."

"Then you'll have to stall them." With that, Trevor took off up the steps.

"Ugh," Levi muttered and followed the others downstairs.

Trevor was about to get himself murdered.

Chapter 16

A Spy in Armor

Levi pushed through the crowd to the pages posted beside the Ping-Pong table.

"I have to camp with that little sissy. No way." Hunter's voice carried over the chattering campers as he fixed Levi in a steely glare.

Levi's stomach tightened into a hard little ball. *No, please don't let Hunter mean me.* Hunter elbowed past him, knocking him backward a few paces. Suzanne followed, her nose scrunched like Levi had forgotten his deodorant for the past two months.

When he reached the list with his name, the hard ball in his stomach dropped and bounced around by his ankles. He, Lizzie, and Sara were grouped with Hunter and Suzanne. The other campers in their group were Luke, Gabrielle, and a few new kids, including Morgan and Braden. They would be the first to camp in the mountains. It was going to be a nightmare.

Worse yet, he wouldn't be back from the mountains in time to call home this Sunday, and he needed to call, especially since nobody had answered the phone when he'd tried last Sunday. Maybe Levi could make a trade and camp near the castle this weekend. His gaze flicked to the second list, of those camping south of the castle the first weekend. He spotted Trevor's name below Brock's. Maybe Mr. Dominic would let him and Trevor switch spots.

Levi sucked in a breath, suddenly remembering. *Trevor!* He scanned the room. He had to find Hunter and keep him from going back to his room. He had to buy Trevor some time.

He spotted his enemy by the far wall, surrounded by Braden, Brock, Suzanne, Jacqueline, Martin, and a skinny kid named Derrick. Good. All of Hunter's thugs were accounted for. Still, Levi worked his way toward them in case they decided to leave. He hoped they didn't split up because he hadn't had time to enlist the others' help.

"At least you guys get to go to the mountains first," Jacqueline said in a cranky voice as he slipped into the crowd behind her, easily hidden by her bulk. "I've gotta camp in the same old place with the same old idiots who don't know how to hike or pitch a tent or do anything useful."

Hunter snorted. "At least you don't have to camp with that wimp Prince."

Levi's fists clenched.

"At least I'm in the same group with you, Hunter." Suzanne's high-pitched whine made his teeth ache. Could he survive a whole weekend with those two?

"Hey, maybe Braden can put together a little surprise for him," Hunter said, and the others snickered.

Levi wanted to punch Hunter in the nose, but he restrained himself. If only Trevor could find some evidence against the creep.

When the laughter died out, Hunter's voice came again. "I'm heading up to the room to grab my armguard before archery."

Levi's stomach lurched. Trevor couldn't possibly have had enough time yet. He had to do something. Maneuvering out from behind Jacqueline, he accidentally knocked her huge purple plaid backpack from her shoulder. She snarled, but Levi was on a mission. With a challenging tone he knew Hunter couldn't ignore, he said, "Hey, Hunter, I doubt you can handle a camping trip with an outdoorsman like me."

Surprise flashed across Hunter's face, but he quickly recovered his usual smirk. "Oh, I'm looking forward to it. Nothing like a mountain-top weekend with my favorite runt." The smirk stretched into a bare-toothed snarl. "Too bad Mr. Dominic won't be there, huh?"

A brief shiver of fear coursed through Levi, but he kept his face straight. One thing was for certain, he couldn't switch groups with Trevor now. Hunter would think he'd chickened out.

Jacqueline whacked Levi on the arm with her backpack. "Sounds like lots of fun, especially if he's anywhere near as good at camping as he is at drawing." She turned her small, piggy eyes from Hunter to Levi and let out a honking laugh. "I notice you're not in art class this year, Levi. What's wrong? Not feeling creative?"

He shot her a withering glare.

Hunter laughed and turned away. "This weekend, Prince. I can hardly wait." He tossed a hard glance over his shoulder. "By the way, you'd better be careful on all those mountain rocks. Wouldn't want you to trip on your pretty dress, now would we?"

His ears burned as he watched Hunter swagger from the room. Once his cackling gang slouched away after him, Sara and the others flocked to Levi's side.

Lizzie got in his face, hands on her hips. "What in the world were you thinking, honey? It's not bad enough that we have to spend the weekend with them? You have to make them mad first?"

Ignoring her, Levi grabbed Tommy and Steve by their sleeves. "Come on. The room."

"Huh?"

"The room. We've got to help Trevor." The three sprinted up the stairs, Levi's friends sputtering questions as they went.

As they skidded to a halt on the fourth-floor landing, Levi gasped out a quick explanation.

Tommy's eyes were huge. "Should we go to Hunter's dorm first?"

Clutching his side, Levi glanced between the door to their corridor and the door that led past the chapel to Hunter's. "I don't know."

"I vote we check our room first," Steve said between wheezing gasps. "No point getting pummeled if he's safe."

"Good point." Levi led the way, praying Trevor was in their room and in one piece. With proof of Hunter and company's guilt, of course.

As he swept into their room, wondering vaguely what was different about the hallway, he called, "Trevor?" He stopped cold.

"Is he in there?" Tommy pushed past Levi and froze.

Steve squeezed in between them, still gasping for breath. "What—"

The suit of armor that usually stood guard outside their door lay in the middle of the floor. Its leg moved. Steve let out a little shriek and grabbed Levi's elbow. When its other leg moved, this time with a loud creaking squeal, and somebody said, "Help," Steve nearly wrenched his arm off.

Levi shook him loose and knelt beside the fallen knight. "Trevor? You in there?"

"Get me outta here." The muffled voice definitely came from inside the armor.

Ignoring Steve's frightened moans and Tommy's stifled giggles, Levi lifted the visor. Trevor's bulging eyes stared out at him.

His friend's face shimmered with sweat. "I'm stuck."

"Yeah, I can tell." Biting back a grin, Levi yanked piece after piece of armor from Trevor's body. Steve and Tommy helped with the more stubborn pieces.

By the time they got Trevor free, all four were drenched with sweat.

Levi flopped onto the floor, helmet in hand, and looked at Trevor. "What in the world were you doing?"

Blushing, Trevor sank onto the steps beside Steve's bed. "I was going in disguise."

Steve blinked repeatedly. "How'd you get the thing on by yourself?"

At the same time, Tommy said, "As a suit of armor?"

Trevor gave a sheepish nod.

"You've gotta be kidding. You thought you could sneak into Hunter's room in that thing?" Levi dropped the helmet onto the pile with a dull *thunk*.

"It seemed like a good idea at the time. There're knights all over the place. Who's gonna notice another one?"

"Did you really think," Tommy said slowly, "Hunter and his

roommates wouldn't notice you in their room dressed like that?"

Trevor's sigh shook the hangings on Steve's bed. "Okay, so it was a bad plan."

Levi sighed as well. "So you didn't make it to Hunter's room?"

"Nope. I got the armor on, and that was hard work, let me tell you." He blew out a breath. "Then I started for the door and . . ." His neck turned fiery red. "Well, maybe it's just a little too big right now. Maybe in another year or so . . ."

Tommy rolled his eyes. "So much for getting evidence."

Steve, who sat on the floor gathering the armor, looked anxiously up at them. "Guys, we can't worry about that right now. We've got to get this thing put back together before Mr. Sylvester notices it's missing."

Fueled with panic at what the hall chaperone might do if he saw the mess, Levi shoved himself up from the floor and scooped up armor.

Tommy snagged an arm. "This isn't going to be easy."

"Yeah, I know." Trevor crawled over and carefully hefted a leg. "But be gentle with my man, okay? He's an antique."

Levi shook his head. "Trevor, you are so weird."

Tommy gave a sage nod as Steve giggled, but Trevor merely frowned. "What did I do?"

Levi laughed, letting the tension of the past few days drain away.

Chapter 17

Thor and Loki

The tension returned full force the next morning. Levi knelt on the sand beside Steve, spiral notebook open and pen in hand, being especially careful to keep his roommate between himself and the lake. It had taken the boys more than an hour the previous afternoon to get the knight put back together and set in place. Then at archery lessons, they'd had to explain to the three irritated girls why they'd run off from the great hall without a word.

Now they were on a science field trip on the Castle Island beach, which, despite his fun swim on Sunday, wasn't a particularly comfortable place for him.

Mrs. Austin held up a beaker for the class to see. "Lake Superior contains more water than all the other Great Lakes combined."

A movement caught Levi's peripheral vision, and he turned to watch Mrs. Sylvester, arms hugged to her waist, pause beside the steps they'd taken from the cabin area. Why was she standing way over there when Mrs. Austin had brought her along to help keep track of the class? She wasn't even looking at the campers, just staring beyond them at the water through mournful eyes.

"Levi," Steve whispered, digging an elbow into his ribs.

"What?"

"Mrs. Austin called you, like, three times already."

His gaze shot to the teacher, who was glowering at him. "Yes, ma'am?"

"I said, come here." Her eyebrows nearly disappeared into her gray-streaked brown hair. "Please."

He walked to her, keeping his distance from the lake.

"Get one of those buckets and that shovel." She pointed to a pile of supplies near the stairs. "Scoop up that dead fish so we can study it in the classroom."

He looked at the rancid, half-rotten wad. A wave rolled to within inches of it, leaving frothy bubbles in its wake.

"Hurry now, before the water takes it."

Levi scampered to the supply pile, passing near Mrs. Sylvester. He grabbed the bucket and shovel.

In his hurry, he almost smacked her with the shovel when he turned. He said, "Excuse me," but she didn't even blink, her eyes fixed on some distant point on the horizon.

He followed her line of sight. Nothing there. Just blue-green lake meeting bright blue sky. With a shrug, he hurried back to the dead fish, vaguely aware of the others receiving similar orders from Mrs. Austin.

With his back to the lake, he knelt by the fish. Ew, it was gross. It smelled disgusting. He averted his gaze, fighting his gag reflex. Taking a deep breath through his mouth, he forced himself to look back. The fish's eye was missing, and jagged teeth marks marred its belly. What had bitten it?

A shadow fell over him from behind. He froze, straining his eyeballs to see what cast the shadow. Was it the lake monster come to finish him off?

Something icy coated his knees and rear. Letting out a screech, he leapt to his feet. He whipped around to find a wave retreating with his dead fish, a cloud blocking the sun, and no lake monster in sight. He glared down at his soaked jeans while his classmates laughed at him.

Levi stood on a makeshift stage at one end of the great hall on Thursday afternoon. The Ping-Pong, pool, and foosball tables had been shoved into the far corner near the French doors, leaving plenty of space for play practice. Outside, rain dumped from the leaden sky. Grayish-brown puddles pockmarked the short grass in the courtyard. Water splattered so hard against the stone walkway that the door and windows appeared to be weeping.

Levi felt like crying himself—out of sheer frustration. Why hadn't God given someone else—anyone else—red hair? No matter what his dad said about manning up, he did not want to play Thor. Arms jammed across his bony chest like puny body armor, he made himself listen as Mr. Austin explained the scene.

"Thor is so mighty, so muscular, so powerful—" He glowered at Hunter, Martin, and Suzanne, who were sniggering on the opposite end of the stage. Hunter immediately straightened his face and even sent disapproving looks at his cohorts. Hypocrite.

When the three finally shut up, Mr. Austin harrumphed. "As I was saying, Thor is the god of thunder. He's so big and strong and masculine that when Heimdall tells him he has to wear a wedding gown and pretend to be Freyja, he absolutely refuses."

Levi released a quiet snort. Couldn't blame the thunder god there.

The dwarf's beady eyes fixed on him. "You have the belligerent refusal part down pretty well, I'd say."

Levi scuffed his shoe against the rough wood.

"Soon we'll get to the part where you give in." Both bushy brows lifted. "For the good of the group."

Levi slouched, stuffing his hands deep into his pockets. What choice did he have?

Thankfully, Mr. Austin turned his attention to the smirking Hunter. "As Loki, you'll stick close to Thor."

Hunter's brow lowered into a scowl.

"You're the one who found out Thrymr the giant—" Here he gave Martin a pointed look. "—stole Mjolnir and hid it eight leagues beneath the earth." The teacher then turned to Levi, looking suddenly and inexplicably upset. "We'll have to give you a hammer, of course. Mjolnir is a mighty weapon."

Okay, so he got a hammer to go with his gown. Bob the Builder in a prom dress. Yippee.

"Loki," Mr. Austin said, sweeping a stubby hand toward Hunter. "You will accompany Thor to Jotunheim to help with the gown and the deception."

Great. Him and Hunter, partners. This was going to work out well.

"Now remember." Mr. Austin yanked Hunter to where Levi stood. "Though you're working together on this, Thor doesn't trust Loki." He half-closed his eyes and gave Levi a significant nod. "And with good reason, too. Loki's not to be trusted. He changes form to suit his purposes; he's sneaky and devious."

Levi breathed a mirthless laugh. Sounded like the perfect role for Hunter. He had sneaky and devious down pat, shifting effortlessly between model camper and big bully. A shape-shifter, just like Deceptor.

But as the teacher turned to instruct Luke on his part as Heimdall, Levi felt an uncomfortable twinge in his belly. He'd been so certain last summer Hunter was Deceptor impersonating a camper, but he'd been wrong. His error had cost Miss Nydia her life. He'd best remember that.

And that this was just a play—a nightmare of a play with Hunter as his sidekick and himself in a dress—but a play, nonetheless.

No more rash judgments or ridiculous assumptions for him.

Chapter 18

Crossing the Mountains

Saturday morning, Levi tramped through the woods beside Sara. He didn't need to ask why she was so quiet because he knew she probably felt the same eerie sense of déjà vu that plagued him. The sky was overcast, darkening the path beneath the thick trees. In fact, it was almost as dark as last summer when she'd been dragged down this same trail by her kidnapper, and Levi, Trevor, and Monica had gone after her.

Except for Lizzie, the other campers were oblivious to his and Sara's feelings. Even Luke and Gabrielle knew nothing of what had happened. They may not have even noticed Miss Nydia's absence from camp this summer. He doubted they knew about Terracaelum at all.

Suzanne and Hunter . . . he didn't know about them. Hunter knew where they were. He'd known all along, but how much had he told Suzanne? And what about Braden, who, so far, had kept to himself? Maybe Mr. Dominic's threat had him too scared to blow anything else up. Or maybe he didn't know how to act without his brother at his side.

Levi tried to ignore the little shivers that kept coursing through him every time he thought he recognized a certain patch of forest. But when, after more than two hours, Sara let out a muffled gasp, he couldn't deny the goose bumps on his skin.

They were there. Just beneath the mountains. In the place Deceptor had attacked them. He would've killed them, too, if not for the mysterious windstorm that had driven the demon-sorcerer away. The only thing missing was the cave where the shape shifter had disappeared, trailing silvery blood. Levi caught himself searching the grass for traces of silver. After a moment, he froze, his eyes riveted on a thick patch of darkened grass. He inched nearer. It couldn't be, could it?

He squatted down, sensing Sara beside him, and peered into the dark area. "No, of course not. It'd be long gone by now." The words came out quieter than breath, but he could tell she heard him because she gave his shoulder a gentle squeeze. She knew what he'd thought it was . . . the stain of Miss Nydia's life blood pooled on the ground.

"All right then, campers," Mr. Drake called over the rumble of excited voices. "Find a clear patch and settle down."

Here? We're camping here? A rushing sound filled Levi's ears. They couldn't. It was . . . wrong. He glanced at Mr. Sylvester, who was helping Morgan untangle her hair from the straps of her red backpack.

"I can't." Sara's whispered plea and stricken face brought Levi out of his stupor. "Especially not with him here." She nodded toward Mr. Sylvester.

Levi attempted to reassure her with a smile then approached Mr. Drake. "Sir?"

"Yes?" Mr. Drake glanced up from the bag of supplies he was rummaging.

"Sir, we can't camp here," Levi began, then stopped at the irritated look on the elf's face. "I mean . . . is there any way we can camp somewhere else? This is where . . . last summer . . . Sara—" He gestured toward his friend, who stood stiffly at the edge of the clearing.

As Mr. Drake peered at Sara, his expression softened. "Ah, yes, I see." He glanced at Mr. Sylvester. "Does he know?" The question was almost inaudible.

Levi waited in silence.

After a moment, Mr. Drake's mouth tightened. "Don't worry, we're not sleeping here. We'll just eat a quick lunch and keep moving." He gave Levi's shoulder a pat. "We have a mountain to climb."

"But . . . are we sleeping up there?" He jutted his chin toward the gray boulders with low clouds enshrouding the peaks. Not a cheery prospect.

"No, no." The elf's lips curved into a small smile. "We'll camp on the other side of Mount Midland." He peered up at the slopes. "Fog's rolling in. We're losing light fast." He turned away and gave a single sharp clap. "Lunch, folks. Eat quickly."

Levi made his way back to Sara. "We're not staying here." His lips felt stiff.

She smiled for the first time all morning. "Good." Then she frowned at his dazed expression. "What's the matter?"

Levi pointed a trembling forefinger at the mountain. "We've still got to cross that."

In the dense fog, Levi moved a grasping creeper so Sara wouldn't trip on it. When she'd passed, he let it flop back in the path. "Watch the branch," he called over his shoulder. Let Hunter help Suzanne . . . if he was gentleman enough.

When he caught up with Sara, he called ahead to Albert, "How much farther?"

The pixie paused his steps. "Can't rightly say. With this low cloud, I can't see two inches in front o' my feet."

"That's reassuring." But it was either keep climbing or go back and spend the night in that horrible clearing.

"What's wrong?" Hunter's voice came from a few feet behind Levi.

"Did that idiot take us the wrong way?" Suzanne's not-so-quiet words echoed in the fog. "I should've gone with a different group."

"You got that right," Levi muttered under his breath.

Mr. Drake had divided them into groups so they could take separate trails over the mountain, giving each adult only a handful of kids to monitor. It also gave each group fewer people to bunch or straggle on the paths made treacherous by the fog. They'd soon find out whether it was a good plan.

At least he and Sara weren't in Mr. Sylvester's group. Or in Braden's.

Albert jutted a stubby thumb upward. "Let's keep movin', people."

The five of them trudged on, wheezing and panting as the path steepened. Levi tried to stay alert for dangers on the trail, but he was distracted. Blinded by the thickening mist and with cold moisture clinging to his skin, he had a creeping sense of terror. It was almost as if he were back in the underground tunnels, wandering lost in the damp darkness, heading straight for Deceptor.

He shook his head. That was dumb. He was above Terracaelum now, not below. And he wasn't alone with Regin; he was with friends. He glanced back at Hunter. Well, some were friends; others, not so much.

Stopping suddenly, Albert raised a hand and whispered, "Don't move."

Though Levi could barely make out the pixie's face, he could tell it had turned as white as Regin's. He inched nearer Sara. "What is it?"

She shook her head.

"Did you hear that?" Albert whispered.

"What's wrong now?" Hunter's voice was loud and harsh. "Can't we just keep going so we can get there already?"

"Yeah, this fog's doing nothing for my hair." Suzanne's voice was equally as loud and twice as shrill as she smoothed her frizzy locks.

Who cared what her hair looked like? Levi sure didn't.

"Hush," Albert hissed. "Listen."

Without Hunter and Suzanne's yammering, he heard a flapping, rustling sound. "What is it?"

Albert put a forefinger over his lips. They all stood silent.

Several loud cracks came from somewhere to the right. Then came what sounded like a giant clearing a wad of phlegm from its throat. Suzanne yelped, Hunter grunted, and Sara grabbed so tightly to Levi's arm he let out a squeak.

Albert motioned for them to follow then pressed his finger to his mouth so violently Levi feared he'd bust his lip, but this time the warning was unnecessary. Levi wasn't about to say a word. He doubted even Hunter and Suzanne would be brainless enough to speak.

He'd only taken a few cautious steps when panting breaths on his neck nearly made him bolt headlong into Sara. He swiveled his head, half-expecting some hideous monster. Instead he found Suzanne's panic-stricken face centimeters from his shoulder. Behind her, Hunter's face—minus its usual sneer—hovered in the thickening fog as if disembodied. Shivering, Levi turned and followed close behind Sara, who tiptoed at Albert's heels.

Once they'd slipped up the path a few yards and rounded a boulder, Albert faced them. "Here's the thing," he whispered, "we gotta get over this mountain in absolute silence."

"What exactly was that thing?" Hunter jerked his chin toward the path they'd climbed.

Albert cut his eyes toward Suzanne, who stood sniffling beside Hunter, and Levi knew what he was thinking. If Suzanne didn't already know about Terracaelum, Albert wasn't permitted to let on that the thing they heard might be . . . not normal.

"Could be a bear," he said with an unconvincing shrug.

Levi rolled his eyes.

Albert shot him a look that said, *Explain it yourself then, ya snot-nosed kid.*

Sara gasped, staring past Levi with her blue-green eyes taking up most of her white face. He wheeled around, as did Suzanne and Hunter.

A large reptilian head appeared above the boulder at their backs. Its black scales glittered despite the heavy fog suppressing the sunlight. Levi stood frozen. Albert's "Move!" registered in his brain. But before he could make his feet work, Hunter shoved the paralyzed Suzanne into him, and she and Levi both crashed to the ground.

He stood and pulled Suzanne to her feet. The creature's fiery, snakelike, yellow-orange eyes fixed on him. A harsh rattling—much louder than his dad gargling—filled the air. The monster opened its fanged jaws. Suzanne let out a shriek like ice picks in his eardrums.

He shoved her behind him as a blast of fire erupted from the monster's mouth.

Chapter 19

Dragon Attack

A sharp yank to his arm sent Levi reeling left. Suzanne toppled into him. The ground where they'd stood burst into flames. Albert gave his arm another wrench. Levi scrambled to regain his balance, snatched Suzanne's hand, and took off running.

After several moments of panic-driven scrambling up the mountainside, Levi doubled over, chest heaving, and massaged his shoulder. Albert had almost pulled it from its socket, but he'd gladly take the pain over being roasted alive.

Suzanne whimpered. "W-w-what was that thing? What is this place? I wanna go home."

Levi might've felt sorry for her, except for the memory of how she'd beaten Lizzie with her sword hilt the year before. He turned to Albert, no longer caring what Suzanne did or didn't know about Terracaelum. "Is that a dragon?"

Albert's small face puckered into a frown. "It don't make no sense, see? That was Middie, and I ain't never seen her act like that before. All rattly and spitting fire at folks." He shook his head.

"You've never seen . . ." Suzanne's face went chalk-white.

Sara touched Albert's arm. "You recognized her?"

"Sure, didn't you?" Albert looked from her to Levi.

He shook his head.

"She was in the rules play we put on for you back in June. Mr. Drake was ridin' her."

"Oh." Levi frowned. "She seemed so . . . tame then." He shook his head at the absurdity of his own words. "Or at least, under control. Sort of."

"Why is that thing loose," Hunter demanded. "You people should put down monsters like that. Suzanne almost got killed."

She socked Hunter in the gut. "Because you shoved me."

He grunted. "It was an accident." But he didn't meet her eyes. "Levi tripped me."

"I did not!"

"Enough." Albert held up both hands. "We gotta stop bickering and start figuring how to get out of here safely. Whatever's eatin' Middie, she ain't to be trusted. I gotta fetch Mr. Drake. He'll know how to handle her."

"But why didn't she fly after us?" Sara asked in a tiny voice.

Albert cocked his head. "You're right. She didn't. Maybe she's got an injured wing or somethin'. That'd make her awful cranky."

A strange, almost calculating look crossed Hunter's face, but crashing and screams from their left pulled Levi's attention from the bully. Sara grabbed Levi's hand as he squinted into the swirling mist. He couldn't see what caused the sounds, nor would he admit how glad he was for the comfort of her hand in his.

When the screams and crashing died out, Albert said in a shaky voice, "That's that then." He gave each of them a stern look. "You gotta go on without me. Just stay on this path and—"

Suzanne's eyes bugged out. "But—"

"You'll be fine. It's just that I gotta go help them people." He pointed into the forest. "I know a shortcut that you folks are too big to walk. I can't leave 'em to their sufferin'."

Levi didn't want Albert to leave them either, but he said, "Go ahead, Albert. We'll see you at the bottom of the mountain." He squeezed Sara's hand. She met his eyes in silent agreement, released his hand, and started along the trail. He followed close behind.

Yet as Albert disappeared over an outcropping, his stomach writhed. What if they met up with another cranky dragon?

When they reached the summit without incident, Levi's stomach unclenched slightly. Now all they had to do was get down the mountain in one piece. Easy. Yeah, right. The fog had thickened, and a misty rain fell, making the trail slick and his skin prickle.

Several painstaking moments later, he paused in the midst of crossing a particularly slippery ledge. Had he heard something? He looked back at the path they'd traversed.

Hunter glared at him. "Get moving or let me by."

"Shhh."

"Don't shush me. Albert didn't make you boss."

Levi bit back the harsh words he wanted to spew all over Hunter. "Would you shut up a second? Please. I'm trying to hear."

Hunter's eyes widened. He glanced back. Suzanne skittered around behind Levi, up next to the mountainside. He hoped she didn't get nervous and start flailing around, or she'd send him off the cliff.

There it was again. Definitely a rattling sound. Levi dropped to a squat. He glanced over his shoulder and called softly, "Sara."

She'd reached the other side of the ledge. "What's wrong?"

"Dragon's back."

Her round eyes told him she understood. They had to figure out what to do—find a place to hide, run like mad, something. Before he could decide what was best, he got shoved in the back.

Suzanne screamed. Levi slid down the rock toward empty air. His fingers scraped over the rocks until they wedged on an indentation. His body flew over the edge, and he clung by his fingertips. He couldn't hold on much longer.

"Help!" The joints of his fingers and wrists strained and popped. He shot a glance downward, hoping for a nearby ledge, but he couldn't see anything in the fog. Not even a scraggly tree to grab. His fingers slipped toward the edge in the damp earthy rock.

Soft hands grabbed his wrists. The pale faces of Sara and Suzanne appeared above him. With each girl holding him by an arm, they hoisted him upward until he was able to scramble onto the outcropping. The three of them collapsed in a panting pile.

"Thanks," he wheezed, and the girls nodded, breathless.

A horrendous roar rent the air. A dragon with dark blue scales perched only a few feet above them on a ledge. It emitted the same gurgling sound the other one had seconds before blasting fire, a sound like an engine revving, and Levi knew they were in trouble.

"Help us, Hunter," Suzanne screamed toward the far side of the ledge, her expression a mixture of disgust and desperation.

Hunter didn't answer.

Levi rose slowly to his feet, positioning himself between the creature and the girls. He made eye contact with the dragon, whose gurgling grew louder, like an angry gorilla rattling its cage. "Go," he whispered to the girls from the side of his mouth. A rustling sound told him they were moving. He could only hope Hunter would help them get away because he had a bigger problem to deal with at the moment.

He stared into the dragon's eyes—the color of blue flames—and fought the panic fogging his brain. *God, help. What do I do?* The softest imaginable breeze touched his face, like his mom's fingers when she soothed his feverish forehead. Gentle. Soothing.

Gentle. Soothing. It was worth a try. "I'm sorry, Dragon." He kept his voice low and calm.

The creature's throat-clearing noises stuttered to a stop. Its eyes looked a little less angry.

"That's right," Levi murmured, "everything's fine. No need to be upset."

The dragon dipped its head until its snout was less than a foot from his face. Intense heat baked his skin, and an eye-stinging, sickly sweet stench coated his nose and throat. He felt like he'd stuck his head in the oven with a batch of burnt cookies. He could feel his eyebrows singe.

The urge to scream almost overwhelmed him. Instead, he forced out a ragged whisper. "It's okay. We're not here to hurt you." As if they could do any damage to this creature.

Still, the dragon seemed to like what he'd said because it made a humming sound in its throat. Did dragons purr? He slowly lifted his hand. Should he pet the thing?

A sharp squeal from Levi's right brought an abrupt end to the purring. The dragon turned toward the noise, its blue eyes blazing almost white. Suzanne huddled halfway to the edge of the outcropping, cradling her ankle. Beyond her, Hunter snatched Sara's hand and yelled, "Run for your life!"

Sara pulled away. "We can't leave them."

Hunter scampered around the bend. The coward. Sara turned anxious eyes on Levi then inched toward Suzanne.

"No, Sara. Go." How could he distract the dragon from Suzanne? "Dragon, look at me, I'm—"

But the dragon burst from its ledge and dropped to the path beside Suzanne with a tooth-rattling thud, effectively blocking the path between her and Sara. The gurgling came again—definitely not purring this time—louder than before. With a gulp, Levi scuttled past the dragon to Suzanne and rose to his full height. She whimpered in his shadow.

"Stop! Bad dragon!" Though Levi used his firmest voice, the one he used when Cerberus lifted a leg indoors, his knees trembled. Naughty dragons were much more difficult to handle than naughty puppies.

The dragon stopped and cocked its massive head as though confused.

Levi held his breath. "That's right. No fire. Be a good dragon."

The creature eyed him another moment. Levi gestured for Suzanne to go back toward the trail they'd just ascended. He heard her moving, but he didn't look back. He had to keep the dragon's attention on him.

"What's the matter?" He kept his voice quiet and even. "Why are you upset?" This looked like the dragon Mr. Sylvester had ridden in the play. It had to be tame—at least as tame as dragons got.

The dragon's wings flapped open until it hovered over him like a lion over a mouse. Levi couldn't help the terrified squeak that broke from his lips. He stepped back, fully expecting to be flame-broiled. Then he saw it. One of the dragon's wings had a deep gash. Bluish liquid he guessed was dragon blood trickled down and formed a steaming puddle on the rock.

"You're hurt."

Eyes full of pain, the dragon dipped its head.

"What happened to you?" Levi waited a few seconds before realizing how idiotic it was to expect an answer. "I'm sorry you're hurt." He took a tiny step forward. "We didn't hurt you, though, so please don't be upset with us."

A smoky snort greeted his words. He stepped back again.

"It's okay." He held out his hands, palms up. "I don't know how to fix your wing or I would. But I'll get Mr. Drake. Or Mr. Sylvester."

The dragon's eyes narrowed to bluish-white slits. Steam spurted from its nostrils.

Okay, not good. "Or whoever you want, somebody who knows what they're doing." He swallowed hard. "You have to let me go or I can't get you help."

The creature glowered at him several long moments before bursting into awkward flight. It landed on the boulder above, bent double, and bobbed its head in a bow. At least it looked like a bow to Levi, so he bowed in return.

"I'll get help. I promise."

Chapter 20

In Charge

Suzanne refused to speak a word to Hunter, despite his protests that he'd "slipped" on the outcropping. She didn't even acknowledge his offer to help her hike down the mountain. Instead, she snagged Levi's arm and clung to it all the way down.

Now that the danger was past, pain sidled throughout Levi's body. His bloody fingertips throbbed, various cuts stung on his arms and legs, and what felt like a cracked rib throbbed with his every breath.

"That was amazing, Levi." Sara's eyes were bright with unshed tears as she glanced back at him from her place in the lead. "I thought that dragon was going to kill you." She sniffled. "I'm so sorry. I couldn't figure out what to do except pray like crazy."

"It worked." His legs trembled and he longed to rest, but they didn't have time. "We need to get down quick. I promised I'd get help."

"You can't seriously be worried about keeping your word to some beast," Hunter said from behind him.

Levi tossed him a sour glance over his shoulder. "Of course I am. You should be too. If I don't and you find yourself meeting up with that dragon some other time, it'll blast you without even listening to any promises."

"Levi's right," Sara said. "My . . . um . . . I mean, I've been told you have to keep your promises to all creatures."

Levi's eyebrows surged upward. She'd almost given away who her dad was. Hunter certainly couldn't be trusted with that information. And Suzanne . . . Just because she was mad at Hunter didn't mean she'd changed her allegiance.

At the base of the mountain, Levi spotted a cluster of half-raised tents a short distance away. He hurried over, leaving Suzanne to hobble along with Sara's help.

"Is Mr. Drake around? Or Mr. Sylvester?" he asked the few campers piling wood for a campfire.

"They're not here yet." Gabrielle pointed toward a two-person tent. "Mrs. Drake's in there though."

"Thanks." He jogged to the tent and called her name.

She came out, a loaf of bread in hand. "What is it? Is something wrong?" She looked beyond him. "Where's your leader?"

He explained about Albert and the dragons. "I promised I'd send Mr. Drake to help."

Mrs. Drake's dark, thin eyebrows drew together on her high forehead. "You say Nithir's wing was cut?"

"Who?"

"The dragon. I'm pretty sure that's Nithir." She grasped his wrist. "Think. Did the wound look accidental or intentionally inflicted?"

"I don't know." He pictured the wound in his mind. "It was a straight, deep gash, not jagged or anything, but I have no idea what caused it."

The elf woman's lips tightened. "And Middie? Did she have a wound anywhere?"

He remembered what Albert said about Middie not flying. "I didn't see anything, but Albert thought maybe she was hurt."

"Okay, then, it can't be helped." She thrust the bread into Levi's hands. "I have to go. You're in charge until an adult arrives." She started at a brisk trot toward the mountain.

"Me?" He stared after her, his jaw hanging wide. As he hugged the bread to his chest, he wished it was a sword.

First dragons, now this? He didn't want to be in charge. He was only fourteen, for crying out loud.

Hunter didn't appreciate taking orders, especially from Levi, but Levi couldn't help it. He hadn't asked for the responsibility of watching over eight other campers, one of whom had an injured ankle and three of whom were new this summer. At least Sara was there to help. Too bad Lizzie hadn't been in Mrs. Drake's group. She never took sass from anybody, even bullies like Hunter.

Even so, Levi managed to organize the others. Within an hour they had the remaining tents pitched, the fire blazing, and supper cooking. Several times, Levi had to slip away when he saw Morgan bearing down on him. He didn't have time to deal with her right then. As the clouds lowered still more and the drizzle intensified to rain, Levi prayed the others would arrive soon. He didn't want to be in charge all night.

As darkness fell, Miss Althea and eleven grubby campers dragged into camp. Levi sent up a silent prayer of thanks, but Miss Althea's irritability almost made him wish she hadn't joined them. Albert, Mr. Sylvester, and Mr. and Mrs. Drake had sent her to babysit the campers. She clearly didn't appreciate it.

Once the newcomers were fed and settled, the kids huddled in their tents to stay out of the cold rain. Levi shared a tent with Luke and a new kid named Xavier, who wanted to know why they'd been sent down the mountain with only one chaperone.

"Good question." Scrawny Luke frowned at Levi. "Do you know what's going on? Is there something dangerous out there?" He pointed toward the mountain, visible beyond the open tent flap.

Levi tried to look clueless. "Why? What happened to you guys?"

"Well, we were hiking along just fine until Albert ran up and got Mr. Drake, then the two of them took us to Mr. Sylvester's group. After that, we all hiked around to Miss Althea's group." He eyed Levi. "Why did Albert come to us? I thought he was in charge of you guys."

Heat burned under Levi's collar. What should he say? *We thought a dragon was attacking you.* Um, no, probably not. "We heard somebody screaming, so he went to see what was wrong."

Luke nodded. "Yeah, that idiot Braden jumped out from behind a bush and scared everybody. Got all the girls screaming. I thought Lizzie was gonna rip his head off she was so mad." He grinned.

Levi grinned back. He could well imagine Lizzie's reaction.

"Anyway," Luke went on, "we waited with Miss Althea for an eon before Mrs. Drake showed up. Then she ran off, and finally, Albert came back and told Miss Althea to bring us down here." He tossed his hands. "Crazy."

"Sounds like it, but I wouldn't worry about it. They'll get it all worked out soon." He hoped.

His tent mates didn't look satisfied, but tramping around on the mountain all day must've worn them out because they fell asleep early.

When the sickly moon was high overhead, Levi poked his head from the tent. The soggy damp soaking into his bones wouldn't let him sleep. Plus, Luke and Xavier didn't snore. Who'd have guessed he'd actually miss Steve and Trevor's nightly snore-a-thon?

Then there was his worry over the staff dealing with cranky dragons on a rainy night high in the mountain. And Mrs. Drake had acted like the dragons' wounds were intentional. What kind of creature would cut a dragon? Strike that. What kind of creature *could* cut a dragon?

Deceptor, of course. Who else?

With thoughts of the shape shifter heavy in his mind, Levi stared around the dark, quiet campsite. He saw the dull orange glow of the smoldering campfire. Beside it lay Miss Althea, snoring lightly in a sleeping bag. So much for guard duty.

Levi grabbed his rain slicker and slipped from the tent. The pixie woman couldn't be expected to stay awake all night after such an exhausting day. He'd sit up and watch awhile. He couldn't sleep anyway, and Mrs. Drake had made him responsible for the camp. Sort of.

Huddled beneath his raingear by the dying campfire, he stared into the black trees, squinting for any sign of danger. He stared so long his eyelids began to sag.

When Miss Althea's mutterings woke him later, he sat up straight and shot panicky glances around the campsite. The pixie woman mumbled something about dragons and huddled deeper into her sleeping bag.

He shook himself. *Stay alert, Levi.* Next time, it could be more than Miss Althea talking in her sleep. He stretched his achy shoulders. Then paused mid-stretch. What was that? Through the faint smoke beyond the fire pit, was that a shadow? He blinked repeatedly. Was he still half-asleep and imagining things?

No. This wasn't another one of his nightmares. Something was creeping toward the camp.

"Miss Althea?" He stole a glance at her. She didn't move.

But the shadow definitely did.

Chapter 21

A Ship in a Field of Flowers

"Miss Althea," he hissed, this time shaking her sleeping bag until she sat up with a start.

She squinted at him through sluggish eyes. "What are you doing out here?"

"Look." He breathed the word while pointing at the place he'd last seen motion.

She leapt to her feet in a single, silent move. A swish followed by a silver flash told him she'd drawn her hunting knife. She crept into the shadow of a tent. He lost sight of her until a sharp gasp drew his eyes to the creeping figure, now joined by another shadow. Miss Althea's hiss filtered to his ears, "Move and you die."

"It's me, Althea." The words were garbled, like the speaker was being strangled.

A rustling sound followed, and the two figures moved toward the nearly dead fire. Levi held his breath. A sliver of moonlight pierced the clouds, revealing Albert's wild-eyed face.

Miss Althea sheathed her knife and squatted beside Levi, looking exactly like her great-aunt Mrs. Forest, cranky as a wet cat. He was just glad her anger wasn't directed at him.

"Albert, you fool," she said sourly, "what do you mean sneaking into camp like that? I just about slit your sorry throat."

Albert sank to the ground as if his legs wouldn't hold him a moment longer. "I was trying not to wake everybody. Sheesh." He shook his shaggy head, and a twig plopped onto Levi's lap.

Levi picked it up and began breaking it into little pieces. "Where are the others?"

"Still up there." Albert jerked his chin toward the mountain. "It's gonna take some work gettin' them wings healed up."

"So we're on our own here?" Scowling, Miss Althea drew her sleeping bag around her shoulders.

"Yup."

"They should've let me stay." Miss Althea shot Levi a dirty look, like it was his fault she'd gotten stuck with camper duty. "I'm the only one with medical training."

"Now, don't be like that, Althea. You know the elves are better at carin' for the dragons." Albert winced when she turned her glare on him. "I'm just sayin' . . ." He raised both hands in surrender. "I thought Aubrey was gonna have to leave off taking care of Nithir at first, but then the ol' boy settled down some."

"Why? He's cared for Nithir all his life."

Levi hunkered low, trying to stay unnoticed so they'd keep talking.

"I know it, but Nithir almost blasted him when we got there." Albert shrugged. "Probably just skittish, what with his injury an' all."

Miss Althea didn't look satisfied. "I suppose."

"Anyways, we gotta get these kids back to the castle safe and sound come first light." Albert blew out a breath. "Just pray we don't meet no more injured critters on the way."

Levi had to know. "Who did it? Who hurt them?"

Neither answered.

"Was it Deceptor?" He couldn't help the shrillness in his voice.

Still no response.

"Why's he doing it?"

Albert and Miss Althea exchanged looks, then she said quietly, "Back to bed, Levi."

"But—"

"Now. And stay there."

Levi woke in the gray half-light before dawn. Cold and stiff, he peeked from his tent to find the silent camp smothered in what his mom would've called a pea-soup fog. He stuffed his feet into his boots and eased from the tent. He slipped between the eerie masses and blobs of the other tents, not stopping until he reached the edge of the campsite. To the south stood Mount Midland, a shrouded giant.

Since everyone was asleep, he decided to walk north a ways. His footfalls on the wet ground made dull squelching sounds in the gray silence. After a few minutes, the sun rose to his right and sent red rays ricocheting through the low clouds. Still he kept going, warming his clammy skin through exercise.

Shafts of sunlight pierced the fog, gradually burning it down to mere wisps in places but leaving heavy patches in others. When a solid mass blocked the path in front of him, he halted with his heart racing. What was it? The giant from the Rules and Regulations play? Another dragon?

Silently, he inched backward.

A sunbeam burst through the fog, and he blinked at the thing illumined before him. It was the hull of a boat, upside-down in the middle of the grass. He touched the soggy, weathered wood. What was a boat doing here? Was he near water? He stood still and strained his ears. Now that the fog was thinning, he could hear birds twittering nearby and the vague sounds of people walking and talking, probably from camp. But no water noises.

"Hmm." He walked around the hull, studying it, until he came to a string of faded letters upside-down near the ground. He bent and studied the peeling paint. "*Canadian Queen?* What's a Canadian ship doing in Terracaelum?" At his feet, red, purple, and yellow wildflowers sprouted from the plush green grass. "In a field of flowers?"

Hang on, a ship in a field of wildflowers. His mind's-eye flashed to the painting across from his room back at the castle. Could it be a picture of this ship?

He ran a hand over the ghostly prow, hearing Albert's words from earlier that summer replay in his mind: ". . . the world's mash into each other, and boats and them flying machines and such from your world end up in ours."

This must be what Albert meant.

Another memory rose into his mind, this time of Hunter's words from early last summer: "Haven't you ever heard of the Great Lakes Triangle?" Had Hunter known stuff like this happened in Terracaelum? That, like in the Bermuda Triangle, ships and planes disappeared? And that they ended up here?

How could Hunter have known such a thing?

With his brain as muddled as the fog again thickening the air, Levi turned and started back along the track his footsteps had forged through the grass. This whole place was just too fantastic for him to comprehend.

After fifteen minutes of walking among the gray ribbons of fog, Levi paused his steps. The air glistened as the low clouds slowly evaporated. Shimmering mists crisscrossed deep shadows. The trampled grass he'd been following continued ahead beyond his vision. Shouldn't he have reached the camp by now?

A shiver coursed through him. What if those weren't his footprints after all? And if they weren't, whose path was he following? He strained to catch any sounds from camp, but only an echoing emptiness filled his ears, unbroken even by the chirping of birds. The silence felt cold and sinister, making his chest tighten.

Before he could figure out what to do, a huge blast of wind nearly knocked him backward. He bent his knees and braced his body to keep from being flung to the ground. His lashes blew flat against his eyelids. He threw up his arms to shield his face and squeezed his eyes shut tight, sucking in quick gasping breaths against the pressure.

As suddenly as it came, the wind ceased. Levi cautiously opened his eyes and had to squint against the sudden, brilliant light. A short distance ahead was a stand of leafy trees. Above it, the sun glared in the bluest of skies. The ghost of a half-moon hovered not far from the sun, and to his left, a riot of colors stretched across the grass as far west as his eyes could see.

"The flowers," he whispered to himself.

Miles and miles of wildflowers—bluebells, Indian paintbrushes, poppies, cornflowers—covered the meadows like one of his grandma's crazy quilts. His eyes traced the path he'd followed to a dip in the distance. He could barely make out a dark shape that must be the wrecked ship. Twisting around, he saw the mountains far behind. How had he wandered so far from camp?

The trail.

He turned slowly as the eerie feeling crept back up his spine. The path he'd followed to this place continued toward the copse of trees. Almost against his will, his feet carried him farther along the trail. The wind kicked up again, shoving him back, but he pressed ahead despite the spurts of alarm spiking his adrenaline.

He had to keep going because something inside the shadowy edge of the grove drew him, something that looked vaguely familiar. Tiptoeing now despite the fact that the wind noise must cover the sound of his footfalls, Levi inched closer.

Beneath the canopy of trees, a girl sat huddled by a trunk, her face on her knees, her arms hugging her shins. Long golden-blond hair streamed to the ground.

Sara?

Levi ran forward, no longer trying to be quiet, totally ignoring the warning in his mind, and dropped to his knees in front of her. He reached out to touch her, but somehow couldn't, almost as if the wind had frozen his hand in mid-air.

"Sara?" The word came out a raspy whisper he knew she couldn't possibly hear over the noisy gusts.

But her head twitched slightly. Her hands dropped to the ground beside her bare feet, and he noticed for the first time how long her fingernails were. Why didn't she have on her hiking boots? Had she been sleepwalking?

In slow motion, she lifted her head, golden strands of hair trickling back from her bare legs and arms. Levi registered the lacy white fabric she wore, like a nightgown, and then her hands slid up and pushed the hair from her face.

It wasn't Sara.

A girl more beautiful than he thought a girl could possibly be peered at him through purple-blue eyes. Her skin was purest white but tinged pink on her high cheekbones. Her lips were a deep full red.

The wind practically beat him now, sucking him backward like a tornado. Yet he resisted, mesmerized by the beautiful girl. She blinked at him through long golden-brown lashes. Her hair rested in a smooth curve against her pale shoulders as though she sat alone in the eye of a storm. Slowly, those red lips parted into a smile. She reached toward him with one hand, her nails long half-moons at the tips of her pale fingers.

With a grunt, he tried to force his hand, still frozen in mid-air, to take hers. Slowly, painfully, he made it move by millimeters toward her, never taking his eyes from her perfect face. The closer he moved, the more purple her irises became, until no blue remained. Just before his fingertips touched hers, a hurricane wind blasted him so hard he tumbled backward to the ground, landing in the sunlight outside the trees.

He lay on his back, stunned. What had happened?

The girl. He pushed to a sitting position and peered into the copse.

She stood in the shadows, the nightgown flowing to her ankles, and reached for him. But a fear like nothing he'd ever known clawed at him, like a monster trapped inside his gut. He shook his head.

She opened her mouth wide, revealing inch-long fangs dripping saliva, and released a scream that made him clap his hands to his ears.

Chapter 22

The Mormo

Blood vessels bulged on her forehead and corded in her neck. She raked the air with her nails, all the while screaming in fury. With his hands pressed so tight against his ears they ached, Levi half-ran, half-fell away from her. He scuttled back up the slick grass, trying to follow the path without letting go of his ears. No matter how tightly he pressed, the shrill sound pierced through.

After what felt like forever, the noise faded. He dared to drop his hands and peer back. The trees were a distant smudge in the bright kaleidoscope of flowers. The chirp of contented birds and the whistle of the gentle breeze were the only sounds.

Thank you, God, for getting me away from that . . . she-devil.

He sprinted flat-out toward the mountain, praying the others hadn't left without him.

When he reached the camp, Levi found the others preparing to hike back to the castle. He helped take down his tent and grabbed a quick breakfast, then he stood with Sara and Lizzie while the rest finished. He hadn't said a word about his early morning walk. In fact, he hadn't spoken a word at all. Shock kept his brain enveloped in as thick a fog as had covered the earth that morning.

"All right, spill." Lizzie stood in front of him, hands on her hips.

He blinked. Was she talking about the ship he'd found? Or that horrible she-monster?

"Well?" Lizzie cocked her head. "Sara says you talked some dragon into not blastin' Suzanne to smithereens. True?"

Sara frowned. "You think I lied?"

Lizzie pursed her lips. "Of course not, but I want to know why he didn't let the little wretch fry after what she did to me last year."

Levi shook his head. "You know I couldn't do that. Besides, I think she might be realizing what a creep she's chosen for a friend."

Sara hugged her arms to her waist, unfortunately drawing to mind the girl in the copse. "Hunter didn't act very . . . brave yesterday."

Levi scowled. "The jerk left us to die."

"That's not so surprising, y'all," Lizzie said. "Momma always says bullies are cowards at heart. And we all know Hunter's a bully."

Levi nodded, but he wasn't sure that was all there was to it. Hunter had never acted particularly scared of anything before, not like yesterday. But he didn't have time to give it more thought as Luke pushed into their circle, dropped his sleeping bag, and pointed at his swelling left eye. "Hunter is a bully. And he's in a really bad mood this morning."

"He punched you?" Levi's fist clenched. He was sick of Hunter's attitude.

"Yeah, but then I sort of knocked him into the mud when I was rerolling my sleeping bag." Luke smiled sheepishly. "By accident, of course."

Across the way, Hunter tried to clear the muck from his face, hair, and clothes as Braden stood nearby grinning. Levi burst out laughing. "Good going." He slapped Luke's shoulder. "Of course, now he's probably going to try to shove you off the mountain."

Luke's face paled, except for the purple ring around his eye.

"Don't worry about it, honey." Lizzie glared across at Hunter. "We've got your back."

"Yeah, we'll keep an eye out for you," Levi promised.

"And for any other injured dragons wanting to kill us," Sara whispered to Levi and Lizzie after Luke bent to gather his stuff.

"*And* for whatever's cuttin' the dragons," Lizzie said under her breath.

Levi nodded solemnly as Miss Althea approached the campers. "Time to go, everybody. Line up with another camper. We're using the buddy system. You're responsible for your partner. Stick together."

Levi started toward Sara, but Morgan stepped out from behind a nearby tree, headed straight for him, and said, "Levi . . ." just as Suzanne pushed past her.

"Oh no you don't, little girl. I'm hiking with Levi." Suzanne shot a filthy look at Hunter. "At least I know he won't abandon me if something tries to kill me."

With a low growl, Hunter turned away. When Morgan walked over to him and whispered something Levi couldn't hear, Hunter shoved away from her, scowling. He stalked to where Luke had moved into line with Sara and pushed between them.

"Hike with me, Sara," Hunter commanded.

Frowning hard, Levi caught Sara's eye. She gave her head a small shake and lined up with Hunter. Morgan ended up with Luke. Lizzie brought up the rear with Braden. She didn't look pleased.

Suzanne gripped Levi's arm, squeezing the new scab on his elbow, and he sighed. It was going to be a long day.

Levi had never been so glad to see the castle, not even last year after the horrible night with Deceptor. And it wasn't because of the danger, because there hadn't been any. At least nothing more than the usual hazards that went with climbing a rain-slick mountain trail with twenty kids and only two adults, both of whom were shorter than the average six-year-old. Even Braden behaved himself, possibly because Lizzie looked like she'd gladly throw him off the nearest cliff if he didn't.

No, it was the company that made Levi's hike torture. Suzanne hadn't shut up the entire time, and if he never had to listen to a fourteen-year-old girl's list of troubles again, it would be too soon. Between that and watching Sara chat with Hunter like they were the best of friends, he felt like his head was about to explode.

The moment Levi crossed the threshold, his body sore and his back aching from the weight of his gear, Mr. Dominic drew him away from his friends and upstairs to his study. As soon as the door closed behind them, the director faced Levi. Dark circles shrouded his eyes, and a deep wrinkle creased his brow.

"Albert and Althea tell me you met Nithir and Middie."

Levi nodded. Would Mr. Dominic be offended if he put down his stuff? He'd really like to sit. Better yet, he'd love to forget the whole thing and go take a nap.

The director blew out a breath, his eyes intense. "Tell me exactly what happened. Don't leave out a single detail."

"Yes, sir." Levi sighed. *No rest for the wicked, and the righteous don't need none.* Wasn't that what his grandpa always said? With a longing glance at an overstuffed chair, Levi ran his tongue over his parched lips and opened his mouth to begin.

Mr. Dominic's expression softened. "Wait, son, I apologize." He took the pack from Levi's back, accidentally scraping the scab from Levi's arm and making it bleed again. "I'm sorry." He dropped the pack into a corner and fetched a tissue from a box on a bookcase. He gave it to Levi, gestured for him to sit, and poured water from a pitcher in the corner. He offered a cup.

"Thanks." Levi slurped the liquid, set the cup on the floor at his feet, and pressed the tissue against his bleeding elbow.

"I'll let you get cleaned up and rested soon," Mr. Dominic promised. "But I really must ask for the full story first."

Levi launched in, recounting everything as best he could remember. "You say the cut was straight and deep? Perhaps like a knife wound?"

"Yes, sir."

"And Nithir actually stopped his attack when you told him to?"

Levi nodded.

Mr. Dominic studied him so closely he squirmed. What was the big deal? He knew dragons were horrifying and all, but these were trained dragons. Surely they were used to taking orders from people. Or at least from elves, which was pretty much the same thing, right?

"That's it?" The director's eyes were twin probes. "Nothing else happened out there?"

He swallowed hard. Should he mention the shipwreck? What about the purple-eyed she-devil? Would he get in trouble if he did? Miss Althea had told him to stay in his tent and he'd disobeyed. Besides, the whole thing was probably a hallucination of his sleep-deprived brain. At least that's what he kept hoping.

He feigned a big yawn, a delay tactic he'd used more than once with his parents. "Sorry, I'm wiped out." Maybe Mr. Dominic wouldn't ask any more questions.

The director stared at him in silence, his gaze sharp, suspicious. After a few moments, though, the intensity lessened. "Fine, you may go." He rose and opened the door. "Probably wouldn't hurt to stop off at the infirmary for a bandage or two." He indicated the tissue stuck to Levi's elbow.

Levi hefted his pack.

Mr. Dominic scrunched his sunburned nose. "A bath wouldn't hurt either."

Levi bent his lips into a smile and grabbed the doorknob. Then hesitated. Maybe he should mention the freaky purple-eyed girl. Maybe if he told Mr. Dominic, she wouldn't join the other monsters in his nightmares. Besides, he was tired of hiding things from the adults in his life. He needed their help.

Then his brow constricted at a new thought. What if the monster girl was Deceptor in yet another form? If so, he absolutely had to tell Mr. Dominic.

The director touched his shoulder. "Levi, something else happened. What is it?"

The truth, Levi. All of it. "This morning, early, I left camp to go for a walk." Heat climbed his neck, and he studied his freckled fist on the doorknob. "It was real foggy. After a while I ran into this shipwreck thing." He glanced at the director, whose expression stayed neutral.

"And then when I tried to follow my tracks back to camp, I ended up by these trees, and there was this . . . girl . . . sitting under them."

"What girl?"

"She had her face down. At first I thought it was Sara because her hair was really long and blond and all. The wind was blowing me backward really, really hard, but—"

Alarm entered Mr. Dominic's eyes.

Levi's throat tightened. Yep. He'd been stupid to ignore the warning. "I . . . I was afraid something was wrong with her, so I called her name and she looked up. I saw it wasn't Sara, but she smiled at me and reached out her hand." He paused. Would the director think he was nuts? Making up stories? He rushed ahead anyway. "Before I touched her hand, the wind knocked me down, and she turned into this monster thing with fangs and purple eyes, and I thought she was going to attack me. So I ran away." He stopped, sucked in a breath, waited. *Time for the loony bin.*

"A mormo? Has he brought them in?" the director said in a hoarse murmur. His gaze drifted from Levi's as if he'd forgotten he was there. "But it's been more than a month since the last attack. Surely she isn't really here . . ." He fixed his eyes on Levi and grasped his shoulders with both hands. "It had purple eyes? Are you certain?"

Levi gave a hesitant nod.

"Why didn't you stop?"

"Sir?" Because he was running for his life maybe?

"When the Spirit blew you back, why didn't you listen?"

He blinked several times. The wind. It had tried to stop him. Just like when he went down to the cellar. Just like last summer. Would he never learn? "I . . . didn't think."

But Mr. Dominic seemed to have forgotten him again. He muttered in a barely audible voice, "Maybe it's a trick. I pray it's a trick."

"Sir?" Levi finally said, unable to bear Mr. Dominic's fingers biting into his shoulders any longer. "Sir, your hands . . ."

With a shake of his head, the old man let go and apologized. "There's nothing to be done but check it out. You say it was near the shipwreck?"

"To the east of it, I think. I was sort of lost when I met her."

"I understand." He reached around Levi and opened the door.

But Levi didn't step through it. "Mr. Dominic?"

"Yes?"

"What was she?"

The old man's sigh bespoke extreme weariness. "A very evil creature. If you had touched her, she would've been freed to attack you." He met Levi's eyes. "Be thankful you escaped her. That God spared you. Never disregard His warnings again."

Levi nodded, too scared to ask for details.

"One thing is certain." Mr. Dominic straightened to his full height. "All campers will be restricted to the castle grounds from here on out. We'll double our security. I'll make a scouting trip to the mountains myself as soon as I alert the staff." He stopped ticking off items on his long fingers and graced Levi with a gentle smile. "I'm sorry you met up with her, my boy. Try to put her from your mind."

Again Levi nodded, though he doubted it would be so easy to obey.

Chapter 23

Fit to Rule?

Gasping for breath, Levi pushed open the door to the fourth floor. Had the spiral staircase grown steeper while he was gone? He staggered along the hall, dragging his stuff behind him, weighed down by thoughts of the mormo. Would Mr. Dominic find her? Could she come into the castle? He firmed his quivering jaw and forced the sound of her scream from his ears. He refused to think about the dripping fangs surrounded by her blood-red lips. He had to get a grip. He couldn't . . . wouldn't . . . let her join the other monsters in his nightmares.

But he couldn't help shivering. Maybe a hot bath would melt the fear from his heart. That and some sleep. His eyes burned like jellyfish stings every time he blinked.

Tired as he was, though, he couldn't resist a look at the shipwreck painting across from his room. He dropped his stuff and leaned in so close his nose almost touched the canvas. He inhaled the scent of old paint and dust as he tried to make out the fine detail of the ship's side. *There*. What did the words say?

Unable to make out the fine print, he huffed.

Something touched his shoulder. He jumped and banged his greasy forehead against the picture. Knocked loose from its hanger, the painting dropped. Levi fell to his knees, hands outstretched, and caught it just before it smashed to the stone floor. His poor knees weren't so fortunate.

Groaning, Levi shoved himself upright, holding the painting with great care, and turned to see what had startled him. Mrs. Sylvester stood mere inches away, her face white against the long blond hair drifting loose around her shoulders. Her blue eyes were wide, and her lips parted like the mormo's.

He barely repressed a shriek. "I . . . um . . . I'm sorry, ma'am." He swallowed against the dryness in his throat.

She didn't move a muscle, her gaze fixed on the painting in his hands. "Have you seen my husband?"

"Oh." He blinked a few times. "He stayed to help with the dragons. Somebody hurt them."

Her eyes darted to his face. "What? Where?" The words came out sharp, like claws.

Levi took a backward step but was halted by the cold stone wall. "On the mountain."

She stared at him a second longer, then spun on her heel and disappeared into her room. Levi released his pent breath.

He looked down at the picture weighing heavy in his hands. He'd better figure out how to get it hung back up right. When he flipped it over, he found a piece of wire looped around two tacks. He straightened it and was lifting the painting toward the nail when small handwriting at the picture's base caught his eye. He stepped nearer the window and peered at the tiny cursive letters. "*The Canadian Queen* by Nydia Sylvester. June 15, 1885."

Nydia Sylvester? Miss Nydia painted this picture? No way.

His gaze flew to the hall chaperones' door as a surge of sorrow for Mrs. Sylvester pushed into his heart. She must be reminded of her dead daughter every time she left her room and saw this painting. Her daughter who had betrayed the kingdom of Terracaelum and put Sara, the girl she'd vowed to protect, in a situation where she would've died if Nydia hadn't repented at the last moment and taken the death stroke instead.

Levi's thoughts returned to one of the many questions that had worried him all year. What had happened to Miss Nydia when she'd died?

Had she gone to Heaven? Hell? Or had she simply stopped existing? What happened at death to the non-humans populating Terracaelum? It was yet another question he wished he could ask his dad.

He thought of the phone call he'd been unable to make that afternoon. He needed to tell his parents the truth. But how could he do such a confession justice on a five-minute phone call surrounded by waiting campers? That would be so selfish, dropping such a bomb on his parents without enough time for them to ask questions or even scold him for his deception.

His shoulders slumped. He'd have to wait until after camp ended to make things right.

With a heavy sigh and another sad look at Mrs. Sylvester's door, Levi hung the painting in its spot and carried his stuff to his room.

If Levi hadn't been so exhausted, he would've walked right back out of his room. A stench filled it, one so strong it made his already-burning eyes feel like somebody had dripped acid into them. "Ugh. What is that stink?"

Trevor didn't remove his nose from the open window. "Steve."

"Steve?"

"Steve," Tommy said through the pair of gym socks he held over his lower face.

Levi wondered briefly if the socks were clean or dirty. With another inhale, he realized it didn't matter. Even socks coated in week-old sweat had to smell better than this stench. He pulled his shirt up over his nose and breathed in the stink of his own pits. "What happened to Steve now?" Surely not another exploding toilet.

"He met up with a skunk." Trevor's expression was pained.

"Actually," Tommy said dully, "he fell on a skunk."

Poor Steve. Poor skunk. "Is he okay?"

"Who?" Trevor blinked his watering eyes. "Steve or the skunk?"

"Or us?" Tommy groaned.

Levi couldn't help but smile. "I was talking about Steve."

The bathroom door opened before either could answer, and Steve walked out wrapped in a thick towel. Red smeared his forlorn face.

"You okay?" Levi stepped toward him. "Is that blood on your face?"

Steve shook his head. "Tomato juice. Supposed to get rid of the smell." He gestured toward the bathroom.

Levi glimpsed the bathtub full of red liquid. "Oh."

So much for a nice hot bath.

Levi flopped beside Sara on the thick grass near the empty archery mound later that week and opened his copy of *A Bride Named Thor.* "I hate this."

She offered a sympathetic smile. "I know."

He smiled back, appreciating that she didn't tell him he was silly for worrying about it. He settled in to studying lines while she read an English translation of *Prose Edda,* a collection of Norse myths, for Literature class.

After a silent half hour, he looked up, his eyes on the distant mountains. "Heard any more about Nithir and Middie?" He and Sara had told their friends about the campout, but only Sara had been with him to face the angry dragons. "Are they okay?"

"Mom said their wounds are pretty well healed. Mr. and Mrs. Drake spent most of the week with them." She looked down at her hands. "Mr. Sylvester came back soon after we did, though, because the dragons were trying to attack him."

"That's weird. I thought he was their trainer."

"He raised them from hatchlings. Most creatures are completely loyal after that." Sara's brow furrowed. "Of course, it's probably best for Mrs. Sylvester that he came back early. She gets anxious when he's gone for very long, ever since . . ."

Levi nodded, but he was distracted with a new and very distressing thought. Why would the dragons attack their trainer unless he'd . . . done something to earn their distrust? And then there was Mrs. Sylvester and her strange behavior. What if his elf hall chaperones had turned traitor like their daughter?

He shook his head. Now he was just being paranoid. "So, did they figure out what happened? Was it Deceptor who cut them?"

"Probably, but we don't know why." She shrugged. "Other than the obvious, of course."

His forehead creased.

She rolled her eyes. "To make them mad enough to attack people so the mountains aren't safe."

"Oh, yeah, that." Levi's cheeks heated. "Did they find any other injured creatures?"

"Not yet."

"Let's hope they don't."

She nodded then returned to her reading. Levi looked back toward the mountains. He could just make out something massive among the upper trees. Maybe Mr. Dominic's friendly giant hunting for his supper?

He glanced at Sara. With her head bent over the book on her lap and her blond hair hanging loose nearly to the grass, she looked almost identical to the she-devil on the other side of the mountain. A shudder tickled his spine as an image of purple eyes and gaping jaws replayed in his mind.

Then there was that lake monster. And Regin. And the dragons. Middie and Nithir were supposed to be tame, like the friendly giant, but they'd attacked. How many other dangerous creatures were there in Terracaelum? How many were supposedly under the Dominics' rule?

He thought of the deep lines and sunken eyes in Mr. Dominic's face and the near-constant trembling of Mrs. Dominic's hands. Could a couple soon to be a century and a half old really control those wild and dangerous beasts? Sure, they'd stepped up security and restricted the campers to the castle grounds. Sure, Albert said the men were taking turns patrolling the mountains in case of attack, but still.

He glanced at Sara again. Should he tell her about the mormo? Or about the lake monster? If he did, he'd probably end up spilling his guts about her parents and how he wasn't sure they could handle ruling Terracaelum anymore.

He didn't need anything else to feel bad about.
Probably best to leave it alone.

Chapter 24

Roommates

Levi galloped down the spiral staircase, hand sliding on the banister. It was finally Sunday afternoon, time to call home, and he was late. He hoped his folks were home this time. Even though he'd decided to hold off on telling them about Terracaelum, he still wanted to hear their voices.

As he barreled around a tight curve, he spotted someone huddled on the third-floor landing. "Look out!" Though friction burned a layer of skin from his palm, he screeched to a halt before he flattened Morgan.

He plopped to the floor, chest heaving. "What're you doing here? I almost squashed you."

Morgan's pale, tear-streaked face poked from behind the arms she'd propped on her knees. "Doesn't matter."

"What're you talking about? I could've really hurt you."

She shrugged, sniffling.

Levi's blood pressure surged. He could've gotten hurt himself. She had no business blocking the steps. But her pathetic expression settled him down, and he managed to keep his voice relatively gentle. As usual, Morgan reminded him of his sister Abby.

He pushed the thought away. "What's wrong, Morgan? Why're you crying?"

She shook her head.

"Come on, you can tell me." He glanced at his wristwatch. Ugh. He didn't have time for girl tears.

"Don't worry about it. Your friends are probably waiting for you."

Why did her words make him feel guilty? He hadn't done anything wrong. And he really wanted to talk to his family. "Yeah, actually they are." He looked at his watch again. "I'm supposed to hike down to the phones with them, but I'm so late they probably left without me." He stood and offered his hand. "Come with me. Talk to me on the way."

Chin trembling, Morgan took his hand and rose.

"So, what's up?" he asked as they walked down the trail a short time later, everyone else far ahead.

"My roommates hate me."

"Why would they hate you?"

She gave a small snort. "They hate me because I'm not rich like them. Ever since I told them about my momma . . ." She shook her head.

"My parents aren't rich." Levi moved a tree branch so it wouldn't scratch Morgan. "Whether or not you have money shouldn't make any-body hate you."

"It's not just the money." Her voice quieted so he had to lean down to hear. "My momma's not a nice lady. That's why I live with my aunt and uncle. Have since I was little."

She was still little. "That shouldn't matter. Plenty of people live with their aunts and grandmas and stuff."

"Yeah. I shouldn't have told them why I don't live with Momma, that's all."

He waited. What was the big deal about her momma? "Well, you can't help who your mom is or what she's done. If your roommates don't get that, they're not worth worrying about."

"Really?"

He shrugged. "Well, yeah."

She smiled, but the corners of her mouth soon drooped. "It's lonely, though, not having any friends."

His heart gave a tug, and he nodded, thinking how his little sister would feel in Morgan's place. "What if I talk to Sara? They have an open bunk in their room you could maybe have."

She looked doubtful. "You think they'd want me?"

"Sure, why not?"

Levi hung up the phone and wandered outside. His family was home this time, but they were so busy with their own lives, he felt more isolated from them than ever. His sister's choral group had a big performance next week, and his brothers were in swim lessons and softball. Grandpa kept having those dizzy spells, which meant Mom spent every spare minute helping out at their place. And Dad . . . well, there was always somebody at church needing him. By the time Levi had listened to everyone else's news, his phone time had been over.

"You ready to head back?" Sara bumped him lightly with her elbow. "We're all finished." She motioned toward the others clustered beside her.

"Yeah, okay." Levi started toward the trail, not feeling much like talking to anyone, when he remembered.

"Wait . . . Morgan." He wheeled around and scanned the area. She stepped from the building at that moment, her face anxious. "Hey, Morgan, come on." He waved her over.

Her expression brightened, and she hurried to his side. He ignored the furrowed brows and soft whispers of his friends as she snagged his arm. They climbed the path in a bunch, the others' usual chatter subdued—by Morgan's presence, most likely. Levi gave a mental shrug. They'd accept her eventually. She was just a lonely kid, and being kind to someone like her was supposed to be what Christians did, right?

"So, Sara," Levi began, sidling up next to her, "without Ashley in your room, you guys have an extra bed, don't you?"

She looked confused but nodded. The other girls went totally silent.

"Morgan's roommates aren't being very nice to her." He glanced at Morgan with his brows raised, and she nodded her approval. He looked back at Sara. "I told her you three would be happy to have her move in with you."

"Oh?" Sara stopped dead in the path, eyes wide. Everyone else halted.

Monica's mouth opened and closed a few times. Lizzie bit her bottom lip as if to keep from saying something she shouldn't.

"Yeah." Levi shrugged. "You guys have the space and all."

Trevor snorted. Levi shot him a dirty look.

"Sure, that's fine." Sara turned questioning eyes to the other girls. "Isn't it?"

"Yeah."

"Okay."

None of them sounded enthusiastic.

Morgan's cheeks pinked. "You mean it?"

Sara gave a slow nod.

"Thank you so much." Morgan grabbed Sara's and Monica's hands and let out a squeal.

Levi flinched as Lizzie speared him with a look. He would probably get an earful later, but what was he supposed to do? He couldn't let the poor girl stay with mean roommates.

"Come on." Steve started up the trail, huffing. "It's nearly suppertime. I'm hungry."

Levi silently thanked him for the distraction.

In the middle of that night, Levi sat bolt upright in bed, t-shirt drenched with sweat. Heart pounding, he darted wide-eyed glances around the dark room. Nothing was there but his roommates sacked out in snoring lumps on their beds. He drew in a deep breath and told himself to relax. It was a nightmare, nothing more.

"*The Lord is my light and my salvation. Whom shall I fear?*" He ran the verse through his mind over and over. When his pulse stopped pounding in his ears, he lay back on his damp pillow and closed his eyes. They instantly shot open again. Why wouldn't those hideous shapes leave his brain? He was fed up with nightmares. They'd been tormenting him for way too long. Now even the Scriptures failed to offer comfort.

He'd thought the troubles of his miserable school year would end when he got back to Terracaelum, but nothing felt right. He hadn't made things right with his parents. He'd gotten himself into trouble at camp a couple of times already. He'd aggravated the girls by getting them to take in Morgan. Plus, he'd added extra monsters to his night-mares, and he wasn't sure he could trust Mr. Dominic to protect him from them. Aargh.

With a grunt, Levi shoved aside his soggy sheet and climbed from bed. He slipped on shorts and sneakers, snagged his flashlight, and crept from the room. Just as he eased the door closed, it popped open. Gasping, he stumbled backward.

Trevor stepped into the corridor, the goofy grin on his face chafing Levi's nerves. "Hey, where you going?"

"Tower."

Oblivious to Levi's uninviting response, Trevor pulled the door closed behind them. "Can I come?"

No. Levi shrugged and headed for the tower staircase. As he climbed, he tried to shove aside his crankiness. Trevor was keeping him company like he usually did on these midnight trips. He probably knew Levi was having bad dreams and didn't want him to be alone.

But Levi wanted to be alone. *Why, God? Why won't you make these dreams leave me? Why won't you make everything right?*

"So, how's your family?"

Levi rolled his eyes in the darkness. "Fine."

"Did you tell them hi for me?"

"Forgot. Sorry."

A pause, then Trevor said, "Did you tell your dad about me winning that fencing match against Martin?"

Ugh. Another reminder of Levi's puniness. "No."

"Oh."

The note of disappointment in Trevor's voice drove his aggravation up another notch. Even though they were almost at the top of the steps, he wheeled around and glared at him in the lantern light. "Why not call your own dad and tell him?"

Trevor glowered at him, lips pressed into a thin line.

Levi spun around and took the remaining stairs in two large steps. He shoved open the door and stomped halfway across the roof.

"What's with you anyway?" Steel edged Trevor's words.

Levi folded his arms over his chest, hands fisted, and glared at the cloud-choked moon. "Nothing's with me."

"Yeah, right."

He twisted around. "What's that supposed to mean?"

"It means you need to get over yourself."

"Get over myself?" His voice cracked. "Get over myself?"

"Yeah." Trevor's fists balled. His face reddened, and the muscles bulged in his bare upper arms. "Get over yourself."

Snarling like a junkyard dog, Levi flew at Trevor and punched with all his strength square into his best friend's chin.

Releasing a bellow and a spatter of blood, Trevor snatched Levi in a headlock and punched him in the stomach.

Sucking wind, Levi dropped to his knees. Trevor stumbled away a few paces.

"What do the two of you think you're doing?" an angry voice demanded from near the door.

Blinking the fireworks show from his eyes, Levi watched Miss Althea grab Trevor by the scruff of his neck. A trail of blood dripped from his friend's mouth.

"Up, you." The tiny woman hauled Levi from the ground. His breath came in ragged gasps. With both boys gripped in her iron claws, she yanked them toward the stairs. "You're going to Mr. Dominic's office."

Levi wheezed along, bent double from the pain in his middle and the short woman's grip on his collar. He tried not to fall down the steep staircase as she continued her rant. She reminded him more than ever of her great-aunt Mrs. Forest—minus the gray hair. At least she didn't have him by the earlobe. "Out of bed in the middle of the night. And on the roof fist-fighting like a pair of hoodlums. Shame on you! I thought you two were friends."

Levi was ashamed. What had possessed him to throw a punch at his best friend? The last time he'd slugged somebody had been when Zeke broke his Darth Vader action figure four years earlier. His dad had made him promise he'd never hit anybody like that again.

When they reached the bottom of the steps without breaking their necks, Miss Althea slammed the door with a sharp kick. "He should send you both home for this one."

Levi's head jerked up. Would Mr. Dominic expel them?

Chapter 25

Awaiting Judgment

Levi and Trevor sat side-by-side on the stone floor outside Mr. Dominic's office, where Miss Althea had commanded them to wait. Neither spoke for several moments. Only the muffled sound of voices from the office and the occasional scrub of Trevor's hand across his bloody mouth filled the silence.

After the fifth swipe, Levi asked quietly, "Still bleeding?"

Trevor grunted. "Bit my tongue." He stuck it out.

Levi cringed at the bloody tear in its tip. "I'm really sorry." He looked away. "I shouldn't have punched you." He glanced back at Trevor.

"You got that right." Trevor leaned against the stone wall and grimaced. "But I guess I got you back." He smirked. "Didn't think you were ever gonna quit sucking wind."

Levi rubbed his sore belly. "You hit me hard."

"Don't pick a fight if you can't take the licks. That's what my dad always says when my brother beats the mess out of me." Trevor shrugged. "He never cares that my brother picks the fights just so he can cream me."

What could Levi say? His dad would never treat him or his brothers so wretchedly.

"That's why it gets on my nerves so much."

"What?"

"The way you take your family for granted."

"I don't take—"

"You do." Trevor frowned, cracking the blood crusted in the corners of his mouth. "You act like they're a collective pain in your precious little neck."

"That's not true." At least not since he got back to camp. "Besides . . ." Levi jerked his back away from the wall as anger coursed through him again. "What do you know about it? I've been to your house. You've got everything, computers and cars and stuff. And all brand new. You have a flat screen plasma TV in every room of your house. We've never had a new TV in our lives."

"So? That's just stuff."

With a hand slash, Levi dismissed the statement. "You don't have somebody breathing down your neck every second, making sure you're doing what they want, not listening when you tell them you should be able to do what you want. I mean, your dad lets you do anything."

Trevor shook his head like he was talking to a particularly dim-witted child. "That's because he doesn't give a rat's behind what I do."

"Exactly."

"Yeah. Exactly. He doesn't care what I do because he doesn't care about *me*." He looked like he wanted to slug Levi again. "You're so dense you don't even see that your folks pay attention to what you're doing because they actually care about you."

Levi's ears felt scorched. "They treat me like I'm an infant. Not like a guy who's battled a sorcerer and survived a trip through the underworld with a dark dwarf and . . . and a dragon and . . ." He trailed off without mentioning the lake monster or the mormo.

"Did you tell them about any of those things?"

Levi couldn't maintain eye contact. "No."

"Why not?"

"Because if I told them, they'd never let me come back." There. He'd said it out loud. The real reason he still hadn't confessed, which had almost nothing to do with how hard it'd be for his family to learn about Terracaelum over the phone, and everything to do with his own selfishness.

Trevor popped him lightly on the arm. "I know your mom would probably freak, but that's just 'cause she's your mom. But your dad? He's always really cool, the way he listens to people. Really listens."

Levi studied the wistful expression on his friend's face. Trevor had spent a lot of time with Levi's dad when he'd come to their house over Thanksgiving and spring break. He'd even gone with them to their grandparents' house for Christmas. When Levi's mom had thrown a family party for Trevor's birthday, complete with his favorite homemade chocolate cake and a birthday hug, Levi had seen the tears on his lashes. He'd once asked Trevor if his dad minded him spending all those school holidays and special occasions away from home, and the answer had been, "You've got to be kidding. Dad doesn't *do* special occasions. Not since Mom died."

"But your dad drove us to camp," Levi whispered now, knowing how feeble his words sounded. Trevor's dad hadn't spoken any more than necessary on the entire trip and had left before the ferry even arrived.

"He couldn't exactly refuse when your dad called to say he had to preach a funeral, now could he? And my brother flat-out told him no way he was gonna drive us."

Levi pressed his lips together.

"I called him," Trevor whispered.

"Your dad?"

His face reddened. "No, yours. When you were late for the phones with that Morgan girl."

Now Levi's face heated. "I couldn't just leave her crying on the stairs, could I?"

Trevor grinned and shrugged, brows lifted.

Not going there. "So why'd you call my dad?"

"Just wanted to talk to somebody who gave a rip, you know."

"Yeah." Levi fell silent, the buzzing conversation in the Dominics' office suddenly loud in the stillness. He shot a glance at the door. "You think they'll actually kick us out?"

Trevor sighed. "I hope not. I sure don't want to spend the rest of the summer at my house."

"I should send you two packing." Mr. Dominic sat behind his huge antique desk, hands folded as if praying for strength. Beside him, Miss Althea glowered down on them like a judge on convicts.

Levi shifted in the cushioned chair. Here he sat, in trouble again. The fire blazing nearby had felt good after an eon of sitting on the cold stone floor, but now sweat trickled from his armpits. In the chair next to him, Trevor squirmed.

"Fist fighting on the tower roof?" Mr. Dominic's tone was sharp. "Who gave you permission to be out of your beds at this hour?"

Uh-oh. "It's my fault, sir." Levi met the director's gaze. "I . . . I couldn't sleep and Trevor . . ." He glanced at his friend then back to Mr. Dominic. "Trevor was just checking on me when I got up."

Miss Althea grunted. "That wasn't checking. That was punching."

His eyes flew to hers then back to the director's. "That was my fault, too. I picked a fight. I'm sorry."

The grandfather clock ticked away the silent seconds, then: "Althea, why don't you go on to bed. I'll deal with these two." Mr. Dominic fixed them in a stern glare.

"If you insist." Miss Althea huffed as she strode toward the door.

When she was gone, Mr. Dominic sat tapping his steepled forefingers together. "I must assume you two think the rules don't apply to you?"

"Sir?" Trevor shrank back in his seat. "No, sir, we don't think that."

Levi shook his head, eyes wide.

"There's a reason hall chaperones do room check every night. Do you know what it is?"

"To make sure we're in our rooms?" Levi couldn't keep the tremble from his voice.

"To make sure everyone is accounted for." The director's gaze fell heavy on him. "If anyone is not safe in his bed, we must assume something has happened to him. We must search for him."

Like they'd had to do for him more than once already. "Yes, sir."

"I won't ask how often these midnight trips to the roof have occurred," Mr. Dominic said sternly. "But I will demand that they not occur again."

"They won't, sir." Trevor's face was white.

Levi nodded, but the thought of having to stay in bed with his nightmares nearly overwhelmed him. He stared down at his white-knuckled hands clenched in his lap. "It's just that sometimes I have these dreams, and I need to get away." Several moments of silence met his words. Finally, he couldn't stand it and peeked up at the director, careful to avoid Trevor's eyes.

"Sometimes," Mr. Dominic said softly, "our thoughts and memories can crush us beneath their weight."

Levi felt a sudden stinging behind his eyes. He nodded.

The director's lips curved slightly. "I'd imagine a boys' bathroom isn't conducive to clearing your thoughts of such evils."

Trevor snorted as Levi let out a relieved chuckle. He shook his head.

"All right then. I'll grant you permission to visit the chapel when such dreams attack. Then, if you aren't in your room, I'll know to look for you there."

The chapel? Why hadn't he thought of that? Talking to God would be a lot better way to handle things than punching Trevor. "Thank you."

"You're welcome, but . . ." The steely tone returned. "Don't ever disobey my rules again."

Trevor made a loud gulping sound. Levi nodded hard.

"Now for your punishment."

Chapter 26

Torture

After another play practice/torture session in the great hall the next afternoon, Levi scooted toward the hall, ready to escape the humiliation. He could still hear Hunter and company making skirt jokes from over by the foosball table. But Morgan caught up with him before he could reach the door and instantly began chattering, oblivious to the fact that he wasn't in the mood to chat. He looked behind him, hoping to foist her off on Lizzie, who'd been cast as Freyja.

Lizzie only smirked at him, tossed her mane of pink-ribboned hair, and paraded through the open French door on the opposite side of the room. Shoulders slumped, he turned away. Since Sara and Monica had refused to be in the play after last summer, there wasn't anybody else to pass Morgan off on. He trudged into the hall with her practically skipping along at his side.

"It's so exciting. Lizzie's so beautiful, she'll make the perfect Freyja, don't you think?"

He sighed. "She was great as Helen of Troy last year."

"I can imagine. I'm just so glad you talked to them about letting me be their roommate." Morgan's small hand clasped his. "They're so sweet."

"Yeah." He tried to pull his fingers free without being obvious.

As they neared the kitchen doorway, a loud thumping noise erupted from within.

Morgan's grip on his hand tightened. "What's that?"

Levi shushed her and peeked around the doorframe. Mr. and Mrs. Forest hovered by the closed cellar door, him with a butcher knife, her with an iron skillet.

When Morgan gasped, he squeezed her hand to silence her.

"Do you think it's that nasty Dvergar again?" Mrs. Forest's skillet trembled.

"Hard to say. It rained awful hard this morning—here and down under. Could be a sailor." Her husband inched closer to the cellar. A violent barrage rattled the wood. He jumped, dropping the knife millimeters from his wife's foot.

"Eek! You put that thing away." She flew—literally—to the far side of the work island. Levi yanked Morgan back, hoping she hadn't noticed that Mrs. Forest's feet hadn't touched the floor as she fled.

"I'm so sorry, dear," the pixie cook was saying as Levi pulled Morgan down the hall, his finger to his lips. He finally stopped beside a tapestry of the Greek god Hades tossing a screaming, writhing soul into Tartarus.

Morgan stared at Levi, her freckles standing out on her pale face. "What was that all about?"

He shook his head and pried her fingers from his hand. Red half-moons stood out where her nails had dug in.

She planted her small fists on her hips. "You disappeared somewhere a few weeks ago." A shrewd look entered her eyes. "You went down in the cellar, didn't you?" She didn't give him a chance to answer. "What's down there? Some sailor? Or a . . . what did she call it?"

His gaze flicked to the tortured soul in Hades's grasp. He could totally relate. "Dvergar." He bit his lip. Why had he told her the name?

"Dvergar? What's that?" Her eyes glittered with an intense curiosity that made his stomach perform an elaborate tap dance.

"It's nothing. Don't worry about it."

"Whatever." She folded her arms across her chest. "I'm not a baby, you know."

He put his hands on her shoulders and bent to meet her eyes. "I mean it, Morgan. Leave. It. Alone."

"I said okay." Bottom lip poked out, she stomped up the stairs without him.

He heaved a sigh. At least she hadn't noticed the flying cook.

"She's always listenin' to our private conversations," Lizzie whined two days later. She crossed her arms over her chest, bottom lip poked out, looking just like her new roommate had when she'd stormed away from Levi after the kitchen incident. "We had to sneak out just to come up here without her tagging along like some stray dog we shouldn't have fed." Lizzie flopped down on the stone tower rooftop then grimaced as though she regretted the flop, melodrama or not.

Levi rubbed a hand across his mouth to smother a snigger. Tommy, Trevor, and Steve didn't even try to hide their cackles.

"It is not at all amusing to us." Monica pursed her lips. "Imagine, if you will, the difficulty of accomplishing one's tasks when one's roommate talks without ceasing." Her eyes sparked like coals about to burst into flame.

Uh-oh. Monica's snobby tone only came out when she was nervous . . . or furious. And her flaring nostrils told him she wasn't feeling at all nervous.

"Okay, I'm sorry." He sat cross-legged on the floor beside Sara, hoping she'd be more sympathetic. "I felt bad for her. She's lonely and homesick and her roommates were being hateful to her." He met each girl's eyes in turn. "All because her momma made some stupid decisions and left her with relatives."

"Her momma left her?" Lizzie's rigid shoulders dropped a notch. "Really?"

He nodded, knowing Lizzie's dad had abandoned her and her mom when she was little. "Yeah, and when her roommates found out, they acted like it was Morgan's fault somehow."

Lizzie thumped a fist into her palm. "It's not her fault what her momma did."

"She didn't tell us any of this." Monica settled next to Trevor, who raised both eyebrows at Levi.

"No, she didn't," Sara said softly.

"She was probably scared you'd be mean, too." Levi clucked his tongue. "But I knew you'd be nice to her." He studied their three flushed faces, not even a little sorry for the guilt trip he was laying on them. "That's why I suggested she room with you."

"Oh, all right, I'm sorry." Lizzie let out a windy sigh. "I'm being petty again."

"Me, too." Sara met Levi's gaze. "We'll be nicer to Morgan."

Monica shrugged. "She's probably trying too hard to fit in. Once she realizes we're not here to judge her, she'll relax and be herself."

"I'm sure you're right." Levi tossed Trevor a victorious glance.

Trevor grinned and shot him a thumbs-up behind the girls' backs. "She'll probably end up your very best friend."

Lizzie whacked him on the arm. "Shut up, Trevor."

He gave her a wide-eyed look of injured innocence. "What?"

"Should I go find her and bring her up here?" Sara asked Levi.

He peered around the tower rooftop, the place they liked to hang out, just them. Thankfully, Mr. Dominic hadn't said they weren't allowed up here at all, only not after room check.

But to include Morgan in their circle . . .

He felt the weight of six pairs of eyes on him. They were clearly leaving the decision to him. He didn't want that responsibility. Sure, Ashley wasn't in their group anymore, which should mean there was room for Morgan. But she was different. He gave his head a tiny shake. He didn't want anyone else in their group. They were comfortable. They fit together.

"You can't leave her out because she's a little annoying or awkward." Steve stood, his cheeks as red as Lizzie's nail polish. "Otherwise, you'd have to kick me out too."

"We're not gonna kick you out, you goober." Trevor slugged Steve lightly on his oversized gut. "Sit back down."

Steve shot him a dirty look. "I'm serious. If you're going to leave Morgan out because she's a pesky little kid, then a fat kid like me doesn't belong either."

Sara stood and touched his arm. "We aren't trying to leave people out, Steve. Certainly not because of how they look. It's just . . ." She turned to Monica and mouthed the word *help*.

Monica sighed. "It changes the dynamics. To add anybody to a group makes it different." She shrugged. "And it has nothing to do with appearance. I mean, look at me." She held out her black hand to Steve.

"That's right." Tommy stuck out his yellow-brown hand beside hers.

"Yeah, and me." Levi smacked himself on the scrawny chest. "Do you know, the old ladies at my church are forever telling me they wish they had my hair?" He yanked at one of his curls. "Why anybody would want an orange afro like Bozo the clown, I'll never get."

Guffawing, Trevor smacked Levi's tennis shoe. "Yeah, and as for awkward and annoying . . ." He grinned at Steve. "Levi's got us all beat."

"Hey, look who's talking, you big gorilla." Levi reached around Sara and popped Trevor on the back of the head. But then he laughed, and everyone else joined in, Steve included.

Hours later, as they descended the tower steps for supper, Levi realized they'd never decided how much to let Morgan into their group. If they included her fully, they'd have to tell her all about Terracaelum and Deceptor and everything. Otherwise, they couldn't talk about anything ever. Besides, Mr. Dominic had told them not to tell the new kids about Terracaelum. They couldn't disobey the director again, or he and Trevor would get kicked out.

Despite his logic, an uneasy guilt nibbled at his insides.

The next afternoon, Levi stuffed soiled tablecloths and smelly sheets into the washing machine. Only two industrial-size washers and dryers for all these people. He'd be doing laundry until he was Mr. Dominic's age. Grumbling under his breath, he slopped in some detergent, slammed the door, and spun the dial. Then he turned, jerked open the dryer door, and tugged a wad of hot towels into a basket.

He lugged the basket to the folding table and peered out the open window as he folded. The humid air from outside did little to cool the sweltering laundry room. Steam seeped from the kitchen where a couple of the Forests' grand-nieces and nephews were finishing the lunch dishes.

He blew upward to dislodge a sweat droplet from his left eyebrow. It fell, straight into his eye. "Grrr." Why couldn't he have gotten Trevor's job? Levi could see him out there, trimming the undergrowth in the woods nearest the castle. Surely it was cooler in the shade than in this sauna.

When Mr. Dominic had meted out punishment for their midnight fight on the tower roof, he'd been thankful for the grace. Now he didn't think grace had anything to do with it. If he'd been sent home, at least he could sit in an air-conditioned house. He'd probably melt into a puddle of stinky goo in this stifling torture chamber by the time he finished out his sentence. Every Thursday afternoon until the end of summer. Four more Thursdays.

After another hour of careful folding—he'd learned the hard way to be careful when Mrs. Forest made him redo two baskets of sheets that weren't up to her standards—Levi knew he'd die of dehydration if he didn't stop for a drink. He slinked to the door leading to the kitchen and peeked around the corner. Surely Mrs. Forest wouldn't begrudge him a cup of cold water, but who knew? She could be downright nasty. Not that he could blame her, working in these horrible rooms all the time.

Levi sighed when he saw the empty kitchen. He crept to the cabinets in search of a cup. When he found one, he opened the huge refrigerator and rummaged for something to drink. Ahh, lemonade. After another quick peek around the room, he pulled out the massive glass jug and carried it carefully to the work island. He poured the beverage and watched sweat bead on the glass. Eager for that first swig, he rushed the heavy pitcher back to the refrigerator.

Before he reached it, a loud banging came from the back corner. He startled so violently he lost his grip on the slick handle. Though he scrambled to regain his hold, Levi could only watch it fall to the stone floor.

He stood slack-jawed, covered from head-to-toe in lemonade, staring at the sticky liquid coating every surface of the kitchen. Shattered glass sparkled on the floor. Fury filled him so the lemonade practically sizzled on his skin. Heedless of the broken glass, he stomped to the still-rattling cellar door. "Regin!"

The clatter ceased.

"You idiot, quit banging on the door all the time!"

The clanking started in again, even louder than before. Eyes bulging until a twitch started in his right lid, Levi grabbed the handle. He'd show that stupid dwarf.

But a high-pitched squeal from across the kitchen froze Levi in his tracks.

Chapter 27

Spilled Lemonade

Slowly, with a dread so great he thought the blood must have congealed in his veins, Levi turned. Mrs. Forest stood purple-faced and sputtering, gaping from the mess to the now-still door, and then to him. He yanked his hand from the knob and backed up a few paces.

"You . . . you . . ." Veins bulged in the little woman's neck.

For a wild moment, he considered plucking open the cellar door and leaping down. Surely another trip through the underworld was better than this nightmare. Any moment now, she'd regain her powers of speech and then—

"What do you think you're doing?" Mrs. Forest's soft whisper scared him more than the shriek he'd expected.

His mouth opened and closed several times before he could speak. "I . . . I'm sorry. I just got so thirsty." A traitorous burst of saliva coated his tongue. "It's hot." He swept a hand toward the laundry room. "It was an accident. I was putting away the lemonade when Regin started . . ." He gestured to the silent door. "He startled me, and I dropped it." His gaze lowered to the mess on the floor. "I'm sorry. I'll clean it up right now."

Levi turned to look for a mop, shoulders tense, waiting for Mrs. Forest to snag his earlobe and drag him to Mr. Dominic's office again. He'd be sent home for sure this time. No more mercy.

As he pulled a bucket from its hook and trudged to the sink, thinking of how he'd have to tell his friends goodbye and of how he'd never see Terracaelum again, the complete silence caught his attention. He peered around. Mrs. Forest had disappeared. Was she fetching Mr. Dominic?

Or could she possibly be letting him off?

"Please, God . . ." As the bucket filled with soapy water, he swept the broken glass into a pile.

Forty-five minutes later, he left the spotless kitchen and returned to the laundry room. He sighed at the silent washer and dryer and the piles of reeking towels waiting for his attention. It was going to be a long evening. He moved toward the dryer, the heat an almost visible presence, and his parched throat reminded him he'd never gotten that drink.

But at least it didn't look like he'd get kicked out of camp.

"How is it your mom and dad always know when to open the door for us?" Levi murmured to Sara as they climbed the path to the castle, their friends trailing them. They'd passed an uneventful week and had just spent the night camping on the south side of the island. No one had been allowed to camp near the mountains since the dragon and mormo incidents. "I mean, they don't have time to hang out on the doorstep all day."

Sara shrugged. "They keep a pretty tight schedule with the staff. Plus, they have people watching to tell them when we're coming." She nodded toward the castle that appeared as she spoke. Atop the southwest tower, Albert waved at them.

Levi waved back and started across the drawbridge, his thoughts on that day in June when he'd willed the castle to appear and it hadn't. "Can the watchmen see Castle Island when the castle's not visible?" He glanced at Sara out of the corner of his eye. He hadn't mentioned that incident to anyone, not even Sara or Trevor.

"There are spy windows in a few places, so they can see even when the castle's not seen, but they don't usually man them when no one's expected."

Levi smiled at Mrs. Dominic and waited until they'd passed out of her hearing before he asked Sara his next question. "What if you got locked out and your folks were . . . not available . . . not around . . . to let you in? Shouldn't there be a key or something?"

"Oh, there is. We keep one just in case—" She halted, face flaming and eyes wide, and gripped his upper arms with both hands. "Don't you dare say a word about that, Levi Prince." As the other campers neared, she lowered her voice still more. "It's treason for me to even mention it."

"Don't worry. I won't say anything to anybody. Promise."

Her breath left her in a hiss. "Thanks."

He offered her a reassuring smile and fell into step with Lizzie and Morgan, who were giggling over the way Mr. Austin bellowed when Morgan had knocked the tent down on him in the middle of the night.

"I couldn't help it." Morgan's cheeks pinked, but she grinned. "It was so dark, and I had to use the bathroom. I tripped over the peg."

Levi chuckled at the memory then glanced at Sara. She trailed the group, worrying her lower lip. What was her problem? Did she really think he'd tell anyone about the key when he'd promised he wouldn't?

Chapter 28

Dead Fish

Later that week in Science class, Levi yawned so big his jaw popped. He was worn out because he, Sara, and Steve had gotten permission to stay up late the night before to finish their science project on the animal life in Lake Superior. He leaned back in his desk and peered at the cloth-covered aquarium his group had painstakingly filled with specimens from the lake. They'd taken such care researching each creature—what it ate, how it lived, whether it was endangered. They deserved top grades for their efforts.

From the desk in front of him, Steve turned to give him a sleepy smile and a double thumbs-up. Levi smiled back.

Trevor flopped into the desk beside him. "You guys finish in time?"

"Yep. You?" Trevor, Tommy, Monica, and Lizzie had been assigned an in-depth study of the weather patterns on the lake.

"Yeah, you know Monica. I just had to keep my mouth shut and follow orders. We'll get an A, easy." He stretched his long legs into the aisle. "'Course not everybody likes to follow her orders." He cut his eyes toward Lizzie, who sat grumbling in her desk two ahead of Levi's.

Levi smirked. Trevor had probably witnessed some serious lightning and thunder in his group—and not just in the weather they'd studied for their project.

"Good morning, children," Mrs. Austin called briskly as she carried several notebooks into the classroom. She had a pencil stuck through her bun. "Presentation time. I hope you've all worked hard." She flashed a steely smile and dumped the notebooks on her desk. "Come on now, who's first?" She clapped her hands. "Chop-chop."

Martin, Suzanne, and Jacqueline meandered to the front of the room and arranged themselves around an oversized poster turned backward on an easel. Martin skulked in the back. Hunter strutted up last, casting a smile at Sara as he passed. When she smiled back, the blood boiled in Levi's veins. Had she told her friend Hunter about the castle key? If so, she should be worried about him giving away secrets, not Levi.

Once Hunter reached the front, he turned the poster and sent Mrs. Austin an ingratiating smile. "We've prepared a study of shipping on the Great Lakes, both past and present." He gestured toward the full-color, professionally printed poster. "As you can see . . ."

By the time Hunter finished speaking, even Mrs. Austin was yawning. The group swaggered to their seats, Martin looking relieved that he hadn't been required to speak. Hunter threw Levi a smirk that said *top that*. Levi smirked back. He knew his group's project was way better. And they'd done the work themselves instead of plagiarizing some guy's master's thesis and sending to the mainland for an expensive print job.

"Next?" Mrs. Austin called, her eyes still slightly unfocused.

Levi, Sara, and Steve walked to the front.

Sara lifted their handmade poster from its perch behind the aquarium and held it up for the class to see. "We studied the animals native to the Castle Island area." She indicated the neat block letters she'd printed the night before. "We gathered a sample of some of the smaller ones and brought them to show you." As she motioned toward the aquarium, she nodded to Levi. "The cover?"

He and Steve lifted the sheet. The second the cloth cleared the tank, a gasp went up from the class. Levi grinned. Their work was impressive. Steve flashed him a smile as they dropped the cover in the corner.

At Sara's whispered, "Oh, no," Levi turned to see what was wrong. A groan made its way between his lips—a groan echoed by Steve.

The sparkling clean water they'd left full of healthy lake creatures was now dark lavender and clearly toxic. Several fish floated belly-up near the top. Even as he watched, another died.

Mrs. Austin stomped over to them. "Do you think this is funny?" Her eyes bugged out.

He blinked. "You think we did this on purpose?" Heat started up his neck. He glanced at his project partners. How could she believe they'd do something like this? Especially Sara.

Steve's mouth worked soundlessly before he burst out, "We didn't!"

Sara's nostrils flared. "Of course we didn't. Everything was perfect when we left last night." Her fists clenched and unclenched at her side. "Somebody sabotaged our project."

Mrs. Austin searched their faces another moment before turning her glare on the class. "Does anybody know anything about this?"

No one said a word.

"Because if you saw anything, you'd better tell me now." Her eyes flashed. "This goes beyond messing up another group's work, which is bad enough. This is about killing innocent creatures." She made a swiping gesture toward the aquarium. By now the water was deep purple, and Levi was pretty sure all the animals were dead.

Several agonizing seconds passed, and still nobody spoke. Then, when Mrs. Austin's face had grown so red Levi thought she'd pop a blood vessel, someone near the back raised a hand. He strained to see who it was.

Suzanne stood and said in a sickly-sweet tone, "I didn't want to tattle, Mrs. Austin, but I have to tell you what I saw." Her bottom lip trembled. "Those poor little animals . . ." She shook her head and sighed.

"Yes, yes, I know," Mrs. Austin snapped, "what did you see, girl?"

"I woke up early this morning, and when I got to the stairs, I saw Trevor going into the classroom hallway. I wondered what he was doing, so I peeked through just before the door closed." Her eyes widened. "He was coming in here." Her hand fluttered to her throat. "Of course, I didn't know he was going to do such an awful thing—" She pointed a shaking finger at the aquarium. "—or I would've tried to stop him." An enormous sigh breezed through her cherry-red lips.

Mrs. Austin marched to Trevor and snatched his arm. "Trevor Patterson, how dare you do such a thing?" She yanked him up hard enough she'd have ripped his arm out of the socket if he hadn't been so muscular.

Trevor stood blinking down at her, his mouth working like one of the fish in the tank—before it was poisoned. "Hang on, I didn't do this."

"Likely story. You're off to Mr. Dominic's office."

Levi gulped. Mr. Dominic had warned Trevor and him if they stepped out of line again they'd get suspended.

"But—" Trevor's eyes darted around the room like he was seeking an escape route.

Levi frowned. Trevor looked . . . guilty.

"No buts." Mrs. Austin grabbed Trevor's wrist. "Come."

She'd yanked Trevor almost to the door when Steve said in a breathless whisper, "It wasn't him, Mrs. Austin."

Levi released a relieved breath. Of course it wasn't Trevor.

Mrs. Austin glared daggers at Steve. "Do you have proof?"

He gave a terrified nod. "I saw who did it."

Sara let out a muffled gasp that was echoed around the classroom.

Levi whispered, "Why didn't you stop him then?"

Mrs. Austin stomped to Steve's side, still dragging Trevor by the wrist. "Who did it?"

"B-B-Brock Smith."

The teacher's brow wrinkled. "Brock Smith? Isn't that one of the twins? The, er, slower of the two?" Suddenly pink-cheeked, she cleared her throat. "I mean to say, why would he do such a thing? He's not even in this class."

Steve shuffled his feet. "I didn't actually see him do anything to the water."

"What exactly did you see him do?" Little flecks of spittle flew from Mrs. Austin's mouth.

Steve recoiled. "I saw him come in here about an hour before class."

"And what were you doing here an hour before class?" Mrs. Austin's face was now such a bright shade of purple it matched the aquarium water.

Steve gulped. "I left my Latin folder last night. I had to get it before first hour so I came by before breakfast."

She advanced on him a few steps with Trevor in tow. "That doesn't prove anything."

Steve cowered behind the aquarium. "It's what I saw."

"Fine," the teacher muttered, "I'll get the Brock boy, and they'll both go to the director. I don't have time for this. I have a class to teach." Still grumbling, she dragged Trevor from the classroom.

Trevor shot Levi a half-irritated, half-amused look and allowed the stumpy woman to pull him through the doorway.

Trevor plopped down at the lunch table where Levi and the others sat eating chicken strips and fries.

"So what happened?" Steve asked around a mouthful.

Trevor gave a disgusted shake of his head. "Brock said he didn't do it and, you know, I believe him." He peered thoughtfully at the blob of ketchup on his plate. "When we're camping, he's always watching the birds and squirrels with this goofy grin on his face like he really likes them. I don't think he'd kill any fish."

Tommy nodded. "Yeah, he hasn't gotten in trouble at all on our campouts. Maybe his brother's the troublemaker and he just gets caught up in it."

Levi shook his head. "Braden hasn't really done anything wrong when we're camping either, so that doesn't prove Brock's innocence."

Steve strangled the salt shaker. "They sure did plenty wrong with the toilets."

"Well, anyway," Trevor said, cutting off the discussion. "Mrs. Austin said somebody did it and had better get punished, so Mr. Dominic decided to make me and Brock do an extra science project together." He rolled his eyes and picked up a fistful of fries. "As if I don't have anything better to do."

Monica leaned around Tommy and asked, "What sort of project?"

"Yeah, maybe we can help you." Clearly, Sara believed Trevor was innocent. But Levi wondered.

"Hey, thanks. That'd be awesome." Trevor smiled, a fry poking out of the corner of his mouth. "We're supposed to study up on the ecosystem of the lake. That way we'll learn our lesson if we really did kill those fish."

Levi watched him stuff another wad of fries in his mouth. Trevor claimed Brock hadn't sabotaged the project, but he'd never claimed *he* hadn't. Was it even possible Trevor might've thought putting something in the aquarium was funny? Levi didn't think his friend would kill the fish on purpose, but what if he'd put in a dye he didn't know was toxic?

"Well," Lizzie drawled, "I'm not hanging out with that caveman Brick. We'll have to help you separately."

Trevor frowned at her. "He's not a caveman." He glared at each of them in turn. "And don't call him Brick, he hates that."

Levi's eyebrows shot up. What was this? Were Trevor and Brock big buddies now?

He scowled as a new thought occurred: what if they'd sabotaged the tank together?

"Hunter probably got Braden to put some chemicals in the tank." Trevor's gaze moved to Steve. "That's probably who you saw—Braden—and you thought he was Brock."

Before Steve could reply, Levi asked, "What were you doing up there this morning?" He stared at his half-eaten chicken, hearing the blame in his own voice.

The silence following his question lasted too long. Neck burning, he finally glanced up.

"I wasn't. Suzanne made that up."

Trevor had left their room before any of the rest of them that morning. Where had he gone?

"I'm outta here." Trevor stood, shoving his chair back with a loud scrape, and stalked from the room.

Levi's friends sent him accusatory glances. No longer hungry, he rose, stacked his half-eaten lunch on top of Trevor's mostly full tray, and scooped up both. He crossed to the pass-through counter, set them down, and left the room without looking back.

He was such a jerk.

Levi found Trevor on the tower rooftop, staring across the sundrenched landscape.

"Hey."

"What?" Trevor didn't face him.

"I'm sorry."

This time his friend turned. His face was red, and his eyes looked slightly damp.

"I shouldn't have asked you that," Levi went on, guilt twisting his gut. "I know you wouldn't do something like that."

"No, I wouldn't." Trevor still sounded a little offended. He turned his face away. "It's okay."

Levi moved up to the wall beside him. "Do you really believe Brock, that he didn't do it?"

"Yeah, I do. He doesn't seem to be like his brother, you know?"

"What about the toilet thing?"

"I don't know. It seems like he doesn't have much choice but to do what his brother says." Trevor met Levi's eye. "Their parents like Braden better. Braden's smarter; Braden's more athletic. Brock's just supposed to follow his lead on everything, whether he wants to or not."

Levi looked across the fields to the distant mountains. He couldn't help thinking how similar Trevor's home life was to Brock's. Was that why Trevor felt so sorry for the twin?

Chapter 29

Trevor and Brock

Late the next afternoon, Levi headed along the classroom corridor to the science room where Trevor was working with Brock on their punishment project. He glanced at his wristwatch. The others were bound to be at the archery mound by now, wondering why he and Trevor hadn't arrived. Levi was supposed to get Trevor fifteen minutes ago, but he'd fallen asleep. Another round of nightmares had woken him at midnight, but he'd visited the chapel instead of the rooftop, as he'd promised Mr. Dominic.

"This is really cool," a voice said from inside the classroom.

Levi hesitated outside the barely open door.

"I mean," the voice went on, "I always liked animals and stuff, but to see the way the environment affects 'em and how they affect it." A pause. "It's too bad them fish got killed, you know?"

"You really didn't do it, did you?" Levi recognized the voice as Trevor's, meaning the first speaker had to be Brock.

"Nope, that was my brother. He told me to keep watch outside while he took care of some business. Didn't tell me what. I figured it was something goofy like the toilets and them water balloons. Something that wouldn't do no real harm. But killing animals? That ain't right."

Levi wasn't sure exploding toilets were as harmless as Brock seemed to think.

"So you just stood outside?" Trevor asked. "You didn't actually do any of that stuff?"

"I'm too stupid to come up with that junk, just ask my brother. He's the family genius."

"Did Hunter have anything to do with it?" Trevor's question echoed Levi's unspoken one.

"Yeah, him and Braden are always hanging out together." Even from the hall, Levi could hear the jealousy in Brock's voice. "And it's so dumb 'cause Braden's way smarter than Hunter. I don't know why he does what Hunter says." A snort. "Whenever Hunter thinks nobody's looking, he's got his nose stuck in some prissy purple book that looks like it's about to fall apart. And he says *I'm* dense."

The diary? That faded purple diary from the 1880s Levi had found between Hunter's mattress and box spring the year before? He studied it? Why?

"Oh, man, I'm late."

When Trevor's statement registered, Levi hurriedly pushed through the door. "Hey, man, everybody's waiting for us. Come on."

As they trekked across the grass toward the archery mound a few minutes later, Trevor didn't say a word about Braden and Hunter.

Levi finally tossed his hands. "Are you gonna turn them in?"

Trevor looked at him in complete confusion.

Hot blood rushed into Levi's head. "You know what I'm talking about. I heard what Brick told you in there. They deserve to get kicked out."

Trevor's eyes narrowed to slits. "You were eavesdropping?" He lengthened his stride so Levi had to jog to keep up. "His name's not Brick."

"At least I'm not making friends with the enemy like you." And Sara. She'd actually had the gall to play badminton with Hunter in the courtyard yesterday. She'd never played badminton with Levi.

Trevor glared at him over his shoulder. "Brock is not the enemy. And I don't know what to do about what he told me. If I tell, it'd be like . . ."

"It'd be like getting rid of the people who make life a nightmare for us."

Trevor sighed. "It's not that simple. What about Brock?"

"Who cares about Brock?" Though he longed to stick out his tongue like Jer did when he got mad, Levi simply shot Trevor one last sour look and ran on ahead.

He was so blinded with rage he almost ran over Miss Althea, who stood in the shade monitoring the archers. Her gaze ranged between him and Trevor, who entered the area with a scowl on his face. Levi muttered an apology to her and started away, but she grabbed his sleeve.

"You shouldn't let jealousy come between you." Her eyes, so often stern, were melancholy. "Believe me, I know."

Levi frowned. He wasn't jealous. Besides, what did she know about what was going on between him and his friends?

She tugged his sleeve. "I see more than you realize. And I know more about friendship than you seem to think."

Who was her friend? He rarely saw her talking to anybody.

"Nydia Sylvester," she said as though she'd read his mind. "She was my friend. I know, I know . . ." She fluttered a hand. "We didn't act like friends. That's because I let jealousy of her close relationship with Sara spoil things between us." She flicked her gaze toward the campers. "And now she's dead." She looked back, her eyes filled with pain. "What gets to me is that if I hadn't let my jealousy come between us, maybe she would've confided in me. Maybe I could've stopped her from . . ."

Levi nodded, his heart heavy as he looked across at his friends. He understood what she was saying. But he didn't know what to do about it.

Chapter 30

Cousins

"Hey, Levi, wanna take another little dip in the river? Maybe go splish splash in the lake?" Hunter hip-checked Levi as he bent to tug the canoe closer to the bank for canoeing class on Wednesday.

He teetered a moment but quickly caught his balance. Hunter snickered as he and Martin swaggered away. Levi's eyes narrowed. *Another* dip in the river? Splish spash in the lake? How could Hunter know about Levi's water experience? He'd only told his six friends. Mr. Dominic and Dr. Baldwin knew too, of course. He didn't know which of the staff they'd told, but he couldn't imagine a reason for any of them to tell a rodent like Hunter.

Maybe Hunter had eavesdropped on somebody. Maybe even on Levi himself. His ears heated at the thought. Some mornings his roommates looked at him funny, making him wonder if he'd talked in his sleep about Regin and Deceptor. Maybe even about Pressie, if that's who the lake monster was.

He peered at Tommy and Steve, settling into a canoe. Nearby, Trevor snagged a boat for him and Lizzie. Surely his roommates wouldn't say a word about Levi to Hunter. But . . . he looked extra close at Trevor . . . had Trevor said anything to his new best friend Brock?

No. It had been a few days since Levi and Trevor's fight, and though they still didn't see eye-to-eye about Brock, they hadn't argued again or slugged each other. After Miss Althea's warning, Levi had worked hard to get along. If anything, they were extra polite, which felt weird enough. He didn't need to add extra suspicion to the mix.

And yet, what about the girls? Lizzie was always shooting looks at Hunter and Martin that would scorch the Louisiana sun. And Monica? She tipped that little nose of hers in the air anytime they were near. But Sara . . . he'd seen her with Hunter way too much this summer, all friendly and sweet. He had no idea what they talked about, but he didn't like it.

Surely Sara wouldn't discuss Levi with Hunter. She knew he still had nightmares, knew he dreaded canoeing. She'd helped him overcome his fear to the point that he could survive practice and class, but she knew he avoided the water whenever possible. Levi watched her giggle at something Tommy said as he handed her an oar, and his throat tightened. Yes, Sara knew all about his fear. Would she tell? *Could* she?

"Ready?" Morgan tapped his arm. She jutted her chin toward the canoe Mr. Drake had told them to share.

With a quick nod, Levi eased into the craft. He scooted to the back and held the boat steady while she climbed in and plopped down. He gulped as water splashed in around his sneakers.

As they paddled along the gentle current behind Trevor and Lizzie, the rest of the class farther ahead, the tension in Levi's neck and shoulders began to lessen. He was okay. He could do this. And he knew Sara would never betray him to Hunter or anybody else. She was his friend. He was the one betraying her by even suspecting she could do such a thing.

In that moment, a swooshing sound came from his right side. Levi twisted his head around as a hardwood paddle blade came straight at him. He raised his arm in time to save his face from getting smashed, but the impact with the back of his hand produced instant pain then a creeping numbness. He let out a bellow and blinked through sudden tears, trying to see who hit him.

"Oops, sorry." Martin made an unsuccessful attempt to smother a guffaw.

Morgan, who'd whirled in her seat at Levi's bellow, said, "What happened?"

Hunter gave her a wide-eyed look. "I think Martin accidentally bumped Levi with his paddle."

Levi opened his mouth to tell Hunter off when his paddle dragging in the water weighed on his left wrist so that he had to let go. He had no idea how it happened, probably something to do with Martin paddling his hardest toward the side of Levi's canoe to ram it, but suddenly the handle wedged against the side of Levi's craft and the blade against Hunter's. When Martin gave another hard shove, the handle popped up into the air and landed with a thwack on top of Hunter's head.

A brief look of shock crossed Hunter's features. Then he slumped sideways and splashed into the water on the far side of the canoe. Morgan screamed. Martin looked dumbfounded. For an instant, Levi considered letting Hunter fend for himself. He wore a life vest, after all. But as the current bore the crafts farther away from his silent body, Levi knew he couldn't do it.

Sucking in a deep breath, he sprang overboard and fought free of the current. He couldn't cup his injured hand to scoop water, making it hard for him to swim to where Hunter bobbed, unconscious. To make things more difficult, Levi kept having to blow out, to force himself to breathe, because he felt like he was suffocating in the cold water. What if he drowned? What if he got pulled down the waterfall to that monster again?

Somehow, he managed to reach Hunter and snag the boy's life vest with his left hand. Stroking with his now-numb right hand, Levi struggled to the bank and shoved Hunter onto the grassy edge. His entire body quaking, he surged onto the sand, flopped on his back, and let his pounding heart settle.

For a few moments, only the sound of the rushing water came to him. Then he heard distant voices calling and sat up.

Hunter moaned. "What happened?" He eased into a sitting position and fingered the lump on his forehead.

"You got whacked in the head."

"But . . ." Confusion flashed in Hunter's slightly-crossed eyes. "Martin was supposed to hit . . ." He focused on Levi and clamped his mouth shut.

Levi released a small snort. "Ironic, isn't it?" He held up his swollen, purple hand. "You meant to knock me out of my canoe, but here you are." His lips twisted into a grimace. "Somehow I doubt you'd have rescued me, though."

When Hunter's pale face pinked before he looked away, Levi's jaw dropped a few centimeters. Could Hunter possibly be ashamed of himself?

His jaw snapped shut at Hunter's next words: "I'll have to tell Mr. Drake it was your paddle that knocked me out." Hunter released a gusty sigh. "I'm sure he'll have to report you to Mr. Dominic, and who knows what he'll be forced to do."

Levi's stomach lurched. "You wouldn't."

"Of course I would." He made a show of wincing as his fingertips grazed the lump on his forehead. "Hitting people with paddles isn't acceptable." His eyes widened. "I might've drowned."

"You know I didn't hit you. The paddle slipped and got wedged between our canoes and—"

"Paddles don't act like that." Hunter shook his head in a way that made Levi wish for a paddle. "I have witnesses who'll say you hit me."

Levi popped to his feet. Hunter really was the perfect Loki. "I know lies come out of Martin's mouth quicker than slobber, but Morgan will tell the truth."

"Think so?"

"Of course." Yet the cocky look on Hunter's face made his skin prickle with dread.

Some nearby trees rustled, and Morgan's white face appeared. "There you are! Are you okay?"

Levi started to answer, but she raced past him, almost bowling him over, and dropped to her knees beside Hunter.

"I thought I'd have to call your parents and tell them you drowned." She wrapped her arms around Hunter's neck with a sob.

"I'm okay now, cousin." Hunter smirked at Levi over her shaking shoulder. "Don't worry about me."

Cousin? The sour taste of betrayal filled Levi's mouth.

Chapter 31

Betrayal

Levi strode over and spat the sourness into the river.

More rustling announced the arrival of Martin and a sweating Mr. Drake. When the canoe instructor's eyes locked on Hunter, he swooped in on the big, fat liar. "Are you okay, boy?"

Martin shot Levi a malicious grin.

Grimacing, Levi turned back to the river.

"Levi?"

Morgan's soft voice made his stomach churn. Cousin. He shook his head.

"Levi?" She plucked at his sleeve. Still, he didn't look at her. "Thank you for rescuing him. I know how hard it must've been to jump into the water after almost drowning yourself."

He whipped around and glared at her. "What did you say?"

"I . . . I said thank you."

"No. After that." Ice hardened his tone.

"I . . . I was just saying how I know it had to be hard for you because you nearly drowned a few weeks ago."

Fire filled his gut. "Who told you about that?"

She blushed. "Oh. Um . . ." She looked away from his glare. "I . . . Well, I overheard you talking to Sara and the others about it."

Fury almost stole his voice. "You're a spy."

She shook her head. "No, I'm—"

"You deny you're *his* cousin?" He jerked a thumb toward Hunter, who was holding a whispered conversation with Mr. Drake and Martin.

"Of course I'm his cousin." Her face scrunched in a look of confusion. "I never said I wasn't."

"You never said you were."

Her face flushed as her voice rose. "You never asked. Why would I think you didn't know? Or that you'd care one way or the other."

"What's your name anyway? Your full name?" Why had he never asked such a simple question?

She straightened her shoulders. "Morgan Kristianna Fae Little."

"Little? That's not Hunter's last name."

"Of course not. Hunter's dad and my mom are brother and sister. Little is my dad's last name." Her shoulders deflated slightly. "At least I assume it is. I've never met him."

Levi stared at her for a long moment, fighting a twinge of pity. Lots of people didn't know their dads. That was no excuse for Morgan acting like she had. He huffed out a loud breath. "Forget it. I'm out of here."

He stalked along the riverbank toward the bridge that led to camp. He didn't even turn when Hunter's sarcasm-laden words reached him. "Hey, Prince, you better watch out for injured dragons!"

The tension inched up his shoulders and into his neck as he stomped through the trees. Morgan was Hunter's cousin. She was a spy. She was a liar. She was more of a backstabbing trickster than Loki.

He should go pack his bags.

"What's going on?" Trevor slammed the door to their room, Tommy and Steve at his side. The three had hurried after Levi when he'd appeared, sopping, at the canoe launch site. At Miss Althea's rapid-fire questions, he'd simply said Hunter was okay and the others were coming.

Now Levi trudged to his bed and sank onto the thick red comforter, heedless of his soggy shorts. His rage had oozed away on the long trek back to the castle. It wasn't fair that Hunter, Martin, and Morgan were getting him kicked out based on a lie, but what could he do about it?

In a monotone, he told his roommates what happened. Their indignant responses—especially Trevor's—made him feel the tiniest bit better as he rose and pulled out his suitcase. Part of him was ready to go home, ready to talk straight with his parents, ready to make amends. The other part . . .

Tommy sat down next to Levi's suitcase. "You should put that thing away. Mr. Dominic's not gonna believe Hunter over you."

"I don't know about that," Trevor said slowly.

"Thanks for the vote of confidence."

"Sorry." Trevor gave a sheepish shrug. "I just meant Mr. Dominic warned us, you know." His serious eyes fixed on Levi's. "He said if we got in trouble again, we'd be outta here. And he already cut me some slack with the whole science project thing."

Levi wasn't getting into the science project and Brock again. "Yeah, you're right." He yanked open his wardrobe and started stuffing t-shirts into his suitcase, careful to use only his left hand. He stopped at a thumping sound from beneath his feet. "Did you guys hear—"

Steve's eyes bugged out. "What was—"

The thumping came again.

Trevor said, "Duh, the girls."

"Huh?"

"The girls," Trevor repeated. "They're hitting the floor."

"What *are* you talking about?" Levi said, exasperated.

"The girls are hitting their ceiling—our floor." Trevor spoke each word with loud precision. "You know, to get our attention. They want to speak with us." He opened and closed his fingers and thumb to simulate talking.

Levi glowered at him. "I get it." He chose to ignore Tommy and Steve's snickers.

"Well, come on then." Trevor waved for them to follow him to the door.

Levi hesitated. Was he up to telling the girls he'd gotten kicked out of camp? Could he handle their pity? Would they cry? His own tear ducts heated at the thought.

Steve poked his head around the doorframe, the others already in the hall. "You coming?" He paused, studying Levi's face. "It's gonna be okay, you know. Somehow or other."

Levi offered a half-smile. "Yeah, I guess." He followed his roommates.

"What are you doing here?" Levi stared at Morgan, who was encircled by his friends on the tower roof. *Their* tower roof. Couldn't the sneak at least give him time to say goodbye without her here to spoil it?

"Levi, I . . ." Morgan reached for his hand.

He jerked away and shot Sara a hard look. She lifted her shoulders in apology.

Tears welled in Morgan's eyes as she hugged her arms to her waist. "I wanted you to know I told Mr. Dominic the truth."

His eyes narrowed. Whose version of the truth?

"I told him it was all an accident. That you didn't mean for your paddle to hit Hunter." She took a step nearer. "I said you risked your life to save him. That you're a hero."

Behind Morgan, the girls were smiling at him, as if to say this was why they'd brought her. Levi's tense spine relaxed a notch. "You told him they chased us down to hit me?" He held his throbbing, swollen, purple hand in front of her face.

She winced. "I . . . No, I couldn't. Hunter's my cousin, how can I turn him in?"

"How can you lie for him?" He shoved his hand nearer her face, not backing down even when a soft whimper escaped her.

"Levi, stop." Sara tugged at his arm.

Tears sparkled amid the freckles on Morgan's white cheeks. "I didn't lie. I told them you didn't do it."

Venom filled his veins. "You didn't tell them who *did* do it."

"You don't understand." Morgan sighed. "I owe everything to Hunter and his parents. They took me in when my own momma threw me away like—" She hiccoughed. "—a used Kleenex." She covered her face with both hands and sobbed.

Lizzie put an arm around Morgan, giving Levi a dirty look. As if he were the sneak and the liar.

After a moment, Morgan's weeping tapered and she lowered her hands. "I know Hunter can be . . . not so nice sometimes." Her eyes begged for understanding. "But he and his family take care of me. I can't betray him. And you don't know what his life's like. Except for me, he's got nobody to love him." She bit her lip. "I hate to say that since Uncle Bart and Aunt Cecily give me everything, but they're just so involved in their own stuff, you know? They don't even see Hunter."

Levi ground his teeth as the silence stretched. Even Trevor stared at him like he should say something, but what? So Hunter didn't have the best parents in the world. Trevor didn't either, and he wasn't a jerk who went around trying to drown people and then tattle that the other person was at fault when it backfired on him.

And Morgan . . . so she'd kept him from getting expelled. She hadn't told the truth about Hunter and Martin. And she'd been hiding who she was forever and spying on him and everything. On them too. Why weren't they mad at her anymore? Because of a sob story about her momma? Well, Lizzie's daddy had left her and she didn't go sneaking around pretending to be something she wasn't.

"I know where we are, Levi." Morgan's words pierced Levi's mental tirade.

He scowled at her. "What are you talking about?"

"Hunter told me about Terracaelum," she said softly.

Exactly how did she think that would help? It only proved she'd been sneaky about that, too.

"I thought you might be up here."

Mr. Dominic's voice spun Levi toward the doorway to the stairs.

The director mopped his brow on the sleeve of his aqua-blue Hawaiian shirt. "Whew, I'd forgotten what a long climb that is."

What in the world was he doing up here?

Mr. Dominic smiled at their tense expressions. "Clearly I'm interrupting something, so I won't stay. Two things." He held up two fingers. "Levi, Morgan here tells me you rescued Hunter. That's admirable, young man." He patted Levi's shoulder. "I know the pair of you haven't always gotten along. It's even more admirable to risk oneself for an enemy than for a friend. Excellent behavior. *Excelsior!*"

Levi's mouth worked soundlessly. If Mr. Dominic knew what he'd just been thinking . . .

"Oh my, your hand." The director took Levi's wrist and studied his damaged hand. "You need to go see Dr. Baldwin. That may be broken."

"Um . . . yes, sir."

"My second errand." His brilliant green eyes sought Morgan's. "Your mother is trying to reach you, young lady."

A wrinkle formed between her brows. "You mean my aunt?"

"No, your aunt is the one who contacted us, but it was to say your mother wants to speak with you. Will you come with me? Mrs. Drake will accompany you to the cabin area so you may call her." He pulled a slip of paper from his pocket. "I have the number right here."

Although Morgan's face turned white as death and her entire body shook, she followed him to the stairs.

Levi watched her go. When the door closed behind her, he turned back to his friends. Pity for Morgan and accusation for Levi shouted from each pair of eyes. With an angry headshake, he strode toward the exit. Time for another visit to Dr. Baldwin.

"Whoa, not so fast." Trevor's hand closed in a vise grip on his upper arm.

Levi glared at Trevor's hand until he let go. "What?"

"She apologized and told Mr. Dominic the truth." His hulking friend stood in his path, fists on hips. "I think it's time to let her off the hook."

Levi pinched his lips together.

"In fact—" Trevor glanced around the circle of faces. "—I think we ought to invite Morgan to partner with one of us in the Olympics for the canoe races."

"We are a person short," Sara said quietly. She looked at Levi then gestured toward his injured hand. "I'll work with her until your hand is better, then we can go back to being partners like before."

Levi released an irritable grunt. His hand was probably broken. Then Sara could just keep Morgan for a partner. Forever, for all he cared.

"We have been putting it off all summer," Tommy said, "but we've got to find somebody. The Olympics are, like, a week away. May as well be Morgan."

"She could probably use some extra kindness from us right now," Monica said, and Lizzie and Steve nodded.

"It's decided then. Right, Levi?" Trevor's left eyebrow rose. "Or are you gonna hold a grudge against her for who her family is—like with Brock?"

Levi glowered at the stone roof between his wet sneakers. He knew what his friends were asking, but he didn't want to let Morgan off the hook—or anybody else, for that matter. Why should he always be the one to give in?

Without a word, he took off down the stairs.

Chapter 32

A Game of Chess

"I wondered if you'd forgotten me this summer." Dr. Baldwin held open the infirmary door for Levi.

"Of course not. I've been . . . busy, you know." Levi sat on the edge of a cot, shoulders slumped. "Sorry."

"That's all right, I understand. I was only teasing you anyway. You're at camp to learn and make friends and grow strong, not hang around the infirmary playing chess with an old codger like me." Dr. Baldwin thumped himself on the broad torso then crossed to where Levi sat. "What's the trouble today?"

Levi held out his right hand.

"Oh, yes." Dr. Baldwin adjusted his glasses, leaned in close, and peered at it a moment. He tugged open the heavy drapes he usually kept closed, mumbling. "Let's have a little more light on the subject." He took Levi's hand and maneuvered it, pressing and prodding until Levi winced. "Mmm. I don't think anything's broken." The doctor peered at him over his glasses. "Hurts like the dickens, though, doesn't it?"

He nodded, afraid to open his mouth for fear the pain would make him squeal.

"No," Dr. Baldwin pronounced after manipulating each of his fingers, "nothing's broken. Just a very nasty bruise." He released the hand and met Levi's watering eyes. "How did this happen?"

Cradling his hand against his stomach, Levi launched into the whole sorry tale, glad for a sympathetic ear. The doctor listened in silence. The only sign of his attention was the tightening of his lips, barely visible beneath his bushy, salt-and-pepper beard and mustache.

When Levi finished, the doctor stood and crossed to a cabinet, pulled out a cold pack, broke the crystals, and returned to his side. After settling it on Levi's hand, he sank onto the bed across from him. "That Hunter." He shook his head. "He'll be the death of you one day."

"What can I do about it?" Levi couldn't keep the piteous whine from his tone. "Morgan won't turn him in. And besides, Hunter didn't actually hit me. Martin did." He huffed, his anger growing. "Not that Morgan saw that part. But we both know Hunter's not gonna turn in Martin when he put him up to it. Nobody else saw a thing. Even you . . ." His shoulders jerked in a shrug, sending the ice pack toppling to the floor. "If you told Mr. Dominic what I said, it'd still be my word against Hunter's. So, like I said, what can I do about it?"

The doctor picked up the pack and resettled it. "I don't know. I'll keep a closer eye on him when I can, but I'm usually here taking care of sick and injured campers."

"I know." Levi stared at the ice pack. He shouldn't have snapped at the doctor. "I'm sorry. I'm just so frustrated, you know?"

"I understand."

Levi sat in silence. After a while, a clattering sound told him the campers were going down the spiral staircase to supper. His stomach writhed at the thought of entering the dining hall, where Hunter and his gang were sure to laugh at him.

And where his friends would expect him to pity Morgan, as if her treachery had never happened, just because she got cold feet about getting him expelled. Just because her momma called her.

"Can I stay in here tonight?" The words tumbled from his lips without forethought, but he liked the idea. It would buy him a little time, a little space to think about how to deal with everybody. "I can go get my stuff now." He gave the doctor a hopeful look. "Maybe we could play chess or something."

"Well, now, I don't know." Dr. Baldwin's eyes narrowed, though a twinkle lurked in them. "You're not sick, are you?"

Levi shook his head.

"Then again, no one else is either." He gestured to the row of empty beds, white sheets neat and clean. "I suppose a little rest wouldn't hurt you. Probably shouldn't use that hand too much today."

Levi hopped to his feet, grinning. "I'll move the pieces with my left hand, I promise."

"Fine." The doctor's lips twitched. "Go get your things. I'll have a supper tray sent up for us both."

Levi studied his queen. Dr. Baldwin's bishop was all set to swoop in and take her out if he didn't move her. Then he'd be sunk. He took in the board, figuring out all possible plays for each piece, trying to decide which move to make.

"Got a problem there, boy?" Dr. Baldwin asked in a lazy tone.

Levi shot him a mock glare. "Just a small one." He couldn't afford to lose his queen. Where should he hide her? Stuff her under the mattress maybe? He gave an inward chuckle.

Then he froze with his queen pinched between his thumb and forefinger. Hidden . . . under the mattress . . .

He looked up at the doctor. "Last year you told me Hunter's great-grandma or something was at camp with Mr. Dominic and my Papa Levi."

Dr. Baldwin's bushy left eyebrow shot up above his reading glasses. "What does that have to do with anything? Are you trying to divert me from the game?"

Levi was too busy thinking to explain. "What was her name? Do you remember?"

The doctor scratched his chin. "It would've been his great-great-aunt. Eva? Annie?" He squinted at the ceiling, the only sound the *scritch-scritch* of his fingers in his beard. After several long moments, his piercing beetle-black gaze returned to Levi's. "Anna, that was it. Anna Morgan."

Levi's breath caught in his throat. He closed his eyes. Faded gold letters against washed-out purple fabric floated into his mind: Kristianna Fae Morgan. That was the name from Hunter's diary, he was sure of it. Hunter was still hiding his great-great-aunt's diary. And, according to Brock, poring over it when he thought nobody was watching.

So Hunter's aunt Anna attended camp with Mr. Dominic and Papa Levi, which meant the reference to a Prince boy he'd seen when he flipped through the diary was actually a reference to Papa Levi. Too bad Levi couldn't get hold of the diary again and see what it said about his dad's favorite great-grandpa.

His eyes popped open. Morgan. If she was Hunter's cousin, then she had to be related to this Anna person, too. Besides, didn't Morgan say her name was Morgan Kristianna Little or something like that? She must be named for her great-great-aunt, like Levi was for his great-great-grandpa.

He stared unseeing at the queen in his grasp. Hadn't Hunter said something to Morgan that day in early June about a diary? He'd assumed he'd misunderstood, but what if she knew more than he thought? What if she . . .

"Do you plan to make a move tonight?"

The doctor's growled question brought Levi back to the present. He mumbled an apology and moved his queen two spaces to the right. Out of harm's way.

Levi sat up in bed with his heart thumping. What had awakened him? It wasn't a nightmare this time.

Thunder boomed, the repercussion rattling the windows. He shoved away the covers and ran to move the heavy drapes. Outside a storm raged, one more violent even than the nor'easter that had driven them to the castle their first day last summer. Rain hacked at the glass like a mad knifeman. Screaming wind turned the tree just outside his window into a monster slashing at the panes with claw-like branches.

Fear flooded Levi's veins with adrenaline. That hooded, manacled creature Mr. Austin and Dr. Baldwin led during the Camp Classic Rules and Regulations play . . . where was it now? And the she-monster from beyond the mountains . . . had Mr. Dominic found her? Shivering, he darted glances around the dark room behind him. A loud whiffling snore told him the doctor still slept in his adjacent bedroom. For a moment, Levi considered waking him, but that would be way too babyish.

Forcing his mind from monsters and murderers, Levi peered back out at the storm. Lightning flashed, followed instantly by another boom. The window quivered under the wind and rain's increased assault. Could the squall shatter glass? Another flare, another reverberation, and he inched backward. With this storm, anything was possible.

He glanced at his rumpled cot. No way could he sleep now, not with the storm raging. Too bad he hadn't brought anything with him for his overnight in the infirmary besides a change of clothes. Even Math or Latin homework would be better than sitting in the darkness waiting for the horrid weather to pass.

He wished he could visit the library for a good book. That would distract him from the shivers coursing up and down his spine. But last year's middle-of-the-night trip had gotten him into way too much trouble. He couldn't risk disappearing and having the staff hunt for him.

But what if he left a note telling Dr. Baldwin where he'd gone? Then he could run to the library, snag a book, and bring it back with him. Yeah, that should work.

Ignoring the near-constant flashes of lightning, he yanked a paper towel from the dispenser, jotted "Gone to library. Be right back" on it, and propped it against his pillow. Then he snagged a flashlight from the shelf by the door and hurried along the corridor to the library.

Once inside with the door closed, he hesitated. The darkness of the library was a near-physical thing. Though lightning and thunder rolled with such constancy, they somehow made the shadows feel more inky. What if something lurked behind the puffy chairs before the massive fireplace cube? Or between the bookshelves, as Miss Nydia had done on his visit last summer? What if—

"Stop it, Levi. You're freaking yourself out." His lips puckered in self-disgust. "There's nothing here but a bunch of dusty old books, which is why you came. So quit being a baby and find the one you want."

He strode to the shelves beside one of the massive windows, thinking he'd seen some nineteenth-century classic novels in that section. He flicked on his flashlight and shined the beam over the old covers. There, *Robinson Crusoe*. He loved that book. He tugged it out and flipped off his light.

He eased closer to the window for another glance at the light show going on outside. Was it storming on Castle Island? It was hard to tell, especially if the drawbridge wasn't lowered. He rose on tiptoe and pressed his face to the glass, peering downward.

At that moment, a bomb went off. Ears ringing, Levi dropped to the floor and threw his arms over his head. After a few seconds of stillness, he peeked up. The window hadn't shattered; the stone walls were still intact. Even the books hadn't fallen. But what had happened?

He stood warily and peered outside, this time keeping his face well back from the glass. Then he understood. It wasn't a bomb, at least not one made by humans. God had dropped a lightning bolt on the tree directly across the drawbridge. As though the deafening thunderclap had been a lumberjack shouting "Timber," the massive trunk lay smoking no more than a foot from the bridge. Fire sputtered on its stump.

Levi could only stare. What if the tree had fallen on the drawbridge? Would they have been trapped in Terracaelum, unable to go home, ever? He hugged himself and rubbed at his arms, but the goose pimples wouldn't subside.

Eventually, the rain and wind tapered, the lightning and thunder moved on, and the moon melted the clouds. A branch scratched feebly at the glass. Levi's eyes grew wide as he peered down at the tree just outside, the one that reached well above the second story window. What if lightning had struck *that* tree while he was standing here at the window? What if the tree had shattered the window? Smashed him to bits?

He shuddered. "Thank you, God."

Cradling his book in one arm and holding the lit flashlight before him, he scurried to the infirmary and climbed back into the safety of his bed.

Chapter 33

Mjolnir

By the next morning, Levi had almost forgotten his midnight experience in the library. But a quick peek outside showed the downed tree lined up parallel with the drawbridge. And he knew it hadn't been another bizarre dream.

He spent the morning on precalculus and lines for the play, and he was tired from his interrupted sleep. None of his friends were speaking to him, and throughout breakfast and classes, Hunter and his thugs called Levi an attempted murderer.

Landing in the laundry room for another sultry afternoon didn't help.

He was careful, though, to do everything as Mrs. Forest instructed and managed to finish much quicker than before. Even with his sore right hand. By mid-afternoon, he folded his last towel and headed for the kitchen to report to one of the Forests. Maybe he'd make it outside in time to loll around in the shade awhile. He should probably try to make up with his friends, explain why Morgan couldn't be trusted any more than Hunter. Although Sara seemed to trust Hunter plenty.

When he crossed the threshold, wiping sweat from his brow and longing for a cold drink, which he refused to get for fear of another hour-long mess to clean up, he again found the room empty. *Ugh.* Didn't anybody ever work around here? If he didn't check in with somebody, he couldn't leave the laundry room.

Levi was about to stomp into the hallway in search of a staff member when the thumping started on the cellar door again. He whipped around, fists clenched. "Would you shut up and leave me alone, Regin? I'm not opening the door!"

He stalked across the room and halted dead. Mouth working like a guppy, Levi blinked at Morgan in the act of turning the doorknob. Unfreezing, he snatched her arm and yanked it backward. "Stop! You want to get yourself killed?"

Tears flooded her eyes. He let go of her wrist and felt horrible when she immediately rubbed it.

"Sorry." Levi whooshed out a breath. "I didn't mean to grab you so hard."

"It's okay," she said softly, "I'd better get used to it."

What was that supposed to mean? His aggravation rose, but he had to warn her. "You need to leave that door alone." He hooked a thumb toward the rattling door. "He's mean."

"I think it's somebody stuck down there after last night's storm. You know, because of what Mr. Forest said that day."

Levi shook his head. "I thought so too before, but it wasn't. And I almost didn't get out alive. Trust me, leave it alone."

"If I open the door," she said, reaching out a trembling hand toward the doorknob, "at least maybe I can help somebody. And if I don't make it out . . ." She shrugged. "It's better than what I'm going home to after camp."

Was she playing him again? Like she'd done all summer? "What're you saying, Morgan?" He grabbed her upper arms, more gently this time. "You'd rather die down there than go home?" He gave her a little shake. "That's crazy."

A tear coursed down her cheek. "You don't know my momma. She—" Ear-splitting pounding cut her off.

Levi yelled at the door, "Shut up and go away, Regin!"

When the noise stopped, he turned back to Morgan. "Your momma can't be that bad." His words came out harsher than he intended. "I mean, what did she say when you talked to her?"

"She wants me to come live with her. She's getting married. Says she's gotten herself together and is ready to be a real mom." Morgan's eyes were dry now, her expression blank.

"Isn't that good?" Scorn laced the words. He couldn't bring himself to trust her.

"You'd think so, wouldn't you?" Her voice was flat, dead. "Problem is she's come back into my life a couple times since she dumped me in the street." She hugged her arms to her chest as if freezing in the hot kitchen. "It's never worked out before."

He shifted his weight from foot to foot and softened his voice slightly. "Maybe it will this time."

"Yeah, right." She backed away from him a few paces, her eyes hard. "You don't know what it's like to be ripped from a place you feel safe." She released a laugh that didn't sound at all funny. "I know you don't like Hunter, and his folks aren't great, but they take care of me. They've never hit me or been so high they forgot to feed me or left me outside a crack-house in the freezing cold with—" A shudder wracked her small frame.

Imagining his little sister in such situations, Levi winced. "Morgan, I—" He took a step toward her, reaching out his wrapped right hand.

"Forget it." She turned away, sent him one last tortured look, and fled the kitchen.

Levi stood stunned, hand still outstretched. What was wrong with him, treating her like that? How could he not have forgiven her for being Hunter's cousin?

"For you." Mr. Austin thrust a massive hunk of metal at him after play practice the next afternoon.

Levi flinched. "Huh?" He'd been trying to spot Morgan in the crowds leaving the great hall. She hadn't shown up for practice.

"Take the hammer." The teacher's face looked pained.

He looked down at the long, thick shaft with a huge rectangular wedge with some faint scratches that could've been runes on one end and smudged curlicues on the other. It didn't look like any hammer he'd ever seen. "Uh, okay." He reached out, but Mr. Austin drew it back.

"This hammer is precious beyond anything you can imagine. You will guard it with your life, is that clear?" A tic started in the dwarf's puffy right eyelid.

"Why?"

"You're Thor." Mr. Austin shoved the hammer into Levi's stomach, knocking the breath from him. "You must have Mjolnir!" He had a crazed expression on his florid face.

Levi sucked in a mouthful of air and gripped the tool with both hands. The teacher let go. It dropped like an anvil. Levi steadied it just before it smashed onto his toes. "It weighs a ton." Good thing everyone else had already left. He didn't need an audience for this humiliation.

"Doesn't matter. Thor must carry Mjolnir." Were those tears in the dwarf's eyes?

"Okay," Levi said slowly. "But how am I supposed to use this thing in the play when I can barely lift it?"

Mr. Austin retrieved a strip of leather from his desk. "You will wear it at all times."

Levi couldn't help but recoil when the crazed-looking dwarf came at him with the leather strap. Then he understood it was a belt with a holster.

Mr. Austin hooked the strap around Levi's waist. "Put in Mjolnir."

Levi struggled to keep from dropping the hammer as he shoved it through the loop. Once he was sure it wasn't going to fall and break a hole in the stone floor, he let go. And immediately stumbled to the left several paces. "Owww." His back was going to snap. "It's too heavy." He grunted. "I'm not Thor."

Mr. Austin stopped Levi's fall then tugged him close and eyeballed him. "You are Thor. Get used to it. And get used to this." He tapped the hammer's handle. "You'll keep it on except for bedtime. And even then you must not let it out of your presence." His breath was hot on Levi's cheek. "You must sleep with it. Your hand must not move from it all night."

"But . . ." A droplet of sweat fell from his brow.

"You'll adjust to the weight in time." The dwarf's voice was firm, but doubt lurked in his eyes. "You'll have to."

"Enough's enough. Come on." Levi stood as straight as he could with the heavy hammer at his waist. He glowered at his six friends seated in a corner of the great hall that evening. They stared mutinously back at him.

He sighed, shifting his focus to Sara. "Please. Come to the tower roof. We need to talk."

After a long moment, her expression softened. She turned to the others. "He's right. Come on, guys."

They obeyed her, and ten minutes later, the seven stood or sat in various stiff poses around the tower rooftop. No one spoke. It reminded him of last summer when he'd had to apologize right on this very spot. Would he never learn?

He finally broke the awkward silence. "I'm sorry, everybody." His eyes sought Trevor's. "I was mad and I just . . ." He shrugged. "I'm sorry."

After a couple more seconds of silence, Trevor gave a single nod.

Sara said, "We forgive you, of course."

"Yeah, we don't hold grudges like some people." Lizzie widened her made-up eyes at him.

He bit back a smart-alecky response.

"Now what?" Steve sat down in the shadow of the stone wall. "We still gotta figure out what to do about Morgan." His gaze shifted to Trevor. "Brock, too. Somebody ought to be in trouble for the toilet thing. It's been weeks."

Trevor huffed. "I'm sorry. I told you I'm not gonna tell what Brock said about his brother. Braden and Hunter would make his life miserable."

"Nobody said you should," Levi said in a placating tone, Miss Althea's words about broken friendships ringing in his mind. He'd brought these guys up here to smooth things over, not start back in on Trevor about Brock.

Tommy blew out a loud breath. "What about Morgan, then?"

"She's terrified of going with her momma." Levi reported the conversation he'd had with Morgan by the cellar door.

Lizzie and Sara both had moist eyes by the time he finished. Tommy and Steve both scowled, and Trevor was grinding a pebble into powder against the stone floor. He couldn't make out Monica's expression. She sat on the ground staring down at her clenched hands.

"Monica," he said after a moment, "what do you think?"

When she looked up, the grief in her expression caught him off guard. "I think I'm a horrible excuse for a Christian. Here my parents give up everything to be missionaries for the sake of the gospel, even time with their daughters, and I'm too self-centered to see how badly one of my own roommates needs help."

Levi's breath caught as her words sank in. He gazed around at the others, certain his face mirrored the stricken looks on theirs.

"What should we do?" Steve whispered.

Monica shrugged. "What else can we do but try to treat her as we should have all along."

"I'll apologize to her," Levi said softly, "and I'll invite her to be my canoeing partner for the Olympics."

The others agreed, volunteering ways they planned to show kindness to Morgan.

A half-hour later, Levi started downstairs to look for the girl, his heart heavier than Thor's hammer.

Chapter 34

Fencing with Mjolnir

The next week, Levi staggered into the courtyard, his body listing left. Things had been great between him and his friends since the tower meeting, even with Morgan. The only thing really bugging Levi now was that he couldn't walk straight with the ridiculous hammer strapped to his middle.

At first Hunter and his friends had cackled uncontrollably about him lurching throughout the castle like a drunken sailor, but when he'd hefted Mjolnir to try out his defeat-the-frost-giants pose, they'd scattered. And had left him alone ever since. When he went to the infirmary yesterday for a final check on his hand, Dr. Baldwin appeared shocked Levi had the hammer. He'd questioned Levi about it for a long time and finally mumbled some strange thing about hiding it in plain sight. Then, without any sort of explanation, he shooed Levi with a release to participate fully in activities.

Today, Levi wished Dr. Baldwin hadn't released him so soon. No way could he sword-fight with Mjolnir's dead weight on his hip. He'd asked Mr. Austin that morning if he could take it off, just for fencing class, but that maniacal gleam entered the dwarf's eyes again as he barked, "Absolutely not. This is the perfect time to learn balance and precision. It'll be great for the play."

Great for the play maybe, but Levi knew he'd need another trip to the infirmary afterward.

"Find a partner, everyone. Match up as evenly as you can, please." Mr. Sylvester's waist-length, white-blond hair trailed him as he strode between the campers. He stopped in front of Levi, paired up with Trevor, and shook his head. "No, no, Mr. Prince. You and Mr. Patterson are nowhere near the same height and weight." He put a hand on Levi's shoulder and steered him away. When he halted next to Hunter and said, "Yes, this is more like it," Levi cast an anxious glance back at his friend.

Trevor mouthed *sorry*.

Levi turned to find Hunter glaring at him, probably not pleased the fencing instructor deemed them a match, but Mr. Sylvester simply flashed a smile and strode away to find a partner for Trevor.

"Mr. Serge," the teacher announced after a moment, "you and Mr. Patterson should work nicely." Martin popped his knuckles as Trevor shot him a sour look.

Everyone donned protective gear, picked up their buffered blades, and chose an area to spar. Mr. Sylvester told them to watch for opportunities to try the new disarming moves he'd been teaching them. "Remember, your goal is not to injure your opponent but to remove his sword from his grasp."

He paused at the throat-clearing from Jacqueline. "Oh, yes, pardon me, ladies. Your goal is to remove your opponent's sword from his or *her* grasp."

Jacqueline gave a begrudging nod.

"All right then, on my whistle."

"Any last wishes, Prince?" Hunter's whisper reached Levi's ears an instant before the shrill whistle pierced the air.

Hunter came at him hard and fast, landing strike after strike against Levi's blade. It was obvious he didn't think simple disarming was enough. With Mjolnir weighing him down, Levi soon began puffing and wheezing as he fended off Hunter's onslaught, but the other boy smiled the whole time he jabbed and stabbed without even a drop of sweat on his brow.

Levi's hands soon grew so slick within his gloves the moisture soaked through to his sword handle. He had to find an opening and go on the attack or he'd fall out and die from sheer exhaustion. Desperately, he watched for an opportunity, oblivious to the matches progressing on every side.

Suddenly, Hunter whirled and hacked at Levi's legs. Levi shoved his blade with all his remaining strength against Hunter's hack. But instead of Hunter losing his sword, Levi's went clattering off somewhere to his right. Hunter flashed an evil smirk then came after Levi as though he still had his weapon.

"Hey, wait!" Levi lunged to the left, then groaned when he realized he'd moved away from his fallen sword. He shot a wild glance around, hoping Mr. Sylvester would come to his rescue, but the instructor was on the opposite side of the courtyard watching somebody else's match. Why wouldn't he turn around?

Before he could call for help, Hunter swung at him again. Levi scampered out of range. What should he do? Another sweep of the blade, and Levi feinted right, but Mjolnir threw off his balance. Hunter's sword smashed against Levi's head. Despite the padding on the blade and the helmet on his head, the blow dazed him for a second.

Levi growled. That stupid hammer kept messing him up.

Wait. The hammer. He slipped Mjolnir from its holster at the precise moment Hunter began a two-handed downward slice from high above, clearly intending to knock him out with another blow to the head. Before Hunter could strike, Levi swung upward with the hammer and smashed Hunter's fingers against the handle. With a howl of pain, the bully dropped the sword, which would've fallen into Levi's upturned face had the weight of Mjolnir not pulled him forward, headfirst into Hunter's gut. The two landed in a heap on the grass, the sword near their feet and the hammer driven into the soft dirt inches from Hunter's face.

Hunter's shrieked curses soon drew Mr. Sylvester and the rest of the class. Levi disentangled himself from Hunter while the instructor sputtered, "No hammers in fencing," and Hunter sucked on his rapidly swelling fingers.

Levi shrugged and returned Mjolnir to its holster. "Sorry, sir, but Mr. Austin told me I couldn't take it off for sparring."

Mr. Sylvester scowled. "I'll just have a word with Mr. Austin about that hammer."

"Yes, sir." Yet Levi gave the hammer a fond pat as he turned away. Maybe it wasn't so bad after all. If it kept Hunter from clobbering him, it was worth a few trips to the chiropractor after camp.

Chapter 35

Morgan's Momma

Levi stared at the math problem, trying to make his mind work it out, but he could only think about Lizzie's hurried whisper as they entered class for their final exam: "Morgan's momma's coming. Today. She can't even stick around for the Olympics or the play or anything."

What could they do? It was bad enough they again had an odd number for the canoeing event and that Morgan's understudy was going to have to do her part in the play, but what about Morgan herself? Was her momma really as bad as she said? What kind of mother would yank her child from camp mere days before it ended? Would going home with her put Morgan in danger? Why didn't Hunter's parents do anything to stop it?

Levi cast a glance at his enemy. Hunter chewed on the end of a pencil, his face chalky, his sunken eyes faintly red-rimmed. Was he worried about his cousin? It seemed she might be the only person he actually cared about. Maybe Levi needed to talk to him, find out if there was a way to get her out of the bad situation.

A bitter taste coated his tongue at the mere thought of teaming up with Hunter, but should he? For Morgan's sake?

The bell rang, signaling the end of class, and Levi groaned. He'd barely completed a third of his test, and the problems he had finished probably weren't right. *Great.* He scooped up his paper, slouched to the teacher's desk, and set it face-down on the stack of exams.

Sighing, he started from the room. Hunter was a few paces ahead, walking with slumped shoulders and bent head. Levi doubled his stride and caught up, noticing instantly that Martin and Suzanne weren't around. Hunter must be feeling down if he didn't have his usual gang within commanding distance.

"Hunter," he said quietly.

The boy sent him a glare. "What do you want?"

He chose to ignore the hatred blazing in Hunter's eyes. "Is it true? Is Morgan's mom taking her away? Today?"

"Who says it's any of your business?"

"It sounds like Morgan doesn't want to go with her, that's all." He shrugged. "And I just didn't want her to have to go if it's . . . bad." His ears heated. This was Hunter's aunt he was talking about.

"As if you care. You and your friends treat her like a little pest anyway." Hunter started walking again.

"We do not." Levi swallowed hard. "At least not anymore." He followed after Hunter. "We just . . . don't want anything to happen to her."

Hunter's snort echoed throughout the now-empty hallway. "Well, don't bother your pretty little curls over Morgan." His eyes gleamed molten silver in the dusky corridor. "She's my cousin, my responsibility. I'll take care of her. Without your help."

"There she is," Sara whispered to the others during lunch. She gave a slight jerk of her head toward the staff table.

Beside Mrs. Dominic, whose face appeared pinched and anxious, sat a woman with black hair—thin and wispy like Morgan's, but without Morgan's shine and bounce. The woman's eyes were the same pale blue, though lines etched deep around them. She was so emaciated the skin sagged around her mouth and neck like an old woman's, even though Levi figured she probably wasn't much older than thirty. When she raised her eyes and met his stare, he shuddered. Her eyes looked cold, lifeless. No wonder Morgan didn't want to go with her.

He broke eye contact and scanned the room. "Where is Morgan? I haven't seen her all day."

Monica shook her head. "She was gone when we got up this morning. Her bed was tidy, and all of her luggage was gone."

"I figured we'd see her at breakfast to say goodbye," Lizzie said sadly, "but she didn't show, poor thing."

"Apparently they haven't left yet," Steve said around a monstrous mouthful of ham sandwich. "Her mom's still here."

"Duh," Trevor said.

"I'm just saying." Bits of cheese flew from Steve's mouth and splattered Tommy's tray.

Tommy's nose wrinkled. "That is so gross."

"Sorry," Steve said, more food mixed with spittle spraying from his mouth.

"Steve." Lizzie stretched the word into two syllables. "It is not polite to talk with your mouth full, honey."

Trevor busted out laughing with a mouthful of orange juice that sprayed from his nose across the table onto Sara's and Monica's trays.

"Ugh."

"You are so repulsive."

Levi snickered, but when his peripheral vision caught movement at the staff table, he sobered instantly. Morgan's mom and Mrs. Dominic had risen from their seats and were walking toward the hall.

"Guys." He gestured toward the two women. "We gotta do something to help Morgan."

"We don't even know where she is," Trevor pointed out. "How can we help her?"

"We can start by following her mom." Levi shoved back his chair and stood. "Who's coming?"

The girls jumped up, but Steve said, "What about lunch?" and Trevor nodded.

"Who can eat after you defaced our food?" Monica snatched up her tray and stomped off to the kitchen pass-through, the girls following her.

Tommy stood. "Okay, yeah. I'm coming."

Levi pushed by them all and stuffed his tray onto the counter. He jogged into the hall and looked left and right in the empty corridor.

When his friends joined him, Monica asked, "Which direction did they go?"

He shrugged.

Lizzie put her hands on her hips. "Now what?"

"Do you think they went to my parents' study?" Sara asked. "To take care of discharge papers or something?"

He shrugged again, not knowing what to do. "How about we split up and look for them? And for Morgan? We can meet back here in a little while."

Monica snagged Lizzie's arm. "We'll look in our room in case she's up there."

Lizzie nodded without so much as a protest at Monica's demanding tone. "We'll check out the tower roof, too, y'all. And the classrooms."

Levi faced Tommy and Sara. "Where're Trevor and Steve?"

Tommy rolled his eyes. "Still stuffing their faces, I bet." He jutted his chin toward the dining room. "I'll drag them out of there, and we'll check outside."

Levi nodded. "Okay, Sara, guess that leaves us to check everything else."

They climbed to the second floor and peeked into the library. Then they poked their heads into the infirmary. When they pressed their ears to the Dominics' study door, they couldn't hear Morgan's voice. But the voice Levi knew must belong to Morgan's mom made him shudder. It sounded as dead as her eyes looked. He knew Sara felt the same way when she teared up.

We have to help her, she mouthed, and pulled him from the door.

Next they went down to the great hall where a bunch of kids played billiards and Ping-Pong, but there was still no sign of Morgan. They raced past the still-buzzing dining hall, intending to check the foyer, and if they still hadn't found her, to go out the south door to look in the cabin area. But as he passed the kitchen doorway, Levi skidded to a halt. "Wait. I've got to check something."

Sara gave him a puzzled nod. He peeked around the doorframe and sucked in a breath as Mr. Forest bustled by with a load of dirty dishes. The pixie clunked them onto the counter and, muttering to himself, started back toward the dining hall. No one else was in the room.

Levi crept across it, Sara close behind. When he halted near the dark alcove beside the cellar door, she stared at him, wide-eyed. "What're you doing? We can't go down there."

"Shh." He put his finger over his lips.

Her eyes flashed, but she shut her mouth.

Levi inched into the dim alcove, hoping for some hint of whether Morgan had come that way, and almost fell over something bulky.

His heart skipped into triple time. "Morgan?"

Chapter 36

Back to the Cellar

"What is it? Did you find her?" Sara's nails dug into his forearm.

He bent low. A bag and a bedroll. He felt for a tag.

Sara knelt beside him and gasped. "That's Morgan's stuff."

He squinted at the red sleeping bag and oversized pink duffel. "How can you tell? I can't find a tag."

"Thanks to you, she's been my roommate for the past six weeks. Don't you think I ought to recognize her stuff?"

"Oh, yeah." He stood up straight. The sound of clanking dishes from the direction of the pass-through window told him the kids were finished with lunch. That meant the kitchen staff would be coming in to wash dishes any minute. He had seconds to decide what to do. Because if this was Morgan's stuff, there was only one place she could've gone. He rested his forehead against the old wooden door. "She's down there; I know she is."

"What? In the cellar? She can't be."

He gestured toward the bedroll. "She has to be." He didn't want to go down there again. He couldn't. But what if it was like his dad said . . . sometimes a man had to do a thing, no matter how much he didn't want to? But it was still against the rules, no matter the circumstances. He couldn't disobey again. He was finished with all that. Surely there was another way.

"Your dad." He fixed wide eyes on Sara. "We need to get him. He'll know what to do."

She shook her head. "He's gone. Something got the leprechauns all upset out beyond the Medicollis. He, Mr. Sylvester, and Mr. Drake left before dawn to settle them down."

Levi's shoulders deflated. All three gone? Now? "How about your mom?" He paused. "No, she's with Morgan's momma. We can't get her without . . ."

He slumped against the stone wall, eyes on the cellar door. *What do I do, God? I can't just leave her down there. She'll die.* He pressed his thumbs to his temples, willing himself to think.

Finally, he whispered, "Go get your mom and dad's key."

She flinched as if he'd slapped her. "What?"

"I have to go down after her, but without a key, I can't get back inside the castle. I doubt she can survive the trip down the waterfall like I did." Levi didn't mention the fact that he probably couldn't make himself jump back in that underground river, no matter what was at stake.

"But—"

"There's no time." He grabbed her shoulders and gave her a small shake. "Go."

Sara's mouth opened, but at a loud clatter from the pass-through window, she clamped it shut. With a quick nod, she ran from the room.

Levi huddled in the corner hoping no one would come in before he got the key and went down after Morgan. Because any more delays could mean Morgan's death.

Several agonizing moments later, Sara rushed into the alcove and thrust a piece of heavy metal into his hands. "Here."

"This is the key?"

She nodded, her mouth wobbling at the corner.

Pushing away guilty feelings, he studied the key. It was six inches long and hung on a thick gold chain like an antique necklace. Even in the dusky corner of the kitchen, the green and blue jewels on the key's handle glittered.

"Sapphires and emeralds," Sara whispered.

It was beautiful. "Did you have any trouble getting it? I mean with them in there?"

A crease formed between her eyebrows. "Why would I?"

"Isn't your mom with Morgan's mom in their study?"

She frowned. "The key's not kept in their study."

"Oh. In their bedroom then?"

She shook her head. "It's kept in the foyer."

The foyer? "But everybody's allowed in there."

"I know."

He blinked. "How can they keep it safe?"

Sara's expression turned sly. "Remember? My dad says things are best hidden in plain sight."

Levi started to argue, but the sound of heavy footfalls on stone stopped him. He yanked Sara deeper into the shadows and mouthed the words *I'm going down.*

"Time to be getting on with these dirty dishes, I suppose." Mrs. Forest's high-pitched tones came from someplace way too near their hiding place.

A sigh, then Mr. Forest's deeper voice. "It's a never-ending job."

"I'm going with you," Sara hissed in Levi's ear.

He shook his head violently. "No way. Think what Deceptor would do if he got hold of you again."

"At least let me get somebody—Miss Althea or Mrs. Sylvester, maybe." A beam of light sparkled on her tear-filled eyes, glinting the same brilliant blues and greens as the jewels on the key.

Mrs. Sylvester? What if she and her husband were in league with Deceptor? The cut dragons . . . the unhappy leprechauns . . .

"Did you hear something, dear?" Mrs. Forest's question made Levi suck in a breath. Then she answered herself. "I guess I'm hearing things. That silly old cellar dwarf has me on edge."

"If I'm not back in fifteen minutes, tell somebody," he murmured in Sara's ear. "I have to go now or Morgan might not make it out." He patted the hammer strapped to his waist, thankful Mr. Sylvester hadn't talked Mr. Austin into confiscating it. Then he untucked his shirttail, hiding the hammer beneath it. "At least I have a weapon."

She offered him a weak smile as he pulled the key's gold chain over his head and tucked it beneath his shirt. Levi eased the knob until the door opened with a soft squeal. At least this time that wind didn't slam it in his face. Did that mean he was right to go down?

It wasn't like he had time to analyze the situation. Levi rushed into the blackness and shut the door behind him.

Chapter 37

Darkness

Why hadn't he scrounged for a flashlight or even a candle while he waited for Sara? *Idiotic.* Levi scrabbled with his fingertips against the rough stone wall while inching forward with his toes. He didn't want another accelerated trip down those stairs.

"Just what do you think you're doing, young lady?" Mrs. Forest's raised voice reached Levi from overhead. "Did I just hear that door?" The volume went still higher. "What do you mean Levi Prince went down after Morgan Whitman?" Her tone rose to a shrill squawk that hurt his ears a good ten feet below. Poor Sara.

He tried to hurry. Who knew how long Morgan had been down there. The steps felt endless. When his toes finally struck the floor, he almost fell flat.

Now where? Had Regin taken him left or right the last time he was here? Which way would Morgan have gone? Had Regin, or worse, Deceptor already found her? His stomach clenched.

Levi moved straight ahead, feet shuffling and hands groping, completely blind in the pitch darkness. His breathing grew shallow in the damp dankness. Slowly, fear began to edge into his mind. He couldn't see. Didn't have a clue where he was. Had no idea if he was moving toward Morgan or even whether she'd actually come down at all.

Much later, it dawned on him how foolish he was, rushing headlong into this horrible place with no proof Morgan had ever opened the cellar door.

How long had he been wandering in the darkness? Must be hours. Surely Mr. Dominic would show up any minute with flashlights blazing.

But Mr. Dominic had been called away from the castle. And Levi's only companions were silence and inky blackness.

"Morgan?" Levi's whisper was sucked into the vast emptiness. No echo. No answer. Just dead air.

About then, he realized he'd never been this way before; at least, he didn't think he had. His footfalls no longer clattered on stone. The floor had turned squishy, and he could only imagine the nastiness he walked on. There was no sense of walls with branching tunnels, no scent of water beyond the heavy muskiness. There were no sounds at all, other than his own panting breath and pounding heart. He did his best to make as little noise as possible.

Levi felt like he was in a cavernous tomb. Like he was the only thing alive for miles. How long could he stay alive down here? He tried to pray. He tried to think of Bible verses he'd learned. Anything to get his mind off the feeling that he'd entered an open grave.

A portion of the psalm they'd sung in chapel Sunday replayed in his mind: "Where can I go from Your Spirit? Or where can I flee from Your presence? If I ascend into heaven, You are there; If I make my bed in hell, behold, You are there." He couldn't imagine anyplace more like hell than this.

God, are You here?

His right ear bashed against solid rock, and he dropped to the ground. With a moan, he huddled, clutching his ringing ear while hot wetness seeped through his fingers. When the pain subsided a little, he drew in a deep breath, and the scent of blood filled his nostrils.

Something scuttled not far away. Levi strained his eyes to see through the unrelenting darkness. There it was again, closer than before. His pounding heart made the blood surge from his cut ear, and he pressed harder to stanch the flow. He wished he had a handkerchief or a rag.

The scuttling sounded nearer.

His blood. It smelled his blood. *Not again.* What was it this time? Something worse than Regin?

All the monsters from his nightmares crept into his mind.

He was about to die. Why did he keep getting himself into these situations?

Oh, please, oh, please, oh, please, dear God, get me out of here.

Chapter 38

Morgan and the Dvergar

"Levi?"

The tiny whisper might as well have been a shout. Was God talking to him?

No, that was crazy. Even for a place like Terracaelum.

"Is it you, Levi?" Morgan's voice.

"Morgan?" He scrambled forward a few paces, hand held high to ward off another collision with the rock.

"Yes—"

"What were you thinking coming down here?" He sounded like his mom on a scolding rampage, but he couldn't stop himself as the anxiety of the past hours spewed out. "It's pure idiocy. You could've gotten yourself killed." He flapped his hands. "You might still get yourself killed. Not to mention me. Did you ever think about that?" He ignored the fact that she hadn't invited him down. "Everybody's got to be worried sick about us by now. Sara's bound to have told her parents, and Trevor and the others are searching, and your mom—" Oh. Her mom was what had started all this mess in the first place.

"Have you completed your rant, boy?"

The blood nearly clotted in his veins at the sound of that horrible voice. Regin. Light burst before Levi, and he clapped his palms over his eyes at the sudden stabbing pain it brought. After a couple seconds, he lowered his hands.

Regin held a white-faced, blinking Morgan by the wrist. She looked so miserable Levi couldn't hold on to his rage.

He blew out a ragged breath. "Now what, Regin?"

The albino dwarf grinned at him. "You know the answer to that already, I think."

"You're gonna take us back to the stairs and let us go home?" Sarcasm spiked Levi's words.

Something like melancholy flickered in Regin's eyes, but his grin stayed fixed, like a mannequin's. "I am sorry to say that I cannot."

"Figured as much."

"Come." Regin waved the torch, making the shadows loom and bend in the vast emptiness beyond. "We should go."

Levi followed the two, knowing he couldn't run off and leave Morgan. "How'd you find me?"

Regin gave his head a derisive shake. "You made enough noise to wake all the dead in Hades. How could I not find you?"

Levi grimaced. He thought he'd been pretty quiet.

Besides, did Regin really have to mention the dead?

They marched so long Levi lost all track of time and place. At first he tried to pay attention to the shapes of caverns and tunnels, the areas where moss gave way to clean rock or dirt, the stretches where the walls were rust-colored or dripped moisture from some underground spring. Several times he heard rushing water not far off and wondered if he was hearing the river that had carried him out last time.

He fingered the hammer strapped to his waist, its handle barely covered by his shirttail. How had Regin missed the weapon? Why hadn't he searched Levi?

At least Mr. Austin would be pleased at how much time he was getting in carrying the thing. Not that he'd likely ever know, since Levi probably wouldn't ever get out of this pit. Though the weight of Mjolnir still made the left half of his back throb with every step, he wouldn't give it up now for anything. Because if Regin did bring them to Deceptor, the rusty hammer represented their only defense against the demon sorcerer.

Levi tripped in a small hole and the castle key bounced against his chest. Would he ever get a chance to use the key Sara had pilfered for him? He paused mid-step as another thought struck. Did it even work on the cellar door, assuming he could find his way back there? Why hadn't he asked Sara that question?

And if they didn't get away, would Deceptor take the key from him? Would he know what it was for? Would he use it to enter the castle? A gulp—louder than he'd intended—escaped his stiff lips.

Regin's head twisted around. "What is it? Are you weary?"

Levi shook his head. "I'm okay, but how much farther are we going?" He'd begun to think Regin was leading them in circles. How big could the underbelly of Terracaelum be anyway? Besides, he was worried about Morgan. She'd barely said a word since he found her. Or should he say, since Regin found him? "Maybe we should rest a few minutes. Do you have anything for her to drink?"

Regin peered at Morgan. "Oh, I had not thought . . . Do you need a respite, young lady?" His mouth twisted slightly on the last words.

What was that look about? Levi inched nearer, his gaze flitting to Morgan, who still faced straight ahead, as though oblivious to their conversation. "You okay?" He touched her arm. Regin yanked her out of reach. Levi glared at the dwarf. "She's freezing. Don't you have a jacket? A blanket? Anything?"

Regin glanced uncertainly around the cavern, then back at Morgan with a shrug.

Levi knew he'd have to make a move soon. Morgan was acting so weird she must be going into shock. Should he whack Regin with the hammer? Then try to find the way to the castle steps before he or Deceptor caught them?

Levi peered into the shadows beyond the flickering torchlight. He had no idea which way the castle steps even were.

But the almost inaudible whir and hiss of rushing water somewhere to his right told him the river might be that way. Should he head for it? Try jumping in with Morgan? Could he make himself jump into that water? If he did, what if he couldn't get her out before they went over the waterfall into the lake? Could she survive the plunge? What if the lake monster showed up?

What if it didn't?

A violent shudder coursed through Morgan. With an oddly frightened expression on his face, Regin watched her for several moments, his thumb and forefinger a loose ring around her small wrist. This was Levi's chance, probably the only one he'd get. If he didn't do something now, they'd be led to Deceptor like lambs to the slaughter. And Morgan definitely couldn't survive Deceptor. Neither could Levi.

In one jerky motion, he slipped Mjolnir from his belt and leapt at Regin. Yet he couldn't bring himself to strike the dwarf from behind. Instead, he bellowed, "Let her go," and hovered with the hammer millimeters from Regin's skull.

The Dvergar slowly rotated his head until he saw the hammer, now millimeters from his bulging pink eyeballs. He didn't release Morgan, who hadn't so much as twitched at Levi's bellow. "Mjolnir," Regin whispered, his colorless face somehow losing more color.

Levi frowned. What was the deal with these dwarves and this ancient garden tool? "Okay, so you do know this isn't really Mjolnir, don't you? There's no such thing as a magic hammer. It's a myth."

Extreme annoyance crinkled Regin's mouth. "You know all there is to know about Terracaelum, do you? You, a foolish boy without enough sense to avoid this place a second time, can discern truth from myth?"

Elves, dragons, pixies, Dvergar . . . not to mention invisible floating islands—all were things he'd believed to be mere mythologies before coming to camp. But he'd been wrong. "What are you saying? Thor's real?" The hammer wavered in his grip, almost conking Regin's forehead.

Regin flinched but responded in a cranky tone, "Do not be foolish. Stories of your silly thunder god are mere exaggerations of the true history of my ancestor, Thorn the First. He forged Mjolnir. He used it in mighty battle. In latter days, he adjusted its use to secure peace for his people." The corners of his lips turned down in sudden sorrow. "Now, its purpose . . ." As he trailed off, he turned a look of terror on Morgan and then on to the dark cavern looming ahead.

"What purpose?"

Silence.

"Fine, don't tell me." Levi had to focus on the problem at hand anyway, not whatever was going on in this crazy Dvergar's head. He had to get Morgan out of this place. "Let her go."

Regin released Morgan's arm and raised his hands high, as if Levi had a submachine gun trained on him.

Levi snagged Morgan's wrist and pulled her to his side, not taking his eyes from Regin. "The torch. Give it here." He let go of Morgan and reached out.

Regin thrust the torch toward him.

Levi hesitated. How was he going to carry the hammer and the torch and drag Morgan around? He couldn't trust her to stay with him. She still seemed to be in some sort of trance.

"I'll carry the torch."

Morgan's guttural whisper made Levi forgot to keep his eyes on Regin. Was her voice that hoarse from being underground so long? She held out a trembling hand, and Regin gave it to her. Levi really hoped she didn't drop it.

He had other problems to consider, though. Like the fact that he didn't have any rope to bind Regin. Morgan didn't even have ribbons in her hair that he could use.

"Don't follow us or I'll have to bash you with this thing," Levi said, waving the hammer around in what was supposed to be a threatening manner.

Regin backed up a few more paces, his eyes lingering on Mjolnir in a look that was part hunger, part fear.

"Come on." Levi took hold of Morgan's upper arm, feeling the goose bumps on her skin. Too bad he didn't have a jacket for her. He started toward the muffled sounds he prayed came from the river, shooting glances at Regin for as long as the torchlight reached him. Regin didn't move, but Levi was well aware that the Dvergar could follow them with a stealth he'd never detect. That meant he couldn't put the hammer in its holster no matter how much his hand ached from carrying it.

As they walked, Morgan's trembling increased along with Levi's anxiety. What was wrong with her? Was she that cold? Could she be hypothermic? He wasn't exactly hot in the chilly damp of the tunnels, but his nerves made his hands sweat. Hopefully he wouldn't drop the hammer.

Maybe Morgan was just scared. Maybe if he talked a little she'd calm down.

"Don't worry, Morgan. We'll get out of here okay." He whispered so he could still hear the river and, if the little creep tried it, Regin sneaking up behind them.

Plus, in this creepy place, who knew what other monsters might follow his voice?

Though Morgan's upper arm tensed beneath his hand, she didn't speak.

"I'm hoping we can follow the river back to the castle or maybe through some tunnel to the outside. Worst case, we have to jump in and let the water carry us. I made it out that way before, so we should be okay." *I hope.*

Her silence grated on his raw nerves. "What's wrong?" He spoke more sharply than he intended. "You think I can't handle this? Well, I have the hammer." He held it in front of her. His irritation grew as she kept walking in silence. "You don't think I'll use it if I have to? I can and I will. I'm just not some Neanderthal who likes hitting people over the head if I can help it."

Still no answer.

Fine. If she didn't want to talk, so be it. He stomped along, listening to the growing hum of water and the *drip, drip, drip* in caves and tunnels they passed. He didn't hear shuffling or any other hint of Regin's presence.

After a while the silence and shadows got to him, as did his hollow stomach, which growled loudly. "I *can* get you back inside the castle, you know." Again her arm muscle tightened. "It's true." He glared at her as though she'd challenged him. "I have the key." He released her arm and smacked at his chest where the key dangled from its chain.

Her head whipped around so fast his jaw dropped.

"Show it to me."

Again her voice sounded strange, deeper and raspier than he'd ever heard it. And her eyes . . . they were cold and hard, the blue so pale they almost looked silver. Levi's skin convulsed into solid gooseflesh, as though a million insects crawled up and down his back. He half-expected her pale lips to open and show fangs like the she-monster across the mountains.

She relaxed slightly and glanced away, but he watched her with care, tension filling his every muscle. *Creepy.*

"I mean, show it to me, please, Levi," she said in a higher-pitched, gentler voice.

Levi frowned at his own overactive imagination. The darkness must really be getting to him. He pulled the key from beneath his shirt, somehow comforted by the cold, hard jewels against his palm. Morgan was okay, probably just exhausted. She must've been awake all night worrying about her momma, and then this.

He held up the key for her to see. Despite the oppressive darkness, the gold and jewels caught the flickering torchlight and flashed it forth, scattering ribbons of light around the cavern.

Morgan gave a sharp gasp, and Levi looked up at her. Her eyes were fixed on the key. She licked her lips hungrily, and her burning gaze flicked to his. For a second he thought she was going to attack him, snatch the key, who knew what else, but she didn't.

Instead, she spun on her heel and ran off into the tunnel ahead.

Shocked, he stood frozen, watching the torchlight bounce away, leaving him in the deepening darkness.

Chapter 39

Basilisks

"Wait, Morgan!" Levi sprinted after her, sliding in damp patches of smut, the key thumping against his chest with every footfall. The torchlight shrank so fast he could no longer see his surroundings. As he chased the fading flame, he could only pray he didn't smash into a low-hanging rock.

What was Morgan's deal? How could she leave him alone in the dark like that? What was she running from?

He tried to quiet his ragged breaths to hear if something followed, but he couldn't slow his pace to look back. He needed to catch Morgan because she sure wasn't acting like herself. She needed to get back to the castle fast.

The underlying hum of water turned into a roar, and the underground river sparkled in the torchlight. His breath hitched at the sight of Morgan on the opposite end of the stone bridge. Holding the torch aloft, she peered back as though waiting for him to catch up. He didn't want to step onto that bridge, but he couldn't trust her not to take off again. So he galloped across the slick stones, praying he didn't slip and fall into the icy water.

When he reached the halfway point, the point where he'd leapt over the edge last time, Morgan darted ahead into the tunnel.

"No, wait!"

She didn't wait. He skidded down the bridge and into the darkness beyond, to where Morgan again paused around the bend. Without any hesitation, he latched onto her wrist, vowing not to let go until he got her safely to the castle.

"Don't run off again," he whispered harshly. "You about gave me a heart attack."

Warily, he peered ahead. The blackness sucked in the flickering torchlight and devoured it whole. That's when it hit him: They'd crossed the bridge Regin had warned him about.

Basilisks! With a gasp, he screwed his eyes shut tight. He squeezed Morgan's wrist and tightened his grip on the hammer.

"Close your eyes." He spoke so quietly he couldn't be sure Morgan heard, so he raised his voice a little. "Shut your eyes, Morgan. There're basilisks over here."

He heard her grunt softly and could only guess she understood. For several long moments, they stood in a silence filled only by the sound of the river behind and the echoing emptiness of the tunnels ahead. What should they do? Keep going or turn back?

"Come back!" The bellow from behind nearly forced Levi's eyes open. Instead, he squeezed them tighter. "You must come back to this side of the river!"

Regin.

Levi couldn't let the Dvergar capture them again. "Come on, Morgan, but don't look." He pulled her forward into the tunnel, shuffling his feet to feel for obstacles, careful to keep his eyes closed.

After a while Regin stopped calling and, other than their own muffled footsteps, heavy silence fell. The air grew thick and smelled rancid like something dead. Levi's breaths grew shallower until he panted like a dog. The desire to open his eyes just a slit was so strong he wanted to cover them with his hands, but he couldn't let go of Morgan. And he wouldn't let go of the hammer.

Suddenly, his feet tangled in something, and he went down hard. The hammer clanged against the stone floor, jarring all the way up his arm and rattling his teeth, though he managed to hang on to it. Morgan toppled to the ground beside him.

"You okay?" he whispered.

She didn't answer, but he could feel her shift beside him. The rancid stink was almost overwhelming now. Hesitantly, he let go of her arm and stretched tentative fingers to find what had tripped him. His fingertips brushed something like ridged, whorled paper. It crackled beneath his touch.

"What in the world?" Levi ran his hand along it, discovering that it extended farther than his arm's length. It felt like a flimsy shell he could easily crumble. Like an empty snake skin.

His groping fingers froze. Basilisk skin. His heartbeats burst into a fireworks finale.

"Morgan, we've gotta get out of here." He stood slowly, pulling her up with him.

Even then, she didn't reply.

Barely shuffling on his tiptoes, he inched to the right, away from the empty skin, hoping the basilisk who'd outgrown it wasn't anywhere near. After he'd moved several feet, the hammer struck the tunnel wall with a dull clank that sent his pulse into triple time. With a gulp, he tucked the hammer into his side and ran his elbow along the stone, seeking a basilisk-free escape route. He'd much rather go back and face the river with that lake monster or even Regin than some horrible basilisk. But how was he supposed to find his way when he couldn't open his eyes?

It was maddening, feeling the heat of the torch Morgan held, seeing its red glow through his closed lids, but unable to open his eyes and use the light to find his way out.

Wait. The torchlight. Could basilisks see fire? Or smell smoke? Would it draw the beast? Or maybe basilisks feared fire?

What should they do? Douse the light? Leave it someplace? Keep it close?

Something heavy scraped against the rough ground, but he couldn't tell which direction it came from. *Oh, please, oh, please, oh, please.* He moved faster, rubbing his elbow against the cold stone so the flesh chafed. He could only pray they were moving away from the monster, not toward it. There had to be a side tunnel around here somewhere.

The scraping sound came again, this time from much nearer. Morgan's wrist trembled beneath his hand. It was all he could do to keep his eyes shut. He could practically feel the monster stalking them, but where was it?

Just keep your eyes shut!

Didn't basilisks have poisonous fangs? Did they strike first? Or swallow their victims alive?

God, help. We're gonna die.

The wall ended so abruptly Levi fell sideways with a stifled yelp. The scraping sound became an excited thumping. Levi imagined the snake-monster writhing at the sound of him, turning its massive body and heading straight for him.

Sweat dripped from his brow as he righted himself and took off, dragging Morgan behind him. After several moments at a blind, panic-driven sprint, he slowed and tried to listen over his and Morgan's harsh breaths. Nothing. Had they lost the beast?

"Enough. Open your eyes."

The hoarse voice Morgan had used earlier so surprised Levi that he peeked at her through his lashes. She stared at him, her eyes wide open. She didn't appear frightened at all, but the emptiness in her eyes scared him almost as much as the lurking basilisk. After a few seconds, she blinked and looked away.

"We should go this way," she said, this time in the higher-pitched voice, and pointed straight ahead.

Too shocked to protest, Levi followed her lead.

They rounded a curve in the tunnel and continued walking, this time with her pulling him. Though she kept her eyes wide, he peeped through slits with his head down, ready to squeeze his eyes shut at the first hint of movement. When they reached a left-branching tunnel, a greenish light caught at the jeweled key resting against his shirt. He risked a quick glance ahead at an opening in the rock. A draft ruffled his hair and made the torch spark.

Could there be an exit nearby? Excited, he forged ahead of Morgan, only vaguely aware that her breathing had changed to shallow, nasal spurts. The tunnel walls brightened to green—not the spongy green of moss, but sparkling green like the emerald in the key—and gradually melded into huge green crystal rods unlike any he'd ever seen.

But there was no exit in sight.

Suddenly, Levi realized he couldn't hear the river anymore, only a soft plinking not far away, as if an underground pool hovered nearby. He glanced at Morgan. Her eyes were fixed on the key, her pupils seeming to suck the light into their depths. He caught a glimpse of small white teeth between her parted lips.

"We need to find our way out of here." His lips felt rigid with a fear he didn't understand. This was just Morgan, after all, but she looked like a wild creature on the hunt. "We should go back." He took a backward step, away from the girl who once reminded him so much of his little sister.

She lifted her eyes from the key and smiled, her expression that of the Morgan he knew aboveground. "It's okay. We'll find our way."

He relaxed a fraction. Maybe he'd imagined her peculiar looks before. Maybe the darkness and the strain were messing with his mind. Still, he took another step back. She glided forward a few paces until the space between them shrank to almost nothing. "We should go." He pointed behind her. "Back that way."

"Yeah." Her voice was soothing.

But she moved still nearer, making him inch backward.

He closed his fist around the key, quelling the rainbows of light. Her eyes narrowed and a hiss escaped her. She lunged at him, capturing his right wrist in a vice grip. Wincing, he watched Morgan's small pale hand force up his forearm with a strength she couldn't possibly possess. She dropped the torch to free her other hand and began prying open his fingers.

He could only blink at her in the flame flickering by her feet, even as one finger after another gave way beneath hers. "What are you doing?"

Her nostrils flared. A flicker of silver like liquid nitrogen blazed in her eyes.

"Who are you?" He whispered the words, though he knew the answer. Deceptor. The shape-shifter had assumed Morgan's form.

Even as Levi fought to keep the key gripped in his right hand, the hammer weighed down his left. Mjolnir. Slowly, he eased it upward into strike position, hoping not to attract Morgan/Deceptor's attention to it.

Whack him! Levi tried, but how could he hit Morgan? Had Deceptor somehow possessed her? What would happen to her if he brained her with the hammer?

Oh, God, I don't know what to do, he prayed silently as Morgan forced open another finger. The hammer trembled in his fist, inches from the back of her head.

A sudden hurricane wind blasted him backward. He fell flat, his back striking hard stone, and his head shattering a pool of frigid water. The wind that had rescued him and his friends last year . . . the Spirit. But Morgan still had an iron grip on his wrist, despite the billows buffeting her small body. He sat upright, ready to fight her off.

Something snatched him by the collar and yanked him into the air. *Basilisk!*

Levi gagged as his shirt tightened across his throat then caught under his jaw. His wrist felt like it would snap as Morgan struggled to keep hold of him, shrieking like a rabid panther, mouth gaping black, eyes fully silver. He dangled in mid-air. How could he ever have thought that snarling, spitting, cursing animal was Morgan?

A jolt exploded in his belly as he dropped. He sucked in a lungful of oxygen before his body fractured the surface of the pool. Plunged into icy green water and propelled through the depths by some unseen force, he could only scream with his mind and fight the urge to open his mouth. Unable to shut his eyes against the pressure, he watched his dizzying rush downward, through a circle of rock, and up toward pale bubbling light. He tried to keep hold of Mr. Austin's hammer, but the force of the water twisted his wrist until he had to let it go.

Just when he thought he must give in to the overpowering urge to inhale, his face broke the surface. Guzzling precious air, he forgot for a moment the thing still thrusting him along, swimming faster than the rushing current of what must be the underground river.

Fighting the speed, he maneuvered so he could peek over his shoulder. After all, instant death from a basilisk's stare had to be better than slow death wherever it was taking him. What he saw forced the air from his lungs: a long, greenish-black scaly neck that disappeared into the frothing water. Twin jets of hot air blasted near his ear. A wave of faintness pulled him under, drowning him in oblivion.

Chapter 40

Pressie

Levi woke to a mouthful of sand. He sat up sputtering and found himself face-to-face with those bright green eyes he'd had nightmares about all summer.

He backpedaled, shooting sand into the creature's face.

It sneezed, shooting monster snot all over him. He wiped gray-green slime from his face, all while propelling himself backwards on his rump. The creature opened its mouth wide, yellow fangs glistening in the sunlight. It was going to eat him!

Levi tried to scream, but only an odd gagging sound came out.

A rumbling wheeze echoed from deep within the monster's huge chest. Its eyes watered. Its horse head reared back and a cackling grunt burst from its still-open mouth. It didn't even try to nibble at him.

Levi stopped his backward crabwalk and stared. Was the thing laughing at him? A sudden surge of anger boiled his blood. "You think that's funny? You scared me half to death. I thought you were a basilisk."

It stopped cackling and bent its neck until it was eye-to-eye with him. Levi gulped. Probably wasn't wise to yell at a fifteen-foot monster with three-inch incisors. It didn't act mad, though; its eyes got watery and soft, almost like it was trying to apologize. Besides, if it had wanted to eat him, it had had plenty of chances. The underground wind blew him straight to the creature, which must mean it was trustworthy, right? Plus, the creature saved him from Deceptor, pulling him through the water to safety and depositing him . . . where? He peered around. Castle Island beach. Again.

He rose to his feet, swaying slightly. The creature leaned in and steadied him with its head. "Thanks." Levi gave it a tentative pat on the neck. A low rumble from its throat made him yank back his hand, but the monster nudged his hand with its head. "You like that?"

The creature whimpered. He patted it again, and the low rumble returned. It was purring like his grandma's cat. He couldn't help but laugh.

"You're something else, aren't you?" He gently scratched down its neck, and the creature closed its eyes, thrumming louder than a boat engine. "How'd you know I needed help, huh?" Earlier in the summer and that day. "How'd you know where to find me?" Deceptor would've killed him if not for the lake monster.

"Morgan—" His hand flew to his chest, where, thankfully, the castle key still rested. He had to find her. No telling what Deceptor had done with her while he was impersonating her.

The creature cocked its head to one side, its green eyes questioning.

"Listen, I have to go, um . . . Pressie? Is that your name?" The monster purred again. "Thanks for the rescue, but I have to go help Morgan."

Levi started down the beach, feet slipping in the sand, soaked shorts and tennis shoes weighing on his legs. He glanced over his shoulder. "If you see a girl in the water, save her for me, will you? Just bring her back here." He felt a little silly giving instructions to a lake monster, but it seemed to understand, like the dragon Nithir had.

Pressie bobbed its head, snorted once, and disappeared beneath the waves.

Despite his shaky legs and aching head, Levi flew up the stairway, passed the cabins, and climbed the hill. He had to help Morgan. She'd been underground too long. No telling if she was even still alive.

He knew he couldn't fight Deceptor on his own. Miss Nydia had given her life to rescue them last year; Pressie had rescued him today.

Without God's help in both cases, they would've failed too. How many more rescues would Levi get? In both cases, he'd almost gotten himself and others killed because he'd disregarded the people in charge. He wasn't going off half-cocked again. He had to somehow get to Mr. Dominic.

With no castle in sight, Levi skidded to a halt at the cliff edge, pulled the chain over his head, and held up the key. Its golden shaft glimmered in the patchy, late afternoon sunlight, the emerald and sapphire at its tip resting against his palm. He stared at the empty space before him, and the problem made itself glaringly obvious. It was all fine and good to have the only key to the castle, but what if he couldn't get to the door?

What if he couldn't even see the door?

Waves crashed below; lazy clouds floated overhead. Seagulls screeched and dove for fish in the shimmering waves, overwhelming him with a frustrating sense of déjà vu. He needed to get into Terracaelum, but he didn't know how. Even with the key. Resisting the urge to yank his hair out in curly orange tufts, he paced the lip of the precipice. Maybe there was some sort of clue he'd missed before. Maybe the keyhole was in the ground or on a tree.

That's when he noticed the massive oak he'd seen get struck by lightning that night in the library. The trunk stretched from the wooded area ten feet from the cliff and then far out into open sky. He squeezed his eyes shut, trying to picture exactly where the tree lay in relationship to the drawbridge. If he remembered right, it ran almost parallel, maybe a foot from the bridge, and extended to within a couple feet of the castle wall.

He opened his eyes. If he walked the length of the trunk and reached out and to the right, he should find the keyhole. Hopefully. He had to try.

He looped the chain back over his head so his hands were free, gripped a branch, and heaved himself up, scraping a deep cut in his shin on the bark. The pain woke him to the reality of what he was doing: scaling a tree that might tip and fall with him into the lake. All on the off-chance that he might find a way inside the castle. He was a moron.

But what choice did he have? Morgan needed help, which meant Levi needed to get to Mr. Dominic as soon as possible. A gentle breeze blew into his face, and he drew it into his lungs. Courage coursed through him, and he began inching his way along, using branches to steady himself.

After several painstaking moments, he reached the twigs at the top of the tree. The trunk trembled and swayed beneath his weight. He gripped two fair-sized branches, but the wood was damp from hanging over the water, though the lake lay a hundred feet below, and his hands were sweaty. He'd never been that fond of tree-climbing, and sideways over a drop-off was so much worse.

Still, he'd made it this far. All he had to do now was let go with one hand and try for the keyhole. Slowly, carefully, Levi released his sweaty death grip and pulled the chain over his head. He reached out and to the right, poking the key into emptiness. Nothing happened. Over and over, he poked, stretching farther each time.

Frustrated, he gave a forceful jab, and his right foot slipped. He fell and wouldn't have stopped until his body smashed into the lake, but a branch snagged his shirt. He hung there a second, feet scrabbling, arms flailing, too scared to shriek. Then his sneakers gripped, and he hugged a branch just as the hem of his shirt ripped.

He stood there shaking and breathing for several long moments.

His fingers were shaking so hard, he felt the key slipping. He readjusted his grip and ended up holding it out by the shaft as a sunbeam flashed through the fluffy clouds. Light flooded the jewels and threw blue and green streamers arcing outward. Brilliant rainbow lights flashed all around, and a gray stone wall appeared a few feet in front of him.

"Yes!" The key . . . he'd been holding it upside down. He grinned as the drawbridge began its slow descent.

"You figured it out," a feminine voice called from the cliff edge behind him.

Heart thumping, he twisted his face around. Morgan stood beside the fallen tree with a smile on her face. Her hair hung in a wet mass; her clothes were stained and sodden.

He sighed with relief. She'd escaped Deceptor. "How'd you get here?"

"Oh, uh, same as you." She eyed the lowering drawbridge, as though wondering if it would disappear when she stepped onto it.

Levi understood the hesitation. He wasn't sure how he was supposed to maintain his hold on the key and actually get inside the castle. "Pressie helped you?"

A frown creased her brow. "Yeah, of course. Now come on, let's get inside." She looked away like she was trying to hide tears. "I really need to find my mom. It was so scary down there."

Levi froze. Why would Morgan want her momma? She'd gone into the cellar all upset because of her.

Unless this wasn't Morgan.

Chapter 41

Battle for the Castle Key

Levi narrowed his eyes. Could Deceptor come to Castle Island? A vague memory of the Austins' conversation he'd overheard the summer before replayed in his mind. "You know he'll go anywhere. Even into the castle if he can get an invite."

"You're not Morgan," he said, then wished he'd bitten his tongue out instead.

She glared at him, the pale blue of Morgan's eyes shifting to an icy emptiness. "Come to me, boy. Give me that key." The voice was hollow, deep, harsh.

Levi shuddered. What should he do? Scream bloody murder in the hopes that one of the staff would hear? Pocket the key so the castle disappeared? He couldn't let Deceptor get inside.

The drawbridge was less than four feet from connecting with the cliff now. Deceptor could jump onto it and run into the castle, but he stood watching Levi instead. Why did he want Levi to come to him? Did he need Levi to get inside? Would that constitute an invitation into the castle?

Levi shot a quick glance toward the castle. If he could somehow jump to the doorway while the light held the castle in place . . . He had to get help. If this was Deceptor, Morgan must still be in trouble.

Or was she? A terrible thought struck him. Had Deceptor been inside the castle all summer? In the form of Morgan? Was Hunter in league with the shape-shifter after all? Levi gulped. Had he insisted that

Sara and the girls share a room with the demon sorcerer who wanted the Dominics dead?

No, couldn't be. Deceptor would've killed them all long ago.

Quit panicking and think! He shot another glance at the castle. Did he dare jump?

"Don't even try it." Deceptor had climbed onto the trunk and was moving toward Levi. A twisted silver dagger glinted in Morgan's small hand. Below the tree, the hundred-foot drop to the lake blurred with a shadowy image of the moat, making Levi gasp. The drawbridge was about to connect the two worlds.

He had to do something, but he stood frozen, dumbfounded that Morgan's face could radiate such hatred. What should he do? He wished he still had Mjolnir.

Then again, the weight of the hammer probably would've sunk him into the lake by now.

"I've been waiting all summer for this." Deceptor advanced slowly, clearly enjoying his fear. "Ever since you paid Regin a visit, thinking you'd play the hero and rescue a poor, pathetic sailor, I've had him pounding on that door." Cruel laughter burst from Morgan's lips. "Just waiting for another fool like you to open it so I could kidnap you."

"But why?" Levi knew why Deceptor wanted Sara—to get to her parents—but why one of the other campers?

"Because," Deceptor said in an almost pleasant tone, "then that doddering old imposter you call camp director would come down to fetch you, and I could kill him and claim the throne for myself. And today that little girl walked right into my clutches. And then you came along. I was about to kill you outright, especially after the problems you caused me last year, but then—" Morgan's mouth twisted into an ugly smirk. "—I decided to have a little fun, try a little deception. That's my specialty, as you may recall."

Levi's stomach roiled. Deceptor was now halfway along the trunk. Levi would have to fight, but with what? He darted glances all around.

"I always knew there was a key." Deceptor's eyes raked the key Levi clutched. "And you brought it right to me." The sorcerer took another step nearer. "I should thank you. This is a much better way. It allows me the element of surprise."

Levi's gaze fell on a partially broken branch. It wasn't much against that knife, but it was better than nothing. As he yanked on it, the tree shuddered under the strain.

"Leviticus Prince!"

He whipped his head up and back toward the castle. Dr. Baldwin's swarthy face stuck out of an open window. "Catch!" He disappeared from view.

Catch? Catch what? Levi glanced at the shape-shifter, now almost to him, then back toward the window.

A flash of gold, and a sword sailed through the air. Levi let go of the tree, stretched out his hand, and, amazingly, the hilt smacked into his palm.

"Get Mr. Dominic. I need help!" Wait, didn't Sara say the director was gone to the mountains? Something about the leprechauns? But that was hours ago. Surely he was back by now. If not, Mrs. Dominic would have to do.

Dr. Baldwin disappeared again. Levi turned as Deceptor's silver dagger arced toward his head. He raised his sword and deflected it millimeters from his face. He backed up a few paces.

"Your prince and princess are a bit busy, I'm afraid." Morgan's face was a mask of mock pity. "I set up a little something to keep them occupied."

"In the mountains?"

Deceptor smirked. "And nearer home."

Faint sounds of yelling and clanking from what sounded like the northern side of the castle made their way into Levi's consciousness. He realized he'd been hearing noises as the drawbridge lowered but had been too preoccupied with Deceptor to pay attention. There came a boom then a shriek. The smell of smoke tickled his nostrils. "What did you do?"

"Merely another small offensive move to distract them from the true infiltration." Deceptor edged in and struck hard.

Levi managed another deflection, but he was off-balance. He swayed. The key slipped from his grasp. And fell. A flash and sudden silence told of the castle's disappearance. He sucked in a breath but couldn't look away from Deceptor, who was slicing downward. Wedging his hip against a branch, Levi shoved his sword upward. Their blades caught for a moment, then the knife broke contact with a zing.

Though fear threatened to paralyze Levi, he knew he had to do something. He needed to stall long enough for Dr. Baldwin to get help. He raised his sword against the next strike and gasped, "Did you do something to the leprechauns?" He frowned. "And what about Middie and Nithir? You're the one who cut them, aren't you?"

Deceptor halted mid-jab and smiled, twisting Morgan's lips into a cold grimace that didn't belong on her face. "You figured that out, did you?" His voice was mocking, almost playful. "My little disruptions up north kept your old prince and his people busy aboveground, didn't they?" He said *prince* with such disdain it almost sounded like a curse word. "It kept them nicely distracted from Regin and our attempts from beneath the castle."

"But how'd you do it? Wouldn't the dragons have attacked you?"

Deceptor released a throaty chuckle. "There's value to being me, boy. Watch and learn before you die."

And in one horrible instant, Morgan's small form elongated until it towered over him. Smoke curled around her. Her face morphed from soft curves to sharp angles. Her black hair swirled into the platinum blond of the fencing instructor, Mr. Sylvester.

Levi couldn't stifle a gasp. The elf's mouth twitched into a smirk.

"But why?" His stomach clenched when he remembered the suspicions he'd harbored against Nydia Sylvester's dad.

"Who better to entice the dragons than their trainer?"

"But that's horrible—"

Deceptor/Mr. Sylvester didn't let him finish. He hooked his left arm around a branch and jabbed the dagger toward Levi's chest with his right. Levi barely blocked the jab. Before he could move away, the shape-shifter thrust again, this time so hard he almost knocked Levi from the tree.

Levi surged away, one hand gripping a projecting twig, the other swinging wildly. He blocked Deceptor's strikes, all but one. Hot blood coursed from a nick below his right eye. Sweat snaked down Levi's back, and his breath came in painful bursts.

Deceptor's eyes burned like dry ice in his fencing teacher's pale, unruffled face. The demon forced him steadily backward until the trunk thinned, swaying and bouncing like a rubber band beneath his feet. Any minute it would snap, and he would drop to his death. He had to do something to push Deceptor back.

Levi thrust forward with a solid, low shove toward Deceptor's belly. For a split second, surprise flashed in those cold eyes. Then they narrowed, and the silver dagger clanked against his sword hilt, so hard Levi lost his grip. Just as the dagger swiped at his head, Levi jerked backward. He glimpsed his sword splashing into the lake below.

He would've despaired, but in that downward glance, he also caught sight of a flash of gold, blue, and green. The key had gotten snagged in some leaves at the bottommost of the tree's hanging branches.

"Defeat." Deceptor eased nearer, knife tip inches from Levi's nose, an evil smile twisting Mr. Sylvester's face. "Too bad you lost the key, or I'd have let you live a few more moments."

Levi shot another surreptitious glance at the key that jiggled with Deceptor's every step. "Why? Can't you use it without me?"

Pure hatred shone in Mr. Sylvester's eyes. "Shut up, you little fool."

He blinked. *Guess that's a no.* He knew what he had to do, but that didn't mean he had to like it. Smashing his lips tight together so he wouldn't scream, Levi let go of the branch and stepped from the trunk. He freefell. At the last possible second, he grabbed for the branch nearest the key.

He caught it. His palms ripped on the twigs and bark. Finally, he stopped himself on the very tip of the branch. His shoulders felt like they'd rip from their sockets at any second, but he didn't let go. The key dangled in front of his nose.

Above him, Deceptor let out a furious howl. *Must've spotted the key.*

Levi's fingers cramped. How could he get the key? If he let go with either hand, he'd surely drop. Not to mention that he didn't have the strength to hang on much longer.

An idea struck—a crazy one, but better than nothing.

Levi worked his lower body until he was swinging gently. The branch gave an ominous creak that sent his heart into his throat, but he kept swaying. Just a little more. And a little more. *There.* He opened his mouth and snatched the key between his teeth.

At that moment, the world exploded. Parallel lines of blue and green light blinded him. Something heavy thudded somewhere overhead. And his branch broke with a loud crack. Levi dropped so fast he couldn't even make a sound around the key clenched between his teeth, knowing any second he'd shatter against the water.

Eyes squeezed shut, he prepared for death.

Chapter 42

Into the Lake

A band of iron closed around Levi's chest, jerking him to a halt. His eyes flew open. He hung in mid-air less than a foot above the lake. A split second later, the tree trunk crashed into the water next to him. Water flooded into his face and up his nostrils. He sneezed, his incisors so tight around the key he felt sure his teeth would break. Blinking hard and with his shirt cutting into his armpits, Levi twisted his head to see what had stopped his fall.

At first, he thought he was hallucinating. Blue scales glinted in the light reflected from the waves. Long white fangs clutched his shirt. Two flame-blue eyes fixed on him around a long snout. Massive blue wings battled the air currents. A ropy scar marred the smooth membrane of the left wing.

Nithir?

Beyond the dragon, Levi caught a glimpse of the drawbridge lowering. A loud ripping sound came from somewhere near his armpits. His already-torn shirt couldn't last much longer.

He moved the key with his tongue and forced out a garbled "Up, Nithir!"

The dragon must've understood because his wings beat harder. Slowly they rose. Levi wanted to flap his arms and kick his feet, as if swimming through the air would help them reach the drawbridge faster, but he resisted the urge, knowing he'd only rip his shirt faster. Instead, he prayed.

The seams gave one last horrifying rip, and he fell. He landed face first on solid wood. Air whooshed from his lungs, and the key shot from between his lips. Loud clanks and snarls echoed above him. He flipped over. His hair fluttered as Nithir flew away, but he had other things to worry about. Like the fact that he lay between the battling Mr. Dominic and Decepter, still in Mr. Sylvester's form. If either sliced downward, Levi would be dead.

The same thought must've occurred to Deceptor. His dagger arced not toward his opponent but toward Levi's exposed belly. Levi rolled to the side, unfortunately into Mr. Dominic's legs. Mr. Dominic toppled, and Deceptor's knife jammed into the wood Levi had just vacated.

Levi scuttled farther away and wound up rolling downhill. Only then did he understand the drawbridge was at an angle because it hadn't yet fully connected Terracaelum with Castle Island.

Mr. Dominic leapt to his feet in a move too agile for a 143-year-old man. Deceptor pulled the dagger free of the wood and swiped at the director's legs. Mr. Dominic hopped over it and swung down. Deceptor blocked his overhead cut then shoved his skull into the director's gut. The director gasped at the impact but lunged with his blade.

"Go! Get to safety!" Mr. Dominic bellowed at Levi, but Levi couldn't move. He watched open-mouthed as Mr. Dominic knocked Deceptor's dagger from his grip. It flashed silver as it fell from the drawbridge and hurtled toward the water below.

Deceptor shrieked something that sounded like a foul word, but Levi didn't recognize the language. He had a split-second vision of his mom washing out the demon sorcerer's potty mouth with a bar of yellow Dial soap. Then Deceptor morphed back into Morgan's form.

And stepped from the bridge.

Levi blinked at the empty spot, the image of Morgan stepping off into nothingness imprinted on his brain. A splash echoed, and he gasped. He peered over the edge. In that instant, the smooth moat replaced the long drop to the lake. Morgan's form was gone. The air left his lungs as though he'd plunged at top speed into the frigid water himself.

"Well, that's that then." The director sheathed his sword and reached out to help Levi up.

He stared at the man's blue-veined hand, his brain waterlogged, uncomprehending. After a moment, he lifted his own bloody palm and grasped the director's. He stood on wobbly legs, feeling like the weight of the entire lake pressed him down.

Mr. Dominic put an arm around him, his wrinkles deep with concern. "Let's go inside, son."

Levi allowed himself to be led into the castle, only to be met by a squeal and arms squeezing the breath from him.

"Thank God!" Sara released his neck and stepped back. "I was afraid you were dead. When you didn't come back, I went for my mom. But Deceptor's army broke into the field, so she and the others had to run out and fight. Mrs. Forest had the kitchen staff gather the campers in the art and music room for a sing-along, since it would be the farthest from the noise of battle and they wouldn't know anything was happening. And then everybody else was fighting. I got Trevor and the rest of our friends, and we ran up to the tower so we could see what was going on, but we couldn't figure out what to do."

Levi frowned at her, completely confused, as she rushed ahead at a frantic pace.

"All these horrible creatures came out of the woods and—" She shuddered. "—then Mr. Forest flew over with Dad. And Nithir swooped after him. Then . . ." She paused, frowning. "Well, it was just strange, how fast Mom and the others routed Deceptor's army. Some of our people were hurt, but I still thought it seemed too easy. But by then you'd been gone forever, and I was so scared." She stopped talking suddenly and stared at his stomach. "Where's your shirt?"

He blinked down at his bare chest and the red welts at his armpits. He couldn't make his mind work. Where was his shirt?

Dr. Baldwin bustled up beside Sara, gently pulled her hands away from him, and raised both eyebrows at the director. "To the infirmary, I think."

Mr. Dominic's lips formed a thin line. He said something about exhaustion and shock, but Levi's mind kept replaying Morgan's body stepping off the drawbridge.

"Morgan . . ." The strangled word didn't sound like it could've come from him. He forced his weary limbs to carry him down the empty hallway as he mumbled to himself, "Have to get her out. No telling what Regin and Deceptor have done to her." He paused in the kitchen doorway. What next?

"Regin?" Mr. Dominic stepped in front of Levi and met his eyes.

Levi stared back at him, too tired to explain.

After a moment, the director nodded, hurried to the pantry, pulled out a second sword, and put the hilt into Levi's hand.

The two strode to the cellar door, and Mr. Dominic opened it. Levi jolted fully alert when Regin burst out. Behind the Dvergar huddled Morgan, water dripping from her hair and clothes.

Levi gasped. Confusion made his temples throb. Morgan? No, Deceptor. But how could he have survived that drop? Didn't matter. He was here, in the castle kitchen!

Levi raised his sword and charged.

Chapter 43

Two Keys

"Wait." Mr. Dominic grabbed his sword arm and shoved him aside.

Levi struggled against his firm grip. "But that's—"

He started to say Deceptor, but was he right? He peered at the dirty, ashen-faced girl. She held her arms clenched around her body as though to keep herself from breaking apart. Beside her, the albino dwarf blinked, wincing as if the dim light hurt his eyes. Mr. Dominic released Levi's arm. His sword sagged to the side.

"That's Morgan, the real one." Mr. Dominic took Morgan's arm and thrust her behind him. Dr. Baldwin moved up beside her as if uncertain whether to offer her support. Sara watched with both hands over her mouth.

Levi scowled at Morgan, hands tightening around his sword hilt, ready to fight at the slightest movement. "Why's she wet then?" It had to be Deceptor, but how did he get here so fast?

Mr. Dominic pressed a heavy hand on his shoulder. "It's the real Morgan, son. Trust me."

How could he be so sure?

"She tried to jump in the river," Regin told Mr. Dominic. "I had to go in after her."

That's when Levi noticed the puddle beneath the Dvergar's bony white feet.

Mr. Dominic drew himself erect, like a statue of a medieval king. He glared at the cowering Regin. "How dare you commit treason against this kingdom."

The dwarf flinched as though struck. "I am sorry, Prince Tobias—"

"Do not speak that name." Mr. Dominic's eyes hardened to green marble.

Regin drew back. "I . . . crave your pardon . . . sir. Deceptor told me he had possession of the key. As you know, my brothers are trapped inside with those . . . creatures, and Deceptor said he would kill the rest of my people if I refused to do his bidding. Still, I never gave him what he wanted. I never got it." His pink eyes darted to Levi's face. "But he had it."

Levi's hand flew to his empty mouth. His tongue searched his aching teeth. Where was the key? Had it fallen into the lake?

Regin pointed at Levi. "Where is it, boy? What happened to the key of the Dvergar?"

Key of the Dvergar? Sara had told him it was the castle key. Levi sputtered incoherently.

Dr. Baldwin placed a hand on his arm. "He's talking about the hammer Mr. Austin loaned you for the play. Mjolnir."

Levi's jaw dropped. "Thor's hammer is your key? To what?"

Regin waved away his words. "We call it Mjolnir as a joking reference to your silly human mythologies." His face reflected desperation. "Clearly, Deceptor lied to me about having the key. I can only hope he lied about my family as well." He held out a hand to Levi. "Please, boy, give me the key."

"I . . . I dropped it." His gaze fell to the stone floor. "When Pressie rescued me from that green crystal cave where Deceptor was trying to make me give him the other key . . ." He looked at the director, who gave a single nod of comprehension.

Sara released a muffled sob, but Levi kept his focus on Mr. Dominic. "Pressie pulled me through the water so hard the hammer broke free. I'm sorry."

"Not your fault." Dr. Baldwin patted his arm, though worry clouded his features as he murmured to Mr. Dominic, "What if he gets it? The prisoners—"

Mr. Dominic raised a hand, palm out. "The key is lost in the underground rivers. Deceptor does not have it." He fixed his glare on Regin once more. "I contained the situation with your brothers and their charges when the, er, incident first occurred this summer. As for the rest of your family, I shall send scouts to determine their situation. In the meantime, we have a more pressing issue to discuss."

Regin's eyes widened as he held out both wrists, showing the thin silver bands around them. "Please, sir, I would never willingly betray you. Deceptor tricked me into thinking my family and the—"

At a slashing motion of the prince's hand, Regin went silent.

Mr. Dominic studied the shackles, stroking his stubbled chin with one long forefinger. "There is a way you may begin to redeem yourself, Regin of the Dvergar." He cocked a bushy brow at Dr. Baldwin. "The injured?"

"Mostly superficial wounds, except for a pair of sprites on patrol in the western woods." Dr. Baldwin's brow lowered. "They were set upon by a werewolf. It's not good. I've done what I can to help their bodies dispel the poison, but I don't know if it's enough. Althea and I moved them to the Isolation Room. She's keeping watch over them now."

Levi shivered. He'd known all along that werewolf would get out and attack somebody.

Mr. Dominic nodded. "Could Regin be of help to them?"

"Regin? How could the treacherous Dverger possibly be of any h—" Dr. Baldwin sputtered to a stop, his eyes widening with sudden understanding. "Oh, yes, that's a very good possibility."

Mr. Dominic nodded. "Kindly prepare the Dvergar for the journey. Do not let him out of your custody."

Levi blinked, bewildered about what injured people and journeys had to do with Regin, but the dark dwarf looked oddly excited.

"Oh, thank you, Pri—, uh, sir." Regin bowed so low his beardless chin brushed the floor.

"Don't mistake this for a reprieve," the director said in a hard voice that chilled Levi.

"No, no, I won't. Thank you, sir." He straightened then peeked around the director to Morgan. "I apologize, young lady, for kidnapping you." He cast a timid glance at Mr. Dominic. "I made sure she was not harmed, even though Deceptor told me to kill her."

Mr. Dominic pointed toward the doorway. "Go."

Nose wrinkled in disgust, Dr. Baldwin took Regin's arm and led him out of the kitchen.

Mr. Dominic closed the cellar door.

"Is he dead this time?" Levi had to ask the question even though he knew from past experience it wasn't easy to kill a creature like Deceptor. He burrowed deeper into the chair in front of Mr. Dominic's desk and cradled his bandaged hands to his chest.

The old man studied him as if debating how much information he could handle. "It's doubtful, I'm afraid."

"But you . . . Mrs. Dominic . . . defeated his army." Wasn't that what Sara said? He thought so, but his brain had been so muddled after Deceptor in Morgan's form dropped from the drawbridge.

Mr. Dominic lifted one shoulder. "Somebody released the minotaur, werewolf, and several of the hags from their prison, and they attacked. That much is true. However, it does seem to have been a weak attempt at battle, one easily quelled."

"And the leprechauns?"

"Someone set fire to their cabbages."

"Their . . . what?"

The old man's mouth quirked. "Leprechauns very much love that particular vegetable. If you want to upset them, simply deny them their cabbages."

"Oh." Levi wrapped the blanket tighter around his shirtless shoulders. "But you won anyway. Right?"

A lengthy sigh filtered through the director's lips. "So it would appear, but clearly the attacks were mere diversions from the true battle." His green eyes pierced Levi's. "To gain entry to the castle."

His answer made Levi cringe, yet Deceptor had admitted as much. "He wanted the key. He thought I could get him inside." When Mr. Dominic didn't comment, he continued, despite his burning stomach. "I lost two keys today. One Mr. Austin told me to guard with my life, and the other I talked Sara into getting for me." The burning turned into an inferno. "Without your permission." How had he fooled himself so completely? First with his attitude toward his parents and their right to tell him what to do. Then with his attitude toward Mr. Dominic and his rules.

The director propped his chin in his hand. "All true, I'm afraid."

"I—I thought I was doing right, getting the key and going down after Morgan," Levi stammered. "Because this time the wind didn't warn me, I don't know why, so I thought it must be okay."

"You hadn't been warned enough already?"

Levi looked away, unable to bear the director's gaze. One warning should've been all it took to make him obey. Yet the Spirit had rescued him by shoving him to Pressie anyway, despite his foolishness. "I . . . I'm sorry, sir." His shoulders sagged. "I don't know how to make it up to you or Mr. Austin." He looked up at Mr. Dominic. "Though I'm not sure why Mr. Austin had the key of the Dvergar. What prisoners were Dr. Baldwin talking about?" Were there other werewolves on the loose now? "And what does Regin have to do with injured creatures?"

"Regin has some . . . special skills useful in treating injuries. That's all you need to know."

"Yes, sir." Levi studied the wood grain of Mr. Dominic's desk. He understood. He'd disregarded the director's authority. Broken the rules. Shattered his trust. How could he make things right? "The water ripped the key from me after Pressie rescued me from that green cave place. Maybe somebody could look for it near there?" He couldn't bring himself to volunteer for the job. He had no desire to step foot in Terracaelum's underbelly ever again.

The director's gaze sharpened. "About that cave, what exactly did it look like? Where did you find it?"

"I don't know exactly. We were on the other side of this stone bridge trying to find the way out without meeting a basilisk when we just kind of ended up in this big cavern with huge green crystals."

"Hmm." He cocked his head to the right. "Pressie. Is that what you called the creature?"

Levi's face warmed. "I started calling her Pressie because Trevor told me that's what Superior's lake monster is called. I assumed that's who she is. Is that wrong?" And when had he started thinking of *it* as *she*?

The director smiled. "That's as good a nickname as any, I suppose, though that's not her real name."

"Oh, well, she answered to it, so I just thought . . ."

"You called and she came?"

Levi nodded. "After she rescued me for the second time—"

Mr. Dominic's hands dropped to the desktop with a thump. "The second time?"

"She's how I got back alive earlier this summer." Levi twined his fingers into the blanket.

"I see."

"Yeah . . . So, after she saved me this time, I figured she must not want to eat me—" He tried not to react to Mr. Dominic's smothered snort. "—so I told her to go find Morgan and bring her to the beach." His gaze shifted to the map of Terracaelum behind the director's desk, homing in on the point at which his world and this one connected. "When Deceptor showed up at the cliff, I thought Pressie had rescued Morgan." His lips twisted. "Obviously I was wrong, since he tried to use me to get inside the castle."

Mr. Dominic was quiet a moment. "When you got the key turned the right way up, the castle opened for you." His tone was casual, but Levi got the feeling he was very interested in the answer.

At his hesitant nod, Mr. Dominic sat back as if stunned.

"Blue and green light flashed, and then the castle was right there. Dr.

Baldwin threw me a sword out the window. I dropped the key fighting Deceptor, though, and then he knocked my sword away." Levi again studied the wood swirls in the desktop, not wanting to see Deceptor's face in his mind's eye. "When I saw the key caught in those low branches, I knew it was my only chance. Then I fell again, and I'd be dead if you hadn't shown up. You and Nithir." He lifted his eyes to the director's. "Did you send him?"

Mr. Dominic shook his head.

Renewed guilt twisted Levi's gut. "I must've lost the key when Nithir dropped me onto the bridge. Do you think Deceptor will find it in the lake and break in? I should never have taken it in the first place. I put Terracaelum in danger."

Mr. Dominic sighed. "You may well have." He gave Levi's forearm a squeeze. "But at this point, I don't know how you can make restitution." His eyes grew distant. "We'll have to see how it all plays out. I know the Great Sovereign has a plan in all things."

Chapter 44

The Olympics and the Play

The next afternoon, Levi climbed into the canoe with Sara. From the next craft over, Trevor said, "Hey, Morgan, I'm glad your mom let you stick around for the Olympics. You and me are gonna whup Suzanne and Jacqueline."

Morgan offered Trevor a sickly smile but didn't say anything. According to Sara, she hadn't spoken more than a couple of words since Regin brought her up to the kitchen. Levi hadn't even tried to talk to her yet.

"Come on, Levi," Sara said from behind him. "It's time to focus on the race."

"Yeah, okay." He gripped the paddles the best he could with his bandaged hands. Dr. Baldwin had released him to participate in the canoeing event, but fencing and archery were out of the question. His shredded palms simply couldn't handle those. He didn't mind. His heart just wasn't in the Olympics this year.

He had cheered plenty for Trevor, though, who won the fencing silver. Hunter won the gold, but he didn't strut about it, probably because of Morgan's situation. Hunter didn't even bother mocking Levi for having to drop the events. Had Morgan told him about her experiences in the cellar? Did he know about Levi's battle with Deceptor? Did Sara tell him?

Levi glanced back at Sara, who adjusted her lifejacket and offered him an encouraging smile. He bent his lips a little in return. He didn't know what to think.

When the starting whistle sounded, he made a half-hearted effort to match Sara's stroke pattern. But as the race wore on and they got farther and farther behind, he couldn't bring himself to care. Of course they lost. Sara didn't say a word of blame, only climbed quietly from the canoe as the crowd cheered for Suzanne and Jacqueline, who won the match.

As Levi passed Mr. Sylvester on the way to the castle, the elf patted his shoulder, his expression sympathetic. Levi tried not to flinch at his touch because Mr. Dominic had reassured him the Sylvesters were trustworthy. He'd said Mr. Sylvester's loyalty was part of why Deceptor impersonated him. But Levi couldn't control a shiver, and Mr. Sylvester smiled sadly, as if he knew what Levi was thinking.

Levi tried to muster sympathy for the elf. In spite of Mr. Dominic's unquestioning trust, he had a lot stacked against him—his daughter's betrayal, his wife's withdrawal, and now Deceptor's impersonation, which made the dragons leery of him. But Levi had been sunk in a sludge of dull melancholy since Deceptor in the guise of Morgan dropped from the drawbridge, and he couldn't pull himself out of it.

His dad would say he was troubled in his spirit. He'd let so many people down.

A slew of oversized, hyperactive butterflies—or were they wasps?— fought a full-fledged war in the pit of Levi's stomach, yanking him out of the doldrums. The hour he'd dreaded all summer had come: time for the play. At least his family wouldn't see him acting like an idiot in a wedding dress. He'd gotten a note at breakfast that his mom and siblings couldn't come because Abby's final choral performance had been postponed until that evening. Then he'd gotten another message that his dad's car had died along the way, but that he hoped to have it fixed in time to meet Levi and Trevor when the ferry arrived at the mainland.

Sara pulled him aside before he entered the wings. "I wanted to tell you I loaned Lizzie my mom's necklace."

Levi frowned. He knew which necklace Sara meant, the one they'd found in the Trojan horse the year before when she'd been kidnapped. "But why?"

"Because Freyja's necklace, Brisingamen, should be special and beautiful, and my mom's necklace is both." She offered him an impish grin. "Besides, I thought it might give you enough courage to dress as the bride, Freyja, knowing you'll be wearing my necklace."

He gave her a sideways look, trying to decide how much she was making fun of him. "Thanks, I think."

Her eyes softened. "Really, Levi, I hoped it might help you not feel so alone up on stage. It's just a play after all. Not life or death or anything."

Levi's mind shifted again to last year's play, the one that had almost been the death of Sara. He looked at the stage set up in the safety of the castle courtyard and again said, "Thanks," this time without any sarcasm underlying.

She nodded and started away.

He touched her arm. "I'm sorry."

Her eyebrows lowered as her smile faded. "For what?"

"For not telling you about Pressie and the mormo. You helped me a lot with that whole water thing, and I . . . well, I should've trusted you with the other stuff." Looking down, he ran the toe of one shoe through the lush grass. "I'm also sorry for talking you into giving me your dad's key." His voice dropped to a whisper. "And for losing it."

When she didn't answer, he glanced up. She blinked away tears and offered a gentle smile. Then she walked off to sit with the other campers and their families—the ones who came over on the morning's ferry to watch the play and then take their kids home. Morgan's mom sat alone in the far corner twisting her hands, clearly impatient to take her daughter and leave.

Levi sighed and entered the wings, the old garden hammer weighing on him in a different way than Mjolnir had. Sure he could walk without swaying like a bowlegged horse, and hefting the thing was so simple he could easily pretend to be mighty Thor instead of wimpy Levi, but still . . . He shouldn't have lost the hammer.

When he'd apologized to Mr. Austin, the dwarf had said, "It's actually a relief to me and the missus. Being responsible for that key has set us on edge these past weeks." Maybe Mr. Austin was just trying to make Levi feel better, but if what he said was true, it explained why the normally sweet Mrs. Austin had been unusually testy this summer.

Now Levi adjusted the strap at his waist, thankful he didn't have to start the play in his dress, and watched the literature teacher in the opposite wings. Mr. Austin was in a frenzy of activity with the performance starting in moments, but the sparkle wasn't in his eyes like it had been before Levi lost Mjolnir. Without the famed hammer/key, the play wouldn't be quite as special in the playwright's eyes.

Levi swallowed his guilt. He'd try to make it up to Mr. Austin by manning up and being the best Thor in a goofy old wedding dress that he could possibly be.

Chapter 45

Forgiven

From his place at the ferry railing, Levi nudged Trevor and jerked his chin toward Braden, who ran a finger up and down the gold chain at his neck and peered into the engine room with a calculating look on his face. "Think he rigged something?"

Trevor grunted. "He wouldn't dare."

"You really believe that?"

"Guess I'd better go keep an eye on him." Trevor released a sigh so gusty it rivaled the wind rippling the lake. "Just call me Spy Guy."

Levi snorted. "Where's your armor, Spy Guy?"

Trevor elbowed him in the ribs and smirked when Levi let out a squeak of pain. Before Levi could retaliate, he scurried across the deck toward Braden.

Levi hugged his sore ribcage and glanced around at the other kids. On the opposite side of the ferry, Morgan propped her elbows against the railing, her gaze fixed on the mainland, growing swiftly nearer. He crossed to stand beside her.

"Looks like we're almost there," he said, then gave himself a mental kick. *Duh!* Of course they were almost there. And there was exactly where Morgan didn't want to be.

Without taking her eyes from the shoreline, she said, "Why'd you come after me?"

"What do you mean?" Levi shot a glance across the deck to where

Morgan's mom stood, arms folded across her chest, watching her daughter's every move.

"I mean, why'd you go below the castle to rescue me?" Her pale blue gaze locked on his. "You and your friends don't even like me."

"That's not true." He flushed at her lifted eyebrow. "At least not anymore." He sighed. "It's just we were friends from last year, and a new person changes things, you know? That's not an excuse; it's just the truth."

"Then why?"

"Why did I go down after you?" His pitch rose slightly. "Because I had to. I couldn't very well leave you down there alone. You could've died." So could he, for that matter. What was her problem? Why not say *Thanks for going after me, Levi. You're my hero, Levi?*

Morgan returned her stare to the looming dock. "You believe in God and all that stuff from chapel, right?" She drew in a breath. "I mean, your dad's a preacher, kinda like Mr. Dominic, so you have to."

Levi frowned. "I don't have to believe because my dad's a preacher. I believe because God saved me."

"Like Jesus dying on the cross and rising from the dead?" She glared at him. "All to rescue us from hell?"

He nodded, baffled by her obvious anger.

"Isn't hell worse than the cellar?"

Levi glanced down at the bandages on his palms then back up at her. "Yeah, it is."

"You rescue me from the cellar but don't care enough to make sure I'm rescued from hell?"

He blinked. He'd never thought of it that way before. He hadn't told Morgan about Jesus. Sure, she'd heard it in chapel, but it wasn't the same as hearing from a friend. No wonder she was upset. "You're right, Morgan," he finally said. "I'm sorry. Jesus is the only way not to spend eternity in a place much worse than the cellar."

She pressed her lips together.

"So what do you think?"

"Can Jesus save me from that?" Morgan cocked her head toward her mom.

"Oh." He swallowed hard. "He can, but he doesn't always . . . If he's in your life, though, it's a lot easier to deal with . . . stuff."

A cynical look crossed her features, making him sad. "Yeah."

Levi opened his backpack, fished out a notebook, and tore off a scrap of paper. "If you want to talk or need something or whatever, you could call or text . . . or whatever." He scribbled his contact information on the page and offered it to her.

She looked at him a moment before taking it. Then she smiled, and a flash of the happy Morgan from earlier that summer appeared. "I'll think about it."

Levi's dad stood waving beside his old green Ford. Levi waved back, hoisted his luggage, and hurried down the ramp. Dad jogged over and scooped him into a bear hug. "I missed you, son."

Levi gritted his teeth against the tears that stung his nose and throat.

"Hey, Mr. Prince," Trevor called, jogging up behind Levi.

His dad pulled back with a grin. "Trevor! Good to see you." He reached out one arm and scooped the bigger boy into the hug with them.

Dad released them both, still grinning, and snagged their sleeping bags. "Ready to hit the road?"

"Yeah," both boys said. They followed him to the trunk to stow their things.

"You know," Trevor said after Dad moved toward the driver's door, "it's a long drive." He shot Levi a meaningful look. "Good time to talk."

"Uh-huh."

"I'll take the backseat." Trevor let out a huge yawn as he opened the rear door and climbed inside. "I could use a nap."

Levi went to the passenger door. Before opening it, he peered around for one last look at his friends. Sara was hanging out in front of a small convenience store, pretending to wait for her folks to arrive. He knew she'd take the ferry back to the island as soon as the others left. Beside

Lizzie's mom's convertible, Monica and Lizzie were clinging to each other in a teary goodbye hug—would wonders never cease? Steve waved at Levi from the back of a minivan, and Tommy entered a nearby café with his family, an Asian-American couple with two little boys.

Levi sighed. He'd see them next summer. If his parents let him come back. His heart squeezed. Maybe he should wait a little longer to spill his guts.

But then he'd have to spend another wretched year like the last one.

He opened the car door, but before he got in, Morgan caught his eye. She was dragging her feet toward a rusty blue pickup where her mom stood beside a short barrel-chested man with black spiky hair and a barbed-wire tattoo around his throat. The man's harsh expression made Levi pity the poor girl more than ever.

"Hey, Morgan," he called. When she looked his way, he held his hand to his ear like a telephone. "Don't forget."

For the barest instant, her sad eyes hardened to silver-gray ice. A shiver started at the base of Levi's spine and snaked its way upward. Before it reached his neck, the moment was gone as Morgan smiled, her eyes their usual soft blue. She nodded once and resumed her trudge toward her mom and new stepdad.

Levi dismissed the freaky incident. Must've been a trick of the light.

He let his gaze shift to Hunter, who stood beside a silver luxury car beyond where Morgan's mom climbed into the truck with her new man. He could tell Hunter and Morgan were looking at each other, though Levi couldn't see her face. Hunter lifted his hand, raised both brows, and gave a single jerk of his chin toward the water. Morgan's head bobbed, then she climbed in beside her momma. The truck tires squealed as her stepdad hit the gas before she even closed the door. Hunter's steely glare latched onto Levi's as he swept into the luxury car and slammed the door.

Those two . . . cousins.

With an even deeper sigh, Levi climbed into the front seat beside his dad.

Sprawled across the backseat, Trevor guffawed, obviously in the middle of telling Dad about Levi's performance in the play that morning. "Yeah, he looked good in that skirt, too, lemme tell you. You should've seen those hairy legs!"

Dad grinned at Trevor in the rearview mirror. "I'm sure his little brothers would've loved every minute of it." After a brief chuckle, he turned serious eyes on Levi. "I wish I could've been there, son. I'm sorry. The alternator went out, and I was just thankful to find a garage that could work me in."

"Trust me, it wasn't worth watching."

Another snort erupted from the backseat.

Levi tossed Trevor a mock-menacing glare. Then he said quietly, "Dad, I've got some stuff to tell you."

"Yeah, like what?"

"First of all, I need to apologize for acting like a creep before I left for camp." Heat inched up his neck. "And for pretty much all of last year."

Dad studied him through gentle eyes. "Forgiven."

A year's worth of guilt released its shackles from Levi's heart. "Thanks."

Dad ruffled his hair. "And second?"

"Second . . ." He raked his bottom teeth across his upper lip. "Well, second could take a while."

Dad started the engine. "It's a long drive. We have plenty of time to chat."

Levi rolled down the window, waved at Sara, and watched her until they'd driven out of view. Now that the time had come, doubts again crept in. He'd kept secrets from his parents for so long, what if he couldn't let go of them? What if Dad thought he was crazy?

What if he refused to let Levi return to camp next summer?

A breeze as soft as his mom's kiss touched his brow. *The truth, Levi. That's the only thing that will set you free.* He filled his lungs with the sweet-scented air and faced his dad. "It's to do with that summer camp Papa Levi used to tell you stories about . . ."

About the Author

Author Amy C. Blake has appeared in many publications, both Christian-based and secular. With a Masters in English from Mississippi College, her work has consistently won praise and awards throughout her writing career, which has included everything from contributing articles to the publication of her full-length novels *Whitewashed* and *Colorblind*. Amy is a pastor's wife and homeschooling mother of four who resides in beautiful Ohio.